PROTECTING HIS CURVY GIRL

A CURVY GIRL ROMANTIC SUSPENSE

ROSE PROTECTION AGENCY
BOOK 1

MARY E THOMPSON

ROSE PROTECTION AGENCY

We hope to never meet, but if we do, we will do everything in our power to keep you safe.

Rose Protection Agency is the place to go when you have nowhere else to turn. When your life is in danger, and you don't know who to trust, they will be there. Always. No matter the time or the day, you can count on them.

Rose Protection Agency is a team of former military, special forces, and organizations you've never heard of. They are here to do what they were trained to do... Keep their country, and its citizens, safe.

No matter the cost.

Meet the protectors at
ROSE PROTECTION AGENCY

BOOK ONE

<u>Protecting His Curvy Girl</u>

Why was he alive?

It wasn't fair. Austin Ward had no one. No wife or daughter or even a damn dog. So why was he alive and his partner, the one with all those things, was dead?

Austin wasn't the only one who wanted answers. His dead partner's sugar-sweet librarian daughter showed up at his house and forced her way inside, demanding the truth. Her tear-stained cheeks and red-rimmed eyes gutted him. He ached to wrap her curvy body in his arms and lose himself in her. Erase his pain and hers at once.

But Lacey MacNeil was off-limits. Forbidden. Innocent and too vulnerable for a man like him to take advantage of in her agony. Even if he understood it, shared it.

So Austin did what he had to do and threw her out.

Right into the crosshairs of the man who killed her father.

To protecting what's yours... even when you don't think you're worthy.

ONE

Austin Ward leaned back in his chair and examined the cards in his hand. Absolute shit. He'd never been very good at poker, or rummy, or any of the other card games his partner and friend, Samuel MacNeil, always wanted to play. Samuel beat Austin on the regular, something the older man took absolute delight in.

"How many cards?" Samuel asked, a smirk in his brown eyes.

Austin rolled his eyes, tossing three cards on the table. "Three."

Samuel snorted and retrieved the cards. He slid them, face-down, to Austin, then focused on his own hand before trading one card.

Austin looked at the cards he had in his hand. Still shit, but slightly less bad shit. A pair of aces was better than the pile of crap he was dealt, but Austin learned a long time ago not to settle for the hand he was dealt. He usually handled things better in life than in cards, but he'd never even seen a silver spoon, let alone had one given to him.

"Show 'em," Samuel said, prompting Austin.

They weren't betting, so there was nothing to lose, but Austin still hated to lose. Hated to know someone else got one over on him. Even if poker was mostly a game of chance, it still rubbed him wrong to always lose.

He flipped his cards, showing the pair of aces he hoped meant more than it usually did. Samuel had a knack for card games. Insisted he didn't count cards and never fixed the deck, he was just lucky as shit.

Austin couldn't disagree. Samuel was lucky. A wife who adored him and a daughter who was as sweet as could be. Not that Austin was allowed to comment on Lacey MacNeil. At all. Samuel would knock him out if he knew how often Austin thought about his precious Princess.

Samuel turned his cards over one by one. A three. A seven.

Austin sat up straighter. So far, he was winning.

Another seven.

Still Austin's game.

Samuel smirked and flipped the last two cards. Two more threes.

"Son of a bitch," Austin said, shaking his head.

Samuel laughed with glee, delighted to have gotten Austin's hopes up and crashed them so fully. "Thought you had me, didn't you? You should know better than to think you're going to beat me."

"Yeah, yeah, whatever. One day I will. And you're not going to know what the hell to do about it. You'll be crying and whining and saying I cheated."

"You probably will have to cheat to beat me. God knows you have no skill."

Austin growled at Samuel and got up from the table. "I'm going to check on Hannah."

Samuel nodded and collected the cards, shuffling the deck as Austin walked away.

Austin knocked on the bedroom door, waiting for Hannah to reply before he opened it. "You doing okay?"

The young woman nodded, looking entirely not amused. "I'm fine."

Austin smiled at her. "I know it sucks. One more day. Tomorrow you testify, and this will all be over."

She drew a breath, her shoulders lifting with the move. She let it out slowly. A nod was all Austin got.

"Are you hungry? Or want to play cards with us?"

"I don't know how to play."

"Neither does he!" Samuel called from the other room.

Austin snorted and flipped off his partner.

Samuel laughed, obviously watching for the response.

"You can't possibly lose more than I do," Austin told her.

She smiled, the first hint of ease coming from her. She was brave as hell, reporting her former boss for embezzlement and money laundering. What she didn't know when she went to the authorities was how much he'd stolen and how deep the entire thing went. She ended up in the middle of an investigation that took the better part of a year. A year Hannah spent in hiding, bouncing from one safe house to another, one agency to another.

But it was almost over. In less than twenty-four hours, she was going to testify, and then she would go into witness protection and have a whole new life.

"Okay. I'll try," Hannah said, swinging her long legs off the bed. She straightened the bulletproof vest she wore, a precaution they all hoped wouldn't be needed. She was only twenty-six, seven years younger than Austin, but he was impressed by how she held herself together. She never once broke down, that he saw, and she was ready to stand up in court and tell everyone what she knew.

Austin grinned and stepped back to let Hannah walk

ahead of him. She walked into the living room to Samuel's cheers.

"All right. Now we have a game. What do you want to play?" Samuel asked.

Hannah shrugged. "I don't really know any games."

"Let's start easy. How about Go Fish?"

Hannah chuckled. "I can probably handle that."

Austin groaned and lowered to his seat across from Samuel. "How come you never let me choose games like that?"

"Because you know how to play, you just suck at the other ones."

Hannah snickered and took her cards.

Austin grumbled and retrieved his, no more luck than when they played poker.

Samuel just grinned.

They played for another hour, with Samuel and Hannah trading wins. Samuel taught Hannah how to play poker, and she won a hand.

Austin went to the bathroom, then decided it was time to make dinner. "What are we eating tonight?"

"I think there's a pizza in there," Samuel said. "I'm getting sick of those frozen dinners."

Austin found two pizzas and turned on the oven. Hannah took her turn in the bathroom, and Samuel cleaned up the cards so they could use the table to eat.

Austin put the pizzas in the oven and went to wipe the table down. "I don't know how she does it," he admitted to Samuel.

"Does what?"

"I'd be out of my mind by now. She's just going along like it's business as usual, and she has a huge thing to face tomorrow."

Samuel shrugged. "It's her normal now. I assume she's not

really thinking about it. Might tonight when she's alone again, but getting her out here to play cards with us was a good idea."

"It's so damn quiet here. I get it, but it feels like we're on a deserted island."

"I don't think even that would be safe for her. She's going to look over her shoulder for the rest of her life. Because she did the right thing and someone else didn't."

"That's pretty much why we have jobs. Assholes want to keep being assholes and will do anything to stay that way."

Samuel laughed. "That about sums it up."

The oven beeped, letting them know it was preheated.

"You already put the pizzas in?" Samuel asked, knowing Austin did.

"Yep. You don't have to wait. It just takes longer. And we're all hungry."

Samuel chuckled, shaking his head. "I can't wait for the day some woman domesticates you. Brings you to your knees and teaches you how to do things the right way."

"I'll get to my knees, all right, but not in the way you're thinking."

Samuel barked a laugh. "Uh huh. I hope you'll do it for that reason, too, but one day, you're going to have to beg a woman to give you another chance after you screw up so royally she won't forgive you for turning that mug on her and smiling."

Austin couldn't stop his smile, or his next words. "You offering someone up for me?"

Samuel rolled his eyes, another chuckle popping out. "You couldn't handle my Lacey if your life depended on it."

"Probably true."

The bathroom door opened, and Hannah stepped out. "What's probably true?"

"That Austin has no chance with my daughter."

"Hey! If I wanted a relationship, I'm sure I could talk her into it."

Hannah laughed. "Yeah, that's how every woman wants to be romanced. Manipulation."

Samuel laughed loudly, and Hannah joined him.

Austin scowled at the two of them, wondering how he was ganged up on, and wondering why it bothered him so much. Lacey was too good for him, and there was no way she'd ever be interested in a guy like him, but that didn't mean—

Hannah screamed.

Glass shattered. Bullets split the walls and windows, raining down on them.

Austin hit the floor, trying to stay below the bullets. Even with a vest on, it would hurt like hell. Samuel and Hannah were twenty feet from him. Samuel was covering Hannah on the floor, but she was bleeding. Arm, maybe.

Austin moved toward them. They had to get to the back door, escape through the yard to the shelter out back. Built to be like a panic room, it was nearly impenetrable. But they had to get there.

"Samuel," Austin called out, the pops and echoes of the gunfire loud in the otherwise quiet area.

"Austin, go. Get to the shelter."

"We're all going to go." Austin made it to them, seeing the slice through Hannah's side, not her arm, where the front of her vest connected to the back.

"Take her and go," Samuel demanded. His gun was in his hand, ready to fire back at whoever the hell was shooting at them.

Not that one gun would make a difference.

The alarms were going off, and someone would be there soon, but not soon enough if Austin had to guess. "We have to go."

"I'll cover. Get to the kitchen, then cover for me to move."

"Okay." Austin turned to Hannah. "Are you ready?"

She shook her head, panic in her gaze.

"Stay low, but move fast. I'll be right behind you."

She nodded, the move jerky.

"Go. Go now," Samuel commanded.

Austin shoved Hannah ahead of him, both of them crouching low.

Samuel's return shots stopped the rain of bullets for a few seconds, but it wasn't long enough. Hannah screamed again, collapsing on the floor just inside the kitchen.

Austin dragged her behind the peninsula and shouted for Samuel. "Let's go."

Austin fired toward the front of the house.

Samuel moved toward him, low and slow. Much slower than he should have been moving.

"We need to hurry!" Austin yelled.

Then everything went dark.

LACEY MACNEIL SMILED at the mother and son in front of her and handed over the books they requested. It was her favorite part of the job. Finding new books for young readers and seeing the joy on their faces when they came in to pick them up.

Lacey took her reading glasses off and let them dangle from the chain her father got her. He was always buying her little things that made her smile. He never once judged her for wanting to become a librarian, or resented her for not being a boy. She had plenty of friends with military dads who were angry when their daughters weren't like them.

Her dad always told her she could be anything she wanted to be, and then he backed up those words with his actions, proudly telling everyone he knew about his daughter the librarian, like the work she was doing was as much a service to the country as his own job. It made her feel special. It made her believe she really was contributing. If someone couldn't read or write, they couldn't serve in the military, so in her way, she was helping.

Lacey moved from behind the desk and nodded to Mike, the man working with her until close. Lacey was in charge, but Mike knew his stuff and was an asset. Plus, he was married with two kids in elementary school and had been in the library almost as much as Lacey over the years for the programs they ran. He was instrumental in getting some of them going and helping Lacey and the other librarians understand what would be good for both young kids and parents.

Lacey pushed the cart toward the fiction section, hoping to get a start on shelving the returns so she could get out of there on time, or at least close to it. She had a full night ahead with a container of leftovers and a movie to finish.

The door dinged, alerting her that someone had entered the building. Lacey looked at her watch and groaned. Five minutes to closing, and someone was just walking in. There went her chance at leaving on time.

A man's voice was quiet, obviously respecting the old rules of libraries to keep voices down.

Mike replied and said her name, making Lacey wonder what was going on.

She turned to go back to the front and stopped short when she saw her father's coworker, Zeke Donovan, at the desk. She must have made a noise because both men turned to her, and the look on Zeke's face told her everything she didn't want to hear.

"No. No! Zeke, no. You can't tell me this. No!"

Zeke hurried to her and sank to the floor next to Lacey. "I'm so sorry, Lacey. We are all sorry."

"He's dead? You have to say it. He's dead?"

"Yes, Lacey. Your father is dead. I'm sorry."

"No!" Lacey shouted and cried and screamed and shook.

Zeke bundled her in his arms and held her while she cried. He didn't make any attempt at calming her or asking her to be quiet. He just let her cry. Let her have her pain.

Lacey didn't know where Mike was, but at the moment, she couldn't care. Her father, her hero, the only man who'd ever loved her, was gone. Taken from her.

"What happened?" she asked, fighting to get the words out. The last thing she knew, her father and Austin were on an assignment. One that was supposed to be fairly routine.

"We don't know yet," Zeke said.

"Austin?" Lacey asked, hating that she prayed at least one of them survived.

"He's in surgery, but he'll be fine."

"But my father?"

"I'm sorry, Lacey. I really am. Montgomery and Kirk went to talk to your mother. I told them I'd come see you. Clay's here, too. He waited outside so we could drive your car for you."

"I thought this was no big deal. He was supposed to be safe. How was he not safe? What happened?" Lacey's sobs were loud in the otherwise quiet building.

Zeke pulled her into his arms once more.

Lacey couldn't wrap her head around her father being dead. It wasn't possible. He was larger than life. A good man who helped people. Why would anyone want him dead?

They had to be after whoever he was protecting.

"Who were they watching? Is that why this happened? They did something stupid and turned on them? Or communicated with someone they shouldn't have?"

"I don't have answers for you, Lacey. I wish I did, but we

don't know what happened. We got an alert, and when we got there, whoever did this was gone."

"What about witnesses? Someone who saw it? What did Austin say?"

"Austin hasn't been able to say anything. He was rushed into emergency surgery."

Lacey's breath rushed out all over again. She wasn't allowed to like her father's partner, but she couldn't stop it. He was charming and funny and so damn hot he gave her book boyfriend fantasies a run for their money. Not that she'd ever do anything about it. A man like Austin Ward would never look twice at a woman like her. "I thought you said Austin was going to be fine."

"I'm just telling you what I know, Lacey. Why don't we get you to your par—mom's house? You need each other."

Lacey swallowed around the lump in her throat. She didn't know how she was going to walk in there without her father home. She knew the work he did was dangerous, but she never thought he wouldn't come home.

Zeke helped Lacey to her feet and steadied her. She saw Mike standing not far from them.

"I'm so sorry, Lacey. Please let us know if there's anything we can do."

Lacey nodded, the move wooden and unnatural. What could anyone do? Her father was gone. She'd never talk to him. He wouldn't walk her down the aisle or meet her kids or scare the hell out of whatever man settled for her.

How was she going to go on?

"I'm supposed to work in the morning. Is there any way—?"

"I'll take your shift. And I'll let everyone else know. We'll cover for you for as long as you need. Take care of yourself, Lacey."

"Thanks, Mike."

"You'll take care of her?" Mike asked Zeke.

"I'll get her home, yes."

Mike lifted his brows at Lacey, asking for her confirmation.

"Zeke works... worked with my dad. He's a good man. And very happily married to a wonderful woman."

Mike's gaze drifted to Zeke's hand, where a ring was tattooed on his finger. "Sorry. We all love Lacey. I didn't know."

"All good," Zeke said, not appearing to take offense. "Are you ready?"

Lacey shook her head. As soon as she stepped outside, everything would change. Her father was gone, her mother would fall apart, and it would be up to Lacey to make sure it was all okay.

Not that it was. Nothing was okay. It never would be again.

TWO

Austin fought against the nurse trying to get him to calm down, thrashing and flailing to stop whatever was being put into his IV. "No more meds!"

"It'll help the pain," the nurse said. Robert was on his name tag. "I know you're in pain."

Austin couldn't argue the point, but he didn't fucking care. He would not let the meds drag him under again. Not until he saw Samuel. "Where's my partner? If you take me to see Samuel, I'll let you drug me up. But I see him first."

"Mr. Ward, I already told you. We aren't allowed to give you any information." Robert's tone was one of a weary parent with a petulant child.

"He's family to me. I know he'd tell you the same thing. Go ask him!"

"He can't," a voice said from the doorway.

Austin looked up and saw his boss, Montgomery Rose. Austin sighed. "Finally. Montgomery, what the hell is going on? They won't let me see Samuel or even call him."

Montgomery nodded to Robert, and Robert left the room. Fast. Closing the door behind him.

Fuck. Bad news was coming. Austin shifted in the bed, *fucking hospitals*, and winced at the pain from moving. His shoulder was torn apart, surgery repaired it but he'd be out of work for weeks if not months. Leaving Samuel alone.

"What's going on?" Austin asked, knowing there was something no one was telling him. "Am I done? Doc said I should be able to get back into the field. I thought—"

"Samuel's dead," Montgomery said. No inflection. No teasing. No hint of a smile on his face.

"Fuck you. What's going on? Really. What the hell happened?"

"You don't remember?"

"Remember? What the hell are you talking about? We were under fire, but Samuel was fine. We were going to the shelter in the back." Austin searched his memory. The gunfire. Hannah was hit. She was bleeding, and Austin called for Samuel to come to them.

"Then what happened?" Montgomery asked.

"Why are you asking me? I must have blacked out. I remember the shot that tore through my shoulder." Austin stared off, then closed his eyes, trying to bring the rest up. "After that, it's dark. I don't remember. Ask Samuel. He was coming toward us. He can fill in the rest."

Montgomery sighed. He closed his eyes and rubbed his neck. He let out a slow breath. "Samuel is gone, Austin. He's dead. So is Hannah. When we got there, they were both dead."

"No. No. It's not possible. This isn't fucking funny, Montgomery. What the hell?"

"No one will tell you where he is or let you talk to him because he's dead, Austin. Shot in the head. Took one in the vest, too, but..." Montgomery shook his head.

"How? Why? What the fuck?" Austin couldn't breathe. His chest tightened like someone was sitting on it. The monitors next to him screeched, and the door flew open.

Robert came back, followed by three others. They shoved Montgomery out of the way and went to Austin.

Austin's shoulder hurt like a fucker when they dropped the bed from under him, letting him crash on it. They yanked the pillow from under his head.

Voices shouted, machines beeped, then everything went dark.

"FUCKING HELL," Austin groaned. He'd never known pain like he was feeling. Did he get run over? What the fuck was going on?

He blinked, forcing his eyes open. Darkness surrounded him. Antiseptic. The squeak of sneakers. He turned his head and saw light in the hallway.

Hospital.

Samuel.

Dead.

"No," Austin whispered.

"You're awake."

Austin turned his head and spotted Walker St. Brown getting up from a chair in the corner. "What are you doing here?"

"Night shift. Montgomery talked the staff into letting someone stay here so you didn't attack them." Walker grabbed something next to Austin.

Austin's head lifted with the bed rising. He closed his eyes. It had to all be a dream. It had to be. "Is Samuel dead?"

Walker hesitated for a minute, then nodded. "Yeah, man. I'm sorry."

"What the hell happened?" Austin asked, his throat dry and rough.

Walker held up a cup with a straw, bringing it to Austin's face. "Drink."

"I can take care of myself," Austin said, reaching for the cup before grunting. Pain ricocheted through him, and his arm fell back to the bed.

"Drink, asshole."

Austin glared at his teammate and let Walker hold the cup and the straw for him. Austin fucking hated relying on others. He hadn't had to in years, and he wasn't looking to start now, no matter what was wrong with him.

Walker set the cup on the table next to the bed. He looked like he wanted to be anywhere but there, which was almost funny because Walker was known as the one of them without a life outside Rose Protection Agency. Single, no kids, no interests. Walker was married to the job, not that he seemed happy about it. He wasn't ever happy about anything.

Austin saw himself in Walker in a decade. He didn't love the thought.

"We've been trying to piece it all together, but there are more holes than anything," Walker said. "Samuel and Hannah are gone. She had a gunshot wound on her side and another one to her leg. Her throat was cut. Samuel was shot in the head."

"Why... where was I?"

"In the kitchen, near the door but inside. Best guess is you were hit, and it knocked you out."

Austin nodded, closing his eyes against the pain he felt. Not the physical pain, but the pain of loss. Samuel wasn't just his partner. He was a mentor, a friend, and the closest thing Austin had to family. "How's Lacey? And Valerie?"

"Not good," Walker said, raising one eyebrow but not commenting on Austin asking about Lacey first. "Zeke and Clay went to see Lacey. She lost it. Montgomery and Kirk told Valerie. It was bad."

"Have they... How long has it been?"

Walker checked his watch. "Two days. It's after eleven, and it all went down dinner time day before yesterday."

Austin closed his eyes. He wanted to be there for Valerie and Lacey. To tell them he was sorry. To honor the man he loved like family. Like family was supposed to love.

"Did you catch the asshole who did this? Obviously, they didn't want Hannah to testify."

"That's the best guess, but Howard was under twenty-four-hour surveillance. Can't tie this to him."

"Fuck," Austin breathed. "So he's going to walk because he took out the best witness, the only witness, against him, and there's not going to be any justice for Samuel or Hannah."

"Probably," Walker said.

Austin wanted to punch the man in the face. It wasn't Walker's fault, but his easy acceptance was infuriating.

"Get some sleep. You're going to need it."

"I need to get the fuck out of here."

"Sleep first. Talk to the doctor tomorrow. But they're saying you need to be here for a few more days."

"Fuck that."

"Take it up with them."

Austin grumbled and nodded, letting Walker go back to his chair in the dark corner of the room. Austin didn't want to sleep. He wanted to remember what happened. Why didn't he go outside with them? Why was he alone in the kitchen? And why the hell was he still alive?

LACEY WOKE up in her childhood bedroom and stared at the ceiling. She felt like someone was sitting on her chest. The weight of her loss was so heavy she couldn't move. *Would it*

ever get better? She didn't think so. How could it when her hero was gone?

Lacey toyed with the book shaped locket her father gave her for a graduation gift. It was a family heirloom that belonged to Lacey's grandmother, her father's mother. Lacey never knew her grandmother, but her father told her stories about the woman she was named after. The first Lacey MacNeil was a strong woman, mother of four boys, avid reader, and alone for most of her life.

Lacey had two things in common with her grandmother. Being alone was the last thing wanted to share with anyone.

The overwhelming feeling of loneliness pressed down harder on Lacey. She'd always been a daddy's girl, latching on to her warm and loving father from childhood. Not that her mother was horrible, but she never understood Lacey. She always pushed her to be something else. Someone else. Someone Lacey never wanted to be.

"You shouldn't be stuck in a library all day. You need to get out and meet people, Lacey."

"Why would you want to dress like that, Lacey? You should exercise more and eat healthier, and show off the figure that's under those frumpy clothes."

"Don't date men like him. You'll never go anywhere with a man like him by your side."

Every choice Lacey made was wrong in her mother's eyes, but her father always said she needed to figure out what was right for her.

The chime signaling someone was at the front door went off, causing a panic to race through Lacey and the family dog to bark loudly. Was someone there? Were they coming after the whole family?

Her father's boss, Montgomery Rose, said they believed the attack was on the woman Samuel and Austin were protecting, but he wouldn't say anything else. More secrets, more silence, more lies.

Lacey sat up and listened for more noises. If someone was trying to sneak up on the house, they were doing a shitty job of it. The front door closed with a loud click, then the lock engaged. Cocoa stopped barking, meaning he either knew who was there or he was hurt.

Lacey swung her feet out of bed and tiptoed to the door. She could see the entryway from her bedroom door, so she opened it quietly, hoping whoever was in the house wouldn't know she could see them.

Her mother set her handbag and keys on the table by the front door, then turned to put her jacket in the closet under the stairs.

"Mom," Lacey said, stepping out of her room. "Why were you out this early?"

"I had something to do." She turned and headed toward the kitchen, leaving Lacey to wonder what the hell was going on.

Lacey rushed down the stairs, rubbing Cocoa's head before they both followed her mother. Lacey stepped into the kitchen as Valerie turned on the coffeepot. "What did you have to do? Was it for the funeral? I would have gone with you? And why did they need to see you so early?"

Valerie looked at the clock on the stove, her gaze holding on the green numbers that read seven-eighteen. "It wasn't for the funeral."

"Okay, then what was it?"

"Just leave it, Lacey."

"What is going on, Mom? I get that you're upset, God, I am, too. But you're keeping things from me. It feels like everyone is. I can handle the truth about what happened."

"Apparently, no one thinks we can. They aren't telling me anything, either."

"Then we need to go see Austin. He was there."

"Stay away from that man," her mom hissed.

Lacey took a step back. "What? Why?"

"He didn't protect your father. He was supposed to be his partner, but he's perfectly fine and your father is dead."

"But that's not Austin's fault."

"Yes, it is. If your father had a partner who could do his job, they would both be alive. Instead, he was given that man-child of a partner. That useless piece of garbage."

"Mom!" Lacey couldn't believe her mother was saying those things. It didn't matter that it was just the two of them and that Austin would never hear the words, putting them out there was cruel.

"You listen to me right now, Lacey. You stay away from that man. He's never been any good. Your father told me all about his past, and he's not the kind of man you need to be anywhere near. He didn't keep your father safe. All his playing around and joking and acting like everything was always fine... It caught up to Samuel, not that trash Austin."

"Mom, how can you say that? Austin's been a friend of ours for years. He's been here for Dad's birthdays, parties, everything. He spent Christmas with us!"

"Because your father invited him. I never... I should have told your father not to invite him. Austin is no good, and he's never going to come anywhere near us again."

"What did you do?" Lacey asked, taking a step back. Could she... Could her mother have killed Austin?

"I told him to stay away from us. If he has any sense of honor, he'll listen."

"Mom." Lacey couldn't imagine how hurt Austin was, and for her mother to reject him was even worse.

"No, Lacey, don't. I went to talk to him. To find out what happened. I asked him why your father died. How he died. I just wanted the truth. But he wouldn't tell me. It was the only thing I wanted from him, and he refused. He refused to be your father's friend. Now we have to bury your father, to say goodbye to him, and we aren't allowed to know anything. So, no, I will not welcome that man back into our home, into our lives, when he doesn't even have the decency to tell us what happened. To share Samuel's final moments—" Valerie broke down and fell to the floor. Her hand stayed on the edge of the counter, trying to hold herself up and failing.

Lacey went to her mother and hugged her tight. Cocoa pressed to Valerie's other side. They all loved Samuel. As much as Lacey was hurting, her mother was hurting worse. Broken and destroyed. He was the love of her life. Before Lacey, her parents were a duo. Married for thirty years and planning retirement together. They were the future Lacey always hoped to find one day. Someone who loved her for every piece of her, who never judged her or questioned her, and who would do anything for her. Just like her dad did for her mom.

Valerie sobbed in Lacey's arms, everything finally breaking. Two days of planning a funeral she never should have been planning. Endless questions and zero answers. Pain and heartbreak and loss that neither of them ever expected to face.

The coffeepot beeped, letting them know it was done, and Valerie drew a deep breath. She squeezed her eyes tight, then let out her breath and removed herself from Lacey's arms. Valerie stood and went to fix her coffee as though her breakdown had never happened.

Lacey wasn't so quick to recover. She needed more time. She sat on the floor with Cocoa and let her tears fall, trying to remember the last time she saw her father. She was supposed to have dinner with him that week, a dinner they planned for after his last assignment.

A dinner they'd never have.

It had been longer than a week since she saw him, maybe

two. A quick visit, shorter than planned when he got called into work.

"Get up, Lacey. We can't sit around and feel sorry for ourselves. Your father wouldn't want that." Valerie carried her coffee to the table and glared at Lacey.

Lacey wanted to roll around on the floor and protest, but she was right. Her father always said there were people who had it worse than them, and that whenever she felt bad for herself, she should think about them. Take her frustration and do something with it.

Lacey knew just what she was going to do with her frustration. Just as soon as she could get away from her mother and confront the one man who could give her answers.

Butterflies took flight in her stomach at the thought of confronting Austin, but she ignored them. Austin Ward might be the sexiest man Lacey had ever laid her eyes on, but he was never going to be hers. Lacey had seen the women Austin went home with, and she didn't come close to any of them. Her crush was definitely one-sided.

But she had to talk to him. He would tell her what happened. He'd always been good to her. She just had to get him alone after the funeral, and he would tell her the truth.

He owed her that much.

THREE

Lacey was exhausted. All she'd done was stand around and talk to people, but she was worn out. The well-wishers never seemed to end. People her father had served with, saved, or affected all poured through the funeral home to say goodbye to him and to offer their condolences to Lacey and her mother. Many of them made their way to the church for the funeral. Choosing to do the wake and funeral together meant an extra long day, but it also meant when it was over, they could move on.

Hopefully without the heels Valerie insisted Lacey wear. They pinched her toes and made her feet ache. She shifted her weight side-to-side to try to get some relief, but it was useless. She tugged on her locket, focusing on the cold metal in her hand instead of the blistering pain from heels she wasn't used to as she walked down the aisle to the front of the church.

"Stop fidgeting," Valerie breathed as they moved into their row.

Lacey dropped her locket and stopped moving her feet. At least the dress her mother laid out for her was comfortable. It was solid black with a subtle lace detail just below her breasts, and the damn thing was flattering on her curvy figure without being indecent or too tight.

If only she'd been allowed to wear shoes that were equally comfortable.

Lacey looked around the church at the people finding seats. Her father's coworkers sat together a few rows back. Zeke held hands with his wife, Nina. Nina's friends filled a few rows behind Rose Protection Agency, including Dawn Patterson. The billionaire heiress told Lacey that Samuel had been there for her at a time when she needed help. He never shared details about his work, so the admission was a surprise to Lacey.

Behind Dawn and the others was another group of men who were definitely military. All of them were paired up with a woman, some of them with kids. The group also seemed to know Samuel, but Lacey wasn't familiar with any of them.

It amazed her how many people were there to honor her father.

And who wasn't there.

Lacey asked Zeke if Austin was coming, but Zeke didn't know. He said Austin had checked himself out of the hospital, so Lacey expected him to show up. That he hadn't was a painful barb. Lacey didn't expect Austin to listen to her mother and stay away. Not for the funeral.

Valerie elbowed Lacey. Lacey spun a look at her mother and earned one in return, along with a nod toward the front where the priest was starting the ceremony. His words were background noise for Lacey. Nothing anyone could say would bring her father back, and no words could make it better that he was gone.

Lacey followed along with the others as they went through the motions of the funeral service. When it was over, six of her father's coworkers stepped forward to carry his coffin outside to the waiting hearse.

Lacey and Valerie followed right behind the coffin, watching as it was loaded into the back of the vehicle. Montgomery and Walker offered their arms to Valerie and Lacey, guiding them to the waiting limousine.

Valerie didn't speak on the way to the burial site, staring out the window as they drove past all other traffic thanks to the police escorts arranged by someone.

The number of things Lacey didn't know or understand continued to pile up until she was ready to explode. Her mother's grief only added to that feeling. Valerie had barely spoken since she broke down in the kitchen the day before. She walked around the house like she was in a daze, going into a room only to stand there and look around before she'd leave without doing anything.

Her mother needed closure, and so did Lacey. After they buried her father, she would find a way to sneak off and confront Austin.

The limo stopped on the road next to rows of graves. Lacey followed her mother out of the limo and accepted the arm Walker offered her again. Her heels dug into the soft spring ground, compliments of an overnight shower. Walker was patient with her, not complaining when she lost her balance and sank into the dirt.

A tent was set up over the hole in the ground. Walker delivered Lacey to the front row of chairs next to the hole, then returned with Montgomery to the hearse for her father.

Tears streaked down Lacey's cheeks as her father came closer. The casket was closed, another mystery she wondered about. She never saw his face in death. She wasn't sure she wanted to, but she hated that she'd never see him again. That he was going to be lowered into the ground and everyone would move on with their lives.

The priest said a few words, then the men who served with her father paid their respects. The flag draping the casket was removed and folded into a triangle and presented to Valerie.

Valerie hugged the flag to her chest and sobbed.

Lacey swallowed roughly and put her arm around her mother, trying to be strong for her. Valerie cried as the casket was lowered into the ground.

The crowd of people slowly drifted away. Kirk and Stephanie Rice were handling the reception of people for the family and had returned to the house after the funeral. Lacey was going to stay as long as her mother wanted to, but she was ready to leave.

Valerie finally stood and looked for Montgomery. He was by her side in a moment, guiding her to the limousine again. Walker led Lacey, and when both women were secure, the limo took off with the two men behind them and a police car in front.

The house was a jumble of noise and people when they arrived. After the silence of her mother in the limo, the activity at the house was jarring. Lacey wanted to go upstairs and get away from all of them, but she knew her mother would be angry if she did. Lacey made her way through the house, accepting more condolences from close friends who'd come.

Someone stepped into Lacey's path, and she looked up to find her best friend, Maggie. Maggie wrapped Lacey into a hug, holding her tight without words. They met in their last year of college, when Lacey was finishing her English bachelor's degree and starting her Library Sciences graduate program. Maggie was another RA on the floor, and the two of them hit it off immediately, sharing a love of books and an affinity for old TV shows instead of bars and reality TV like most of their classmates.

"What can I do for you?" Maggie asked.

Lacey shook her head. "Nothing is going to help."

"It'll get easier. That's what all those people on the documentaries you like to watch would say."

Lacey smiled. "Yeah, yeah."

"When are you going home?"

Lacey shook her head. "I don't know. The library has been really good and said to take as long as I need. I think Stephanie and Kirk are going to stay with my mom for a few days. I'm ready to go home now."

Maggie laughed softly. "I know. You need time for yourself."

Lacey nodded, loving Maggie that much more for understanding what Lacey couldn't say.

An alarm went off in Maggie's bag, and she groaned.

"What is that?"

"I need to go nurse. Owen took the boys home after the funeral, but I wanted to see you. I'll be back." Maggie had a three-month-old and a two-year-old with her husband of five years. She'd checked in with Lacey every day since her father died.

"No, don't come back. Be with your family."

"I want to be here for you, Lace."

Lacey hugged Maggie tight. "I know you always are. But I also know you need time with your family."

"After I nurse, Carter will go to sleep, and it's nap time for Adam. I'll be back. I promise."

"I love you."

"I love you. I'll see you soon."

Lacey nodded and waved as Maggie wove through the crowd toward the front door. When Maggie disappeared, Lacey headed for the kitchen. She was about to step into the kitchen when she saw her mother crying on Stephanie Rice's shoulder.

Lacey quietly backed out, giving her mother a minute. Stephanie and Kirk were close family friends. Kirk worked at

Rose Protection Agency with Samuel, and the four of them had gotten to know each other well over the years. Lacey couldn't remember an event the Rices weren't there for. She knew Stephanie would take care of her mother, which gave Lacey a minute to herself.

She headed for the front door, trying to look like she wasn't making a run for it. She grabbed her handbag and stepped outside, sighing when she saw her car was blocked by three others in the driveway.

"Shit," she breathed.

"You okay?" Walked asked from right behind her.

Lacey spun on him, surprised she didn't hear the massive man come up behind her. "I was going to run out and get some ice."

Walker raised one eyebrow, clearly not believing her lie. His gaze drifted to the driveway. "You're blocked in."

"Yeah. Um, do you have a car I could borrow?"

"I'm not sure that's a good idea, Lacey."

"I just want to get ice."

"He's not in a good place."

"And you think I am."

"That's why I don't think you should go. Give him some time. He lost him, too."

"I'm not going to make it worse for him. He shouldn't be alone, Walker."

Walker sighed, the sound half-groan and half-agreement.

Lacey hoped the agreement half won out, but she knew if she pushed too hard, she'd lose any chance at getting out of there.

"He hasn't been returning anyone's calls."

"All the more reason for me to go see if he's okay."

Walker reached into his pocket and came out with a set of keys. He spun them around his finger and stared off.

"He's like family to me. He should have been here. I don't

want him blaming himself. My mom... He needs to know I don't blame him." Lacey wanted answers, but she also cared about Austin. If Walker knew that...

"Dammit." Walker sighed again, then held out his hand, keys flat on his palm. "Be back soon."

"I will. Thank you, Walker." Lacey grabbed the keys, then kissed the man on his cheek before hurrying down the front steps. She pressed the unlock button on the fob, finding the vehicle that beeped. She hurried to it and got in the driver's side before Walker could change his mind.

Lacey pulled away from the curb, ignoring her butterflies and steeling her spine. She would get answers. No matter what. Her mother deserved that. And so did she.

ALL AUSTIN WANTED WAS to drown his grief and guilt in peace. Shut out the outside world and pretend he was the one being put in the ground.

Austin closed his eyes and saw Valerie's face when she showed up in his hospital room. The pain and grief in her eyes. Austin knew Samuel was dead, but seeing it on his widow's face slammed the reality into his gut once more.

"What happened?" Valerie asked.

Not how are you? Not are you okay? Austin spent Christmas with the MacNeil's last year. Slept on their couch on Christmas Eve and woke up with the family the next morning. He was there for Samuel's birthdays and backyard picnics and every event they'd hosted for years.

But he wasn't family.

"I don't know," Austin said. It was the truth. They were making dinner, then they were under attack. They were heading

for the back door, to get to the panic room outside... The rest was blank. He knew there were pieces missing, but Austin couldn't remember them.

"You don't know, or you won't tell me?"

Austin had never heard that tone from Valerie. Samuel joked his wife could be a ball-buster, but she'd never turned it on Austin. She welcomed him into their home and told him he could stay as long as he wanted.

"I don't know, Valerie. I don't remember."

She swallowed harshly and moved closer. Her arms were crossed around her middle, protecting herself from him. She shook her head, a tear sliding down her cheek before she ruthlessly swiped it away. "I don't want to see you again."

"What? Valerie?"

"I told Samuel taking you on as a partner was the wrong move. That one day you would get him killed. He thought he could save you. Make you a better man. He was wrong."

Austin froze, unable to move or react. All those years, all that time, she thought so little of him.

"Stay away from me. And stay away from Lacey. I see the way you look at my daughter. She's too good for you. You're not going to get her killed the way you did my husband." Valerie turned to leave, then stopped when she got to the door. "And don't even think about coming to his funeral." Then she left, a sob echoing down the hallway.

A knock on his door brought Austin back to the present. He checked himself out of the hospital that morning. Against Medical Advice. Couldn't stand the smells and the sounds and the guilt that pressed down on him. His teammates would have forced him to stay, so he waited until the day of the funeral, until none of them were there to hold him down and force the issue. As soon as he was alone, he called for the doctor and got the hell out of there.

The person knocked again, and Austin ignored it again. Everyone he knew was at the funeral. The funeral he wasn't allowed to go to. Because he survived and Samuel didn't.

Austin played the day over and over again in his mind. He was joking with Samuel when all hell broke loose. If they'd been quiet, would they have heard whoever snuck up on them? If they'd been focused on the task, would it have changed the outcome?

Austin didn't know the answers to those questions anymore than he knew what happened after the first shot tore through his shoulder. Samuel was dead, and Austin only had his guilt and grief to keep him company.

The knocking started up again, insistent and unending this time, so Austin dragged himself to the door, intent on telling whoever the hell dared interrupt his peace to go to hell.

Before he could get the words out, she pushed her way inside, shouldering him out of the way and walking in like she belonged there.

Lacey MacNeil was a vision in her frumpy librarian clothes, with her reading glasses on and her hair in a bun. She tempted Austin on a level no other woman ever had. But Lacey MacNeil in a sleek black dress, red-rimmed eyes, and flowing brown hair was a fucking goddess. A goddess tainted by being in his presence.

"What the hell are you doing here?" Austin barked, hoping his tone and demeanor would put her off and send her running.

Sweet girls like Lacey didn't belong around men like him. He was rough and dirty. She was pretty and perfect. She deserved so much better than him.

"I need to know what happened that day," Lacey said, her voice tilting just enough to show her emotions.

Emotions Austin would use to get her the hell out of his house. "Go home, Princess."

Her dad called her *princess*, and the barb stuck. She sucked in a breath. Her brown eyes watered.

Austin was an asshole, and he knew it, but he couldn't risk putting her in danger. He'd already taken her dad away, and if anything happened to Lacey, Valerie wouldn't survive.

Neither would Austin.

"I'm not going home until you tell me what happened that day. How were you surprised? How did someone get the jump on you?"

Austin cocked an eyebrow. "The jump? You watch too much bad TV."

"Just tell me what happened," she cried, the tears falling freely.

They were far from her first of the day, Austin knew, but dammit if the sight of them didn't make him want to tear his own skin off. His fingers twitched with the need to soothe her, to hold her and console her, to tell her what she wanted to know.

But he couldn't. The black fucking hole in his memory stopped him from telling anyone what happened. Valerie, his bosses, the police, and now Lacey.

"I can't tell you," he said, knowing that was the party line. It didn't matter that he didn't remember. Even with full knowledge, he wouldn't have been able to tell her anything. She didn't have to know he couldn't remember. "It's time for you to go."

"I want to know what happened."

"It doesn't matter what you want, Princess. You're not supposed to be here. I'm sure if your mother came to me and said to stay away, she also told you I'm off-limits. Let's not make mommy mad. Go home like a good girl and forget you ever met me."

Austin crossed his arms and leaned back on the counter, wincing only on the inside so she didn't see his pain.

She glared at him, then sighed heavily. The tears continued down her cheeks, but she ignored them and let them fall.

She turned toward the door, done with him and done with her questions.

He would never see her again. He'd leave town, put it all behind him, and never see any of them again. It killed him to know it, but he had no other choice. He couldn't face his brothers, his team, and know he was there when one of them died and he didn't do every damn thing possible to prevent it.

She reached the door and stopped. Hand on the knob, she looked back at him. "You're a coward, Austin Ward."

Austin didn't argue with her. She was right. Pushing her away, running from his problems, hiding in his house. He was a coward.

She opened the door and stepped back just as a bullet whizzed past her face.

Austin heard the crash as it hit a lamp across the room.

"What the hell was that?" Lacey asked, leaning forward to look.

"Get down!" Austin shouted as another bullet tore through the door.

Lacey screamed, and Austin stopped breathing.

No. Not Lacey.

She moved toward him, thank God, and he grabbed her hand.

"We have to go. Now."

She nodded, determination and fear warring in her gaze.

Austin tugged her down the hallway, neither of them moving as fast as they needed to go. He pushed her into the bedroom just as footsteps sounded in the living room.

"Closet." Austin shoved her toward the closet. He pushed all the clothes to the side and revealed a hidden door at the back.

"What is this?" she asked. Her gaze bounced between him and the door they'd just come through.

Austin punched in the code and sighed when the door opened. "Panic room. Get in. Now. Before they kill us."

"Who is trying to kill us?"

"I don't know, but I'm guessing it's the people who killed your father."

FOUR

Austin leaned against the door to the panic room and looked at the terrified woman across from him. He built the panic room for himself, but there was no way in hell he was going to leave her outside. Even if the space was small for one and microscopic for two.

Lacey looked around the space, eyes wide with fear.

"Are you claustrophobic?" Austin asked.

Lacey didn't reply, just scanned the room. Her gaze jumped from one corner to another, across him, then over to the side.

Austin had to snap her out of it, bring her back to the present. He pushed away from the door, wincing when the pain in his shoulder sent a wave of nausea through him. He paused, slamming his eyes closed. Throwing up was bad enough, but to do so in an enclosed space would be horrible.

"Are you okay?" Lacey asked.

Austin sucked in one more breath through his nose and opened his eyes. "I'm fine. Are you claustrophobic?"

She shook her head. "You're not fine. Your shoulder…"

"I'll live."

Her gaze slid to the door behind Austin. "Will we?"

Austin nodded once. "Door's reinforced steel. The whole thing is. I never planned for anyone else to be in here with me, though. Sorry it's not more comfortable."

"Can they get in?"

"No. The whole place is secure. There's no way in here without the passcode, and when someone is inside, it's automatically locked for four hours unless it's unlocked from in here."

"We're stuck in here for four hours?"

"Are you claustrophobic?" Austin asked, realizing she might not have been answering him earlier when she shook her head.

"No, but..."

"You're not supposed to be here." Austin sighed and hung his head, the reminder of the day washing over him in a flush of cold. For a minute, he'd forgotten what day it was. And that he was MacNeil family enemy number one.

Lacey met his gaze and nodded once. Almost like an apology. Like she knew her mother's order was bullshit, but she went along with it, sort of.

"What's your biggest fear?" Austin asked, desperate to change the subject.

"Well, being shot is pretty much on top of that list right now."

"Hoplophobia. Understandable. Although I'd say maybe not irrational at this moment."

"How do you know that word?"

Austin tilted his head to look at her. "Hoplophobia? It's hard to be in the military and do our jobs without understanding some people are terrified of us, and of what we do. That people have a fear of guns, even if they've never held one or had one pointed at them or anything. Whether that fear is irrational or not is not up to me to decide. It only makes sense to understand how they're feeling."

"Yeah, but you know that word. And you know what it means. That's not normal."

"Who are we to say what normal is? Maybe it should be normal that people learn about things. I would think you'd appreciate that."

"I do, but I'm not used to it."

"You probably assume I have bibliophobia, don't you?"

She snorted, then clapped a hand over her mouth.

It was freaking adorable.

"Sorry."

Austin smirked. "Nothing to be sorry about. Unless you were agreeing with me." He raised one eyebrow in question.

"Not agreeing with you. I know you don't have a fear of books. Dad tells me about how much you read." Her face fell. "Told me." Her hand went to the chain around her neck, her thumb sliding over the back of a locket.

"Is that a book?" Austin asked.

Lacey smiled and looked down, lifting the necklace up to show him. "It was from my dad. It was my grandmother's, the woman I was named for. She loved books, too."

"What's inside?"

Lacey shrugged. "I don't know."

"It's not a locket?"

"It is, but I don't have a key."

"Your dad didn't give it to you?"

Lacey shook her head. "How's your shoulder?"

Austin tried to shrug off the pain and grunted with the movement.

"You're hurt. Let me look at it."

She moved across the already tiny room and stood next to him. He was taller than her by at least five inches, which put his shoulder right at her eye-level. He wanted to fight her, but she gently lifted his arm to remove the sling he wore.

And he let her.

Austin closed his eyes for just a second, allowing her to care for him.

She sucked in a breath, and he tried to pull back, but a hand on his stomach had him freezing in place.

"Sorry," she whispered, removing her hand.

He nearly cried at the loss. She never touched him. Ever. When he first started hanging around their family, she would hug him when he'd come over, but in the last few years, she hadn't touched him.

He missed it.

But he wasn't allowed to miss it, so he stuffed the loss down like he did with all the other losses.

"It looks like you might have pulled a stitch." Her voice was soft, just like her touch. She stepped closer, and her breasts rubbed against his arm. "I think you need to get to a doctor."

"Not really an option right now."

She looked around as though she'd forgotten where they were for a minute, then took a step away from him.

He wanted to grab her and haul her back in against him.

"I... sorry. What... How long...? I can try to do something. Do you have a first aid kit? Maybe I can bandage it better?"

"It's okay," Austin said, tugging his shirt up over his shoulder again. "I'll be fine until we get out of here."

Lacey moved as far away from him as she could get and looked around the room. She lifted one foot and rolled her ankles, then did the same with the other. She smoothed her hands down her skirt.

He upset her. He was rude and gruff and hurt her feelings. She'd been through enough, and instead of offering her comfort, he was pushing her away.

"If you're willing to look at it, there's a first aid kit in the cabinet over there." He pointed to the metal utility cabinet in the corner of the room. When he was outfitting the space, he didn't bother with furniture or anything that would be comfortable long term. He focused only on what was absolutely necessary. A first aid kit was at the top of the list. The kind paramedics carried.

"Whoa," she said when she opened the cabinet and saw the bag. The red bag with the white plus on it was a giveaway that she was grabbing the right thing. She set it on top of a storage bin and opened the top.

"There should be some butterfly bandages in there. Those should work until I can get somewhere to have the stitches redone. Unless you want to give it a try?"

Her wide brown eyes said hell no, but he waited for her to shake her head.

"Are you hemophobic?"

She shook her head. "No. I'm not a huge fan of blood, but I don't have a fear of it. I'm not sure I have the stomach to sew up a person, though. Especially with you being able to feel it."

"The butterflies should work for now."

Lacey nodded. She dug in the bag for the bandages, then approached him slowly.

Austin worked his arm free of his shirt again, trying not to wince at the pain. He glanced at the wound, knowing he should have covered it that morning. The doctor said it didn't have to be all the time but recommended a bandage to keep from anything rubbing until the stitches healed.

Yet again, Austin fucked up.

"Oh. I don't have gloves or anything. Is there hand sanitizer in the bag?" She went back to look, but Austin stopped her.

"I don't think anything is in there. Just do it, Lacey."

She looked over at him, holding his gaze for a long

moment, then closed her eyes and nodded once before she came back to his side.

LACEY DID NOT WANT to touch him again. No, that was a lie. All she wanted to do was touch him again. But it was a very bad idea. A very, very bad idea.

Because touching his warm skin was like touching a live wire. Hot and exciting and dangerous.

Austin Ward was not just off-limits. He was so far out of her league they weren't playing the same game. She was the book nerd with the big ass, and he was the military bad boy with a line of women waiting for him to look their way. Lacey was fooling herself if she thought, even for a second, that Austin might think of her as anything more than Samuel's daughter.

Lacey swallowed the pain of the truth and wiped his skin clean with an alcohol wipe. Blood had smeared around his stitches and caked into the strands. She wasn't sure how much she should clean up, but she was fairly sure where she needed to put the bandages had to be free of blood before they would stick.

She opened the first bandage and held up the tiny thing. It didn't look like it would do much, but she'd been through first aid training at the library and knew they were sturdy. As long as they were applied correctly.

Which meant on clean, dry skin.

Lacey pursed her lips and blew gently on his skin, trying to dry the moisture left behind by the alcohol wipe.

Austin jerked. "What are you doing?" His voice was rough, like he was in pain.

"I'm sorry. I was trying to make sure it was dry. Blood is

seeping out, and I worried if I didn't get the bandage on, I'd have to start over."

Austin closed his eyes and drew another deep breath. "Fine."

The grunted word was all she got, so she blew on his skin once more, then stuck the bandage to one side of his incision, then pulled it tight to the other side, dragging the skin together in the middle.

Lacey waited a minute to see if it would hold and if she would need to add a second one. When it appeared to be good, she stepped back. "I think you're set. Maybe I should put a bandage over the whole thing."

"Yeah. That would be good. If you don't mind."

"Of course I don't mind, Austin."

He grunted. Great. Another alpha male who was more into grunts than words.

Except Austin was different. He was obviously smart and well-read. He was more than muscles, even though his muscles were nice.

Lacey usually went out with men who were more like her. Men who spent more time reading about gyms than actually in them. Who liked books and considered themselves intellectuals. Who were boring as all hell and never lit even a spark inside her.

But they were the ones who gave her the time of day. Men like Austin could set her ablaze with one look, but they never laid hands on her. Or wanted to.

So she dated men who wanted to and dealt with the disappointing side-effects. Like mediocre sex and zero orgasms delivered by another person. Ever. In her entire life.

Disappointing wasn't even the half of it.

Lacey carefully smoothed the gauze pad over his wound, securing it with the medical tape in the massive first aid kit.

"Thank you," Austin whispered when she stepped away.

"You're welcome." Lacey packed the first aid kit how it was and returned it to its place in the cabinet. She noticed there was nowhere to sleep and nowhere to sit, but there was a well-stocked cabinet with medical supplies and shelf-stable food. She hoped that meant Austin planned to get out of there soon. She closed the door and leaned against it, as far away from Austin as she could get. "Why is someone after me?"

Austin paused for a second, then shook his head. "I don't know. And I don't know that they're definitely after you."

"What do you mean? They tried to shoot me!" Her voice was a high screech that echoed off the enclosed space. She drew a shaky breath and held it, not feeling the calm it was supposed to give her.

"You were at my house. They could be after either of us."

"Who are they? Who killed my father? It's time you tell me what's going on."

Austin shook his head again. His eyes closed, or maybe turned to the floor. "The woman we were protecting was a witness. She was supposed to testify the day after..."

"So whoever she was testifying against killed her and my father? Who was it?"

"I can't tell you that, Lacey. The less you know—"

"The better. Yeah, I've heard that line my whole damn life, and look where it got me." She threw her hands up, indicating the panic room they were trapped in. "Someone tried to kill me, or you, or whatever. Someone shot at me, Austin. This isn't curiosity. You have to tell me what happened."

"I don't know!"

Lacey stopped cold. His shouted confession was the only truth he'd shared with her so far. She knew it in her soul. He really didn't know. "You really don't remember?"

He shook his head. "They think I blacked out when I was shot. I don't remember anything after that."

"My father..." She swallowed roughly past the pain welling in her throat. "My father wasn't with you?"

Austin closed his eyes. The pain on his face matched the pain inside Lacey. He was just as lost as she was. "Montgomery told me your father and the witness were outside. Likely trying to get to the panic shelter in the backyard of the house. I was inside, near the back door. After I was shot, your dad must have taken her outside. She was wounded, I know that, and he probably couldn't carry both of us. They were... they were outside, both dead. Montgomery thinks the shooters didn't know I was there, or didn't care, but maybe that's why they're here. Maybe they wanted to finish what they started and leave no witnesses."

"Oh my God. They're not going to leave until we're dead. They're still out there, aren't they? We can't leave. How are we going to get out of here? We can't stay in here forever! We'll suffocate. We'll die of starvation. My mother's going to kill me. Why did I come here?"

"It'll be okay, Lacey. The team will clear the house and let us out."

"What are you talking about?"

"When the panic room door closes, it sends a signal to my team. It's on our security system. I have cameras throughout the house, and Montgomery has access to all of them. They'll make sure it's safe before we walk out of here."

"Why didn't you tell me that before?" She glared at him for withholding information. She was panicking, and he was relaxed and chill because he knew someone knew where they were. How could he hide that from her?

"I thought they'd be here by now and would have let us out."

"Can you see the cameras? From in here?"

He nodded.

"Let me see."

Austin reached into his pocket with his uninjured arm. He unlocked his phone and tapped the screen a few times before he turned it to her.

"No one's there."

Austin nodded. "I know. But if someone is waiting for us to come out, they're going to hide."

Lacey shivered. "You think they're still out there?"

Austin shook his head. "I suspect they're too smart for that, but I'm not going to risk your life on my guesses."

"But you'd risk your life?"

"My life isn't nearly as valuable as yours is, Lacey."

"You're the one who saves people."

"Not this week." Austin took the phone from her and locked it, shoving it back in his pocket ruthlessly. He leaned against the door and sank to the floor.

Lacey toyed with her locket again and stared at the man she'd always admired. Austin was strong, confident, and intelligent. He was someone she thought of with a mix of jealousy and desire. She knew his past wasn't great, not that she knew details, but he had everything going for him that someone like her wanted. All he had to do was give a woman a look, and he had someone to share his bed. Someone to want him. Hell, he didn't even have to give a woman a look for her to want him.

Ask her how she knew.

"It sounds like it wasn't your fault."

"He's dead, Lace. He's not coming back. Someone's to blame, and I'm the only one left." His words were a punch to her gut, a slice through her heart.

Lacey rubbed her thumb along the smooth metal of her locket and remembered her dad. His smile, his encouragement. He always made her feel like she could do anything. He told her to never give up on what she wanted, no matter how impossible it seemed.

But he was gone.

Austin's phone trilled with an alarm that sent all her nerves back to high alert. He dug the phone out and stared at it. "Time to go, Princess. The cavalry is here."

FIVE

AUSTIN COULDN'T WAIT TO GET THE HELL OUT OF his panic room. When he built it, he hoped he'd never need it, but his past proved to him it was better to be prepared than caught off-guard.

He definitely never expected to need to share it with Lacey MacNeil.

Austin watched the live feed as his teammates cleared his house, going through the rooms one-by-one until they made it to his bedroom. Montgomery held up one finger, then spun it in the air on the camera, letting Austin know it was all clear to go.

Austin unlocked the room and stepped back so Lacey could walk out first.

"Lacey?" Montgomery said, his voice suspicious and shocked.

"I have to get out of here," Lacey breathed, attempting to push past Montgomery as Austin walked out of the closet.

"Whoa, you can't leave." Montgomery stopped her with a hand on her shoulder.

Lacey shrugged him off and tossed a glare from Austin to Montgomery. "I never should have come here."

The hit stung, and Lacey knew it. Her chin dropped, tugging her gaze from Austin's, and he wondered what she saw on his face that gave his pain away.

"My mother is going to kill me," Lacey whispered.

"First, we need to know what happened," Montgomery said. "We need to make sure you're safe before we let you go. How did you even get here?"

Lacey's gaze slid past Montgomery, but Austin didn't know who she was looking at until Walker stepped forward.

"I gave her my keys. Said she needed to talk to Austin. Didn't realize it was going to bring all this." Walker was someone Austin would trust with anything, especially his life, but Austin didn't know Walker well. He was quiet, kept to himself, and never seemed to do anything besides work. Good teammate, shitty friend.

"You did what?" Montgomery barked, clearly not aware of the situation. "Fuck. We need to let Valerie know she's here."

"She already knows," Walker said. "I told her when we got the alert. Kirk and Stephanie stayed with her."

"This is... We need to know what the hell happened. Now." Montgomery crossed his arms and glared at Austin.

Austin's defenses rose without warning, immediately wanting to tell his boss to fuck off because he didn't do anything wrong. Austin was trying to get her to leave. He didn't ask her to come over. He didn't tell her anything. Why the fuck did Montgomery think the whole shitshow was Austin's fault?

"I wanted answers," Lacey said before Austin could defend himself. "No one has told us anything. My mom is... She's broken. She needs to know what happened, what went wrong. So, I came here to find out because Austin was there when my dad died."

"And what did he tell you?" Montgomery asked, the threat in his tone directed at Austin, not Lacey.

"He said he doesn't remember anything. He told me he blacked out."

Montgomery's gaze was locked on Austin, cataloguing every movement Austin made.

It didn't matter that she was telling the truth, Montgomery didn't like it. He wanted everything about that day kept quiet. He wanted them all to say nothing.

It was protocol to keep their assignments confidential, but it felt like more. Austin didn't know what else was going on, but he didn't usually fight his boss.

"Then what happened?" Montgomery asked.

"I told her to leave," Austin said. "Valerie didn't want me at the funeral, or around."

The collective gasps in the room said no one was aware of that piece of information.

"That's why you weren't there?" Zeke asked.

Austin hadn't even noticed him, but he focused on Zeke. Montgomery could be cold and calculating, but Zeke had softened since his wife, who was also Montgomery's sister, came back into their lives. Nina was missing for twelve years, believed to be dead, but escaped her captor and called Zeke. Zeke had been in love with Nina forever, and didn't waste any time before he married her. Since Nina returned, Zeke had changed. Austin hadn't appreciated it before, but staring at a room full of his teammates, all of whom probably felt the same as Valerie, Austin was grateful to have someone on his side.

"Yeah. I wanted to respect her wishes and figured she wasn't the only one who felt that way. It's why I'll be leaving soon." Austin met his boss's gaze as he delivered that news, and was surprised when Montgomery swore.

"The fuck you will. What happened to Samuel is not on

you. It's on the son-of-a-bitch who killed him." Montgomery slid a glare to all in the room.

Austin swallowed roughly, the guilt of his inability to have his partner's six not gone but knowing not everyone blamed him was a tiny bit of relief.

"Okay, that doesn't finish the story. You told her to leave, then what?" Zeke asked.

"She opened the door, and a shot came through. Then another. We didn't stick around to see who was shooting at us."

"Us?" Montgomery said. "You don't know who they were targeting?"

Austin shook his head. "My house, but shots were closer to her."

"So, whoever it was could have shot first and worried about questions later, or they could have been going for her." Walker looked between Lacey and Austin.

Lacey shook as they all spoke. She'd wrapped her arms around herself, as if she could protect herself from the conversation and the truth about the day.

Austin wanted to hold her, to wrap her in his arms and hold her until all her pain was gone. But having her in his house was bad enough. She was off-limits. Samuel's one and only kid. Lacey was her father's world, and Austin wasn't good enough for her. Nowhere even close.

"We need answers before we can walk away from this," Montgomery said. "And you two need protection."

"Fuck that. I don't need protection," Austin spat.

Montgomery glared at the bandage on Austin's arm and the sling draped around his neck. He lifted his left arm. "Arm wrestle?"

"Fuck you." It didn't matter that Montgomery was right, Austin didn't like it. He wasn't an invalid.

"Let's get everyone out of here, and we'll figure everything out. Marcus will be here soon, quietly. He's bringing a small team he can trust to keep this under the radar." Montgomery gestured for everyone to move toward the living room.

Austin took stock of his house as they moved through. Holes were knocked into walls, decor smashed. His furniture was sliced or shot. The assholes who tried to kill them wanted to make sure he knew they'd been there, as if he would forget.

"Oh my God," Lacey whispered. Tears filled her eyes as she looked around the room.

Austin never held on to things. Nothing had ever been precious to him. His favorite toy as a kid? Smashed when his dad was mad one night. His bedroom door when he was a teenager? Kicked in when his dad was drunk. Things were just things, but they were safe. That was what Austin cared about. Lacey didn't get hurt.

"You two were lucky you got in there when you did," Walker said.

"Austin..." Lacey's gaze lifted to his. "Austin saved me."

Austin couldn't handle the hero appreciation look she gave him and smirked. "Self-preservation."

He should have been happy with the scowl that replaced her awed look, but all it did was make him feel like an asshole.

It was for the best, though. That was who he needed to be for her. The asshole who let her father get killed. The asshole she needed to stay far away from.

LACEY WAS NOT GOING to cry. She was not. Austin didn't owe her anything. He wasn't her friend, or her anything. He was her dad's coworker. All the feelings she caught for him over the years were one-sided.

She always knew it, but seeing the callous look on his face

and hearing the words he snarled was a reminder that he was only ever nice to her because of her dad. It was never because of her.

Lacey swallowed the tension in her throat and tried to let out a breath. She had to choke back all the things she was feeling. The fear and anger and pain. She could let it all out when she was alone.

"Can I go now?" Lacey asked, directing her question to Montgomery since he was the one in charge.

Montgomery shook his head. "When the police get here, you're going to need to tell them what happened. Then we need to figure out what we're going to do."

Lacey didn't like that answer. Not that she liked the idea of leaving and having to face her mother, either. Maybe she could sneak back into the panic room and live there for a while.

A noise at the door drew everyone's attention and a few guns from the men of Rose Protection Agency before Captain Marcus Patrick called out.

The guns went away, and Montgomery replied. "All good, Marcus."

Marcus stepped inside, followed by two police officers. The three men looked around the house, then settled their gazes on Montgomery, carefully avoiding Lacey. "What happened?"

The simple question set off the next two hours. Lacey and Austin were separated and interrogated by both officers and Captain Patrick. Security footage was apparently reviewed, but nothing was shared with Lacey. She sat on the cushion that wasn't destroyed and waited until she either saw an opening to leave or was told she could go, whichever came first.

She was not happy when neither happened, and the men in the room decided she needed to be in protective custody.

"I don't need that," Lacey argued.

"Your mother just lost your father," Walker said. "Please don't risk her losing you, too."

Dammit, the man knew what to say. Lacey glared at him, but he was right. "Fine."

The next thirty minutes were another flurry of activity where decisions were made without Lacey's input at all. She and Austin were surrounded by others and led to an SUV waiting outside, then driven away.

Lacey wanted to ask where they were going, if she could see her mother or get some clothes from home to change into, or anything, but she kept quiet on the short drive. When they pulled into the garage of a small house, Walker got out without a word and opened her door.

"We'll stay here until we can figure out something more permanent."

Lacey nodded, knowing it didn't matter what she said. The decision was made. She was a prisoner, even if she was being held by the good guys.

She followed Walker and Austin into the house, kicking off her heels as soon as she was inside.

Walker noticed the move and winced. "We'll get you some clothes. I'm not sure what's here."

"It's fine." Lacey went to the couch and curled up on one end, tucking her feet under her. She ached for a book and a bath and some time to herself. After living with her mother for days, doing everything she could to help plan her father's funeral, Lacey hoped to be home that night or the next.

But she just had to go to Austin's.

"Do you want to call your mom?" Walker asked her once he and Austin went through the house and confirmed everything was secure.

"I probably should," Lacey said, even though she didn't

really want to. She wasn't ready for the lecture or the yelling or the pain of knowing she hurt her mother. Again.

Walker tapped the screen on his phone and put it to his ear. After a second, he said, "I have Lacey. Can you get Valerie?"

Another few seconds went by and Walker nodded, then handed the phone to Lacey.

"Mom?"

"Are you okay?" Her mother's icy tone wasn't a surprise, but it hurt.

"I'm fine."

"What were you doing with him?"

Lacey's gaze went to Austin. No matter what he thought of her, or didn't think of her, he saved her. He made sure she was alive. He could have left her to the gunmen, but he got her into the panic room. "I wanted to know what happened to Dad."

"I told you to stay away from him, Lacey. He's no good. He's only going to get you hurt, or killed. I think today proved that."

"He saved me, Mom."

She snorted. "After he almost got you killed."

"Mom..."

"Are you coming home?"

So no one told her what was going on. Not in detail. "I can't, Mom. Montgomery said they need to figure out what's going on first."

"I'm sick of this company running our lives. They put your father in danger, paired him with a man who couldn't do anything when it really mattered, and—" Her sob broke into her rant.

Lacey waited. She couldn't argue. Not really. She knew her father was helping people. She knew what Rose Protection Agency did mattered. They were out there doing what others couldn't, or wouldn't. She was proud of her father, and of the men he worked with.

"Lace?" Kirk's voice said.

"Yeah. Hey."

"Hi, hun. Your mom's... Well, you know. We're going to stay with her, make sure she's okay. Are you safe?"

"I'm with Walker and Austin."

"Okay, good. Let me talk to Walker again, hun."

"Okay." Lacey handed the phone over to Walker without an explanation.

He took the phone and said hello.

Lacey hugged herself tight. She hadn't had a chance to grieve the way she needed to. How did one grieve? She'd never lost the most important person in her life before. She spent her days trying to keep her mother together and her nights collapsing with exhaustion.

And now fear.

Lacey swallowed past the fear and knew the tears were coming. She'd been able to fight them off so far, but she was losing the battle.

She scrambled off the couch and raced down the short hall. There had to be a bathroom somewhere. A place where she could be alone.

She closed the bathroom door behind her and turned on the water. She tried to stifle her tears, hoping Walker and Austin didn't hear her over the rush of the faucet, but she couldn't hold it all back anymore.

Lacey sank to the floor in front of the shower and let the tears come. She let the anguish fill her and ruminate. She let it all in, or out. She didn't care. She went to Austin for answers, and instead of bringing her mother peace, she brought her more pain.

A sob escaped, and another one was right behind it. Lacey let them come, crying harder with each sob. She cried so hard she didn't know anyone was in the bathroom with her until Austin pulled her into his arms.

"No," she said, shoving him away. "Don't do me any favors."

He didn't reply, just yanked her into his arms and held her. He held her without a word, without telling her to be quiet or offering any empty platitudes. He stroked his hand down her back and held her.

And Lacey let him. She realized how exhausted she was from fighting her feelings. She let her grief out, let it consume her. She cried and screamed and let it all out.

Austin's presence brought her a comfort she hadn't felt in days, since Zeke walked into the library. With that comfort came relief, and she let her exhaustion drag her under.

"WANT ME TO GET HER?" Walker asked from the door.

Austin shook his head. "I'm good."

"Your shoulder—"

"I'm good," Austin growled.

Walker didn't say anything, just walked away.

Austin pressed his nose to her hair and inhaled. He memorized the scent of her hair, her skin. He memorized the feel of her weight on his lap. He memorized the sound of her sleeping, her soft snores wrapping around his heart and squeezing tight.

He wondered when she was going to break. He knew it would happen. He hated it as much as he was thrilled to be there for it. For a chance to hold her and let her trust him to take care of her.

Unlike he did for her father.

Austin would never be able to make up for what

happened to Samuel. He hated himself for it, and he deserved all the things Valerie said. As soon as he could, he'd find another job and get the hell out of town. But until then, he'd make sure nothing else happened to the MacNeil family. Especially to Lacey.

SIX

Lacey came awake slowly, one sound waking her at a time. A cabinet door closed. Footsteps sounded somewhere far away. Her stomach rumbled. Breath rushed past her cheek.

That last one had her freezing. She kept her eyes closed and tried to remember when she fell asleep. Where.

There was a weight on her, an arm over her side. A hand holding her stomach. Legs pressed against hers from behind. And a thick erection nestled against her ass.

Was she kidnapped? What the... Austin. The safe house. Her father's funeral.

The crash of despair sent a shiver through her, and the arm around her stiffened. The hips pressed to hers eased back, putting a space between her body and his erection. The fact that she missed it was irrelevant.

The hand over her side shifted slightly, loosening the grip on her until it slid off her altogether. Lacey did everything she could to remain still. To hide the fact that she was awake and cataloging his every move as he got the hell away from her as quickly as possible without risking waking her up.

The bed shifted with his weight, the movement turning her enough that she couldn't hide that she was awake. She startled, pretending that was what woke her.

"Shit, sorry. I didn't mean to wake you up," Austin said, his voice gravely, scraping over all her exposed nerves. He adjusted himself, attempting to hide the erection that had been against her body moments ago.

"It's fine. I..." Lacey stopped. What was there to say?

Austin sat on the bed at her feet. "Are you okay?"

She snorted before she could stop herself.

"Right. Stupid question. You woke up with a strange man wrapped around you and never gave me permission to be here. I apologize. It won't happen again." He bolted to his feet, taking a measured step away from her.

"You're hardly a stranger, Austin. And I'm assuming I fell asleep on you." Lacey looked around the darkened room and tried to guess what time it was. "How long was I out?"

Austin shook his head. "I don't have my phone. I don't know."

"How did I get in here?"

He ran a hand through his hair, his uninjured arm. "I, um, I carried you."

"Your shoulder," Lacey gasped, climbing out of the bed and approaching him before she could think about what she was doing.

He took a step back before she touched him.

Lacey's hands fell, her step freezing. He didn't want her touching him. He was only in the bed with her because she crashed on him and he was being a good man. His erection was a biological reaction. It didn't mean he was interested, and she needed to remember that.

"I'm fine."

Lacey swallowed roughly and nodded, fighting the tightness in her throat. She was the only one in the room struggling with emotions and attraction. Austin was being a good man, not trying to cop a feel. The second he realized how close he was, he moved. She could not forget that.

"I'm going to see what Walker's doing," Austin said, turning to leave the room. Light from the rest of the house spilled in when Austin opened the door, then it was dark again.

Lacey sank to the bed and dropped her head into her hands. Her locket swung free, and she grabbed it. "Why, Dad? Why did you put him here with me?"

Tears trickled down her cheeks, the feeling of being alone more potent than before. Her dad was her hero, and if he were alive, he would have been the one guarding her. He always did. But he was taken from her.

Lacey gave herself another minute to be upset, then shook off the pain. It was going to be with her for the rest of her life. Getting it all out now wasn't possible. She needed to learn how to function, and she needed food if the insistent rumble of her stomach had a say.

After a quick trip to the bathroom, Lacey went to the living room of the small house. It was cozy, in a weird way. It had to be the soft sounds of male voices in the kitchen and the aroma of dinner tantalizing her. It definitely wasn't the bed she shared with Austin.

Walker saw her first and smiled kindly at her. "Feeling better?"

Lacey shrugged. "I guess."

Walker nodded, his gaze holding more understanding than she expected. He was a mystery to her, a man she knew as her father's coworker, but a man she didn't really know. Samuel never said anything bad about any of his teammates, but he had higher praise for some. Walker was never one Samuel shared much about, which made Lacey wonder what Walker understood about her pain.

A question for another time, maybe.

"I made dinner, if you're hungry."

Lacey nodded, her nose drawing her closer to the kitchen. She spared a brief glance at Austin, who was pressed to the wall and giving her plenty of space, then approached Walker.

"I know you like a lot of different food. There was some beef in the freezer, and beef usually sucks after it's frozen unless you know how to handle it. It's just a basic stew with a few extra surprises."

"Surprises?" Lacey asked, her stomach agreeing before her mind. She was hungry, and the scents coming from the pot on the stove were only making the hunger pains more intense.

"Mushrooms. Lots of them."

"I love mushrooms," Lacey groaned.

"I know," Walker said with a smile.

Lacey looked up at him, wondering how the man knew so much about her, then realized it had to have been her father. Lacey might not have known Walker well, but he knew her. He knew what she liked, what was her favorite, and he made dinner she would like. "Are you a fan of mushrooms?"

"Oh, yeah. What's not to like?"

"They're fungus," Austin said from the other side of the room. A full body shiver wracked him when Lacey looked back.

A laugh burst from her at the look of horror on Austin's face.

Walker joined her in laughing at Austin.

Austin scowled, but a hint of a smile betrayed his annoyance. "Mushrooms are gross."

"More for us," Walker said, turning to Lacey and offering her a spoon.

She took the spoon and clinked it to his in a cheers. "Yep."

Walker grabbed two bowls and filled them both to the top. He handed one bowl to Lacey and led the way to the table.

She followed him, sinking to the seat and realizing how heavy she felt. The weight of the last few days was getting to her. A good meal, one she didn't have to think about, was a blessing she hadn't known she needed.

Austin made a sandwich for himself and joined them at the table. The three of them ate without talking, the food soothing a piece of Lacey in need of comfort.

When they were finished eating, Walker encouraged her to sit down while he cleaned the kitchen. Lacey tried to argue, but he insisted.

"Do you want to take a shower or anything? Go to bed? You don't have to stay up with us."

Lacey nibbled her lip and considered what to do. "Is it possible for me to make a call?"

"Who are you calling?" Austin barked.

"We try to keep calls to a minimum. Especially since we don't know who is after you two or how they found you." Walker's response was more measured.

"But that doesn't mean I can't make a call?"

"Will you let me check your phone for any spyware before you use it?" Walker asked.

Lacey nodded. She went to her handbag and retrieved her phone.

Walker plugged it into a computer Lacey hadn't noticed before and clicked a few buttons. He stared at the screen while she stood behind him and waited. She didn't have anything to hide, but she didn't love the idea of anyone reading the texts she exchanged with her bestie.

Lacey didn't know if Maggie had made it back to the house earlier. With the kids, the time they had together was infrequent but no less important to either of them. Lacey was looking forward to more time to Maggie... but then she went to find Austin.

"Your phone's good." Walker handed it back to her. "Can

I ask who you're calling? I think Kirk has your mother's phone so she can sleep."

Lacey shook her head. "I wasn't going to call her."

"Who are you calling?" Austin asked.

Lacey met his gaze, frustrated that he wanted to know. "My friend. Is that allowed?"

"Friend or boyfriend?" Austin asked.

Lacey glared at him and walked away. She didn't want to tell him she hadn't ever had a real boyfriend. The lonely, chubby girl who was more interested in books than boys grew up to be the lonely, chubby woman who felt like she missed out on a lot but still couldn't bring herself to approach the pretty people.

Someone like Austin wouldn't understand. Her dad said Austin was never lacking company. He could have any woman he wanted. He couldn't comprehend what it was like for someone like her. Someone without an abundance of confidence.

Lacey closed the door to the bedroom and sank onto the mattress. She tapped Maggie's name and lifted the phone to her ear.

"Lacey! What the heck happened to you? Are you okay?" Maggie asked.

"Yeah, I'm fine. I guess. I think. I don't know."

"Whoa. What's going on? I was joking. I figured you couldn't handle anymore of your mother's attitude and skipped out while I was gone."

"No," Lacey admitted. "Although the idea has appeal."

"Are you home? Do you need me to rescue you? Owen can stay with the kids. I have two hours before I need to feed the baby again."

"I'm not home," Lacey said. "I'm in a safe house."

"You're what?" Maggie's voice dropped, and the sound on the other end said she dropped with it. "Are you okay?"

"I don't know. I... This is all so messed up."

"Start at the beginning. Where did you go after I left?"

Lacey told Maggie everything, from taking Walker's vehicle to Austin's to someone shooting at them and getting to the panic room to Montgomery refusing to let her go anywhere without protection. And forcing Austin into the same situation.

"So you're there with him right now?" Maggie asked, her tone more cheerful than the news warranted.

"Yeah. He's in the other room."

"How many beds are there? Tell me there's only one."

"I've only seen one. Why?"

"Come on, Lace! One bed? Trapped together? He's protecting you. Use your imagination."

Lacey's cheeks warmed at the memory of how she woke up. Her lack of comment tipped Maggie off that something happened.

"You did it already! Hell, yes. Good for you. I'm so proud."

"I didn't do anything!" Lacey protested loudly. She realized how loud she was and whispered, "Nothing happened."

"Then why did you get quiet?"

"I... Nothing happened. But I kind of lost it and was crying. Austin came in and held me."

"Aw. That's sweet. But I'm talking about the naked kind of something. You have a man you've been lusting after for years at your beck and call. Take advantage of that, Lacey!"

"He's not at my beck and call. He's only here because he got shot and had surgery and they don't want him alone. He tried. He has no interest in being around me any longer than absolutely required."

"I've seen how that man looks at you when you're not paying attention. I don't think he's as resistant to your charms as you think he is."

Lacey snorted. "First, I have no charms. Second, you've been drunk on pregnancy hormones and love hormones and forgot what a man looks like when he's trying to be polite. Austin has zero interest in me."

"I might be drunk on all the love in my life, but you're the one who doesn't know how a man looks at a woman he's going to fantasize about when he's heading to the spank bank."

"Maggie!" Lacey cried with a laugh. She put her hand over her mouth, holding the laughter in.

"Oh, please, you probably have a vibrator named after him. I would, if I were you."

Lacey's cheeks heated. Maggie wasn't wrong, but Lacey had never admitted that to her.

"Oh. My. God. You do! Ha! I love it. Okay, so yeah, you really need to jump the man. Just sneak into the bed when he's sleeping and tell him you'll do all the work so he doesn't hurt his shoulder."

Lacey laughed. "You're horrible."

"You are just scared, my friend. Sometimes you have to take the initiative with men. They can be pretty clueless. You know I had to ask Owen out three times before he agreed, and then he got me lost on my way there. If I didn't know there was something worthy of my effort, we never would have had this family we have. You deserve the same thing."

"I don't know, Mags. I just…" Lacey toyed with her locket, thinking about her dad. She'd just lost the man she thought would always be there for her. Was she really ready to have her heart broken again?

"Nope. Don't go there. I know your dad was your favorite person, and I know losing him is beyond comprehension. For me, too. He was amazing. There will never be another man like him. But he always wanted you to find someone. He said when you least expect it, the one you're meant to be with will come along and will be there for you in a way you never knew someone to be there for you."

Lacey wiped the tears from her cheeks and sniffed. "Yeah, but if there was ever a time I needed someone, it's now, and where is he? Where is this mystery man my dad thinks is going to show up?"

"Maybe he held you when you were crying and stayed with you until you were okay."

"My mom would kill me. She hates Austin. Apparently, she always has and said she only tolerated him because my dad thought he was a good guy."

"Since when does your mom's opinion matter more than your dad's?"

"Since she's the only parent I have left," Lacey whispered.

"Aw, sweetie. Go tell Austin you're crying and need him to hold you again."

Lacey snorted. "You're so bad."

"You love me, and you know it."

"I do. I can't believe I got myself into this mess. And now I'm stuck here for God knows how long."

"Read a book, watch some TV, and jump the sexy man who made you feel better. Sex fixes everything, Lace."

"I'm not so sure about that."

"Then you've definitely been having the wrong kind of sex."

"That's definitely true, but I don't think the right kind is in this house." Lacey looked around the room she was in. Paneled walls, dark lighting, and a squeaky bed that would alert everyone within miles of what was going on if someone tried to have sex on it.

Maggie's baby cooed on the other end of the line, and Lacey's core clenched. She always wanted a family, a baby and a husband and a life that was more full than her books and work and empty apartment.

"Give me a minute," Maggie said to Owen, who responded with a kiss Lacey could hear. Not a quick peck either, a full kiss with smacking lips and a soft moan that was met with a responding sound. Maggie giggled, then whispered something Lacey couldn't hear.

Owen's voice faded with the baby sounds.

"Sorry about that."

"You never have to apologize for your family. How is Carter?"

"He's good. Getting a little fussy, so Owen is walking him around the house."

"You have to go. You have your family to be there for. I just wanted to let you know I'll do my best to keep you updated on what's going on, but I might be unavailable for a little while."

"Think about what I said, Lace. When are you going to get a chance to bang the protector again? Even if it's one night, enjoy yourself."

"That's all I've ever had, so why would it be any different with him?" The question was rhetorical, but Maggie didn't get that.

"Maybe it won't be one night with him. Maybe he'll be different. Maybe he's the one your dad was always talking about you being with, and it took a true tragedy for Austin to pull his head out of his ass and realize what was right in front of him this whole time. All I know is you will regret it if you don't boink that bad boy and get a few spectacular orgasms out of this shitshow you're in the middle of."

"He's injured."

"Even better. You do all the work, show him how good you are, then tantalize him with your tits and rock his world so he never wants to let you go."

Lacey laughed. "God, I love you."

"I love you, too, girl. And I'm sorry about your dad. He was one of a kind. Never to be replaced."

Lacey's throat tightened again. "Thanks."

"Bye, hun."

"Bye."

Lacey hung up the phone and stared at it. If only she had the confidence Maggie had. Maybe then she would actually go for it with Austin. Instead, she was going to hide and pretend she wasn't interested because that was what she did. She couldn't be rejected if she never put herself out there.

SEVEN

Austin listened to Lacey laugh on the phone and fought against his jealousy. He had no right to be jealous of her 'friend.' Or to question if whoever she was talking to was really just a friend. Austin had no claim on her, even if he wanted to.

The door opened, and Lacey looked into the living room, her gaze connecting with his. Whatever she saw had her sucking in a breath, her chest rising fast.

"Everything okay?" Walker asked, diverting her attention to him.

Austin wanted to punch his teammate. Walker had no right to Lacey, either. No right to step between Lacey and Austin. No right to draw her attention.

"All good," Lacey said.

"Did you tell your *friend* where you are?" Austin barked. He sounded like an asshole, and he knew it, but he couldn't pull it back.

Walker's scowl said he needed to try.

"No. I'm not an idiot." Lacey stomped to the bathroom, abandoning her path toward them into the living room.

As soon as the door closed, Walker turned on Austin. "What the fuck?"

Austin glared at Walker, ignoring the question.

"She just lost her father. She's in hiding. She's not fucking used to all this. Get your damn head out of your ass and knock it off, or I'll knock you out."

"Fuck you."

Walker closed his eyes, fists clenched at his sides, and blew out a breath slowly.

Austin couldn't let go of the tension radiating through him. Holding Lacey was a mistake. Having her in his arms twisted his fucked up head into thinking she was his. Definitely twisted his dick into thinking she was his. Waking up with her in his arms, his cock pressed tight to her curvy body, his hand on her soft belly, it fucked with him.

Climbing out of that bed was the right thing to do, but all he wanted to do was climb right back in and finish what he started when he held her. Strip her dress off her and bury himself in her. Claim her, heal her.

But he fucking couldn't because she didn't want him. She was too good for him. He'd been told his whole life he was trash, and Valerie only confirmed those words when she showed up in the hospital.

"I'm sorry about what Valerie said to you," Walker said, his voice quiet and sympathetic.

"Whatever," Austin said, blocking the words and the emotion they tried to stir up. "She wasn't wrong. I let Samuel down. I let everyone down."

"You were shot."

"Not the first time."

"And not your fault. Could have happened to any of us."

"But it didn't. Happened to me. To Samuel. I was his partner. I was the one there. I was supposed to have his back. Instead, he's dead, and I'm stuck here." Austin's words were quiet but angry. He hated himself for what happened, and wanting Lacey only added to that hatred. He'd fucked up enough for the MacNeil family. He had to stay away.

"Is there something I can change into?" Lacey asked, her voice drifting to them from the hallway.

Walker sighed, then walked toward Lacey, ignoring Austin.

It was for the best. Montgomery's words only went so far. Yeah, it helped Austin to know not everyone blamed him, but it didn't mean they trusted him. It didn't mean anyone would want to be his partner going forward. He was tarnished, and as soon as he could get the hell out of there, he had to leave. Start a new life where he couldn't hurt the MacNeil women ever again.

Walker came back into the room, and the door to the bedroom closed. "She's getting changed, then she's going to try to sleep. You want the other room?"

Austin shook his head. "I'm good."

"You can't sleep on the damn couch."

"I slept in the hospital. I can take a few hours on watch."

"You're the one I'm protecting."

Austin's glare must have gotten through to Walker because he held his hands up in surrender and stepped back.

"Fine, I'm not protecting you, but you're not full strength. Do you want something to happen to her because your ego is so fucking big you think you can take care of shit here?"

Austin scowled. Walker was right. Dammit. He didn't want to admit he wasn't at full strength, but he wasn't. "Fine."

"Go rest for a few hours. The more you rest, the faster you're back to good."

Austin wanted to argue, but he was exhausted. He nodded and dragged himself to the bedroom Lacey wasn't in, the one he hadn't slept in with her a few hours ago. The bedroom was plain with a queen bed and an old wooden dresser. The dresser had clothes of a few different sizes for emergency situations, like they were in. Austin hadn't grabbed any of his own clothes when he left his place. He was still in the clothes he'd worn home from the hospital, including the shirt he'd bled all over when Lacey changed his bandages.

Austin dug through the drawers until he found a clean shirt. He normally slept naked, but that didn't fly when there was no telling what they were going to be faced with overnight. He settled for laying out his pants and the clean tee and crashing in his boxer briefs.

The bed squeaked when Austin laid down. He shifted, and it squeaked again. He tried to stay still, willing himself to fall asleep, but the bed in the other room squeaked. Lacey. She was as restless as he was.

She'd slept in his arms, still enough that he drifted off with her. Austin wanted her to have that peace again. To get the rest she needed. He'd seen the circles under her eyes when she showed up at his house. She hadn't been sleeping. He didn't blame her. He hadn't been either.

But Samuel wasn't his father.

Austin stared at the ceiling, listening to Lacey toss and turn in the squeaky bed next door. He closed his eyes and tried to figure out what he should do. A door closed on the far side of the house, Walker doing his check outside.

A sob reached Austin's ears, and before he could stop himself, he was out of bed and knocking on her door.

"Yeah?"

"Lace? Are you okay?"

"I'm fine," she snapped. A sob said she was lying.

"I'm coming in," he said, opening the door and stepping into the dark room.

"What are you doing?"

"I don't want you to be alone."

"I'm always alone."

"You don't have to be, Lace." He walked across the room to the bed on the far wall.

She was in the bed, facing the wall like she'd been earlier. She was curled up into herself, her face buried in the pillow. "Go away, Austin."

"Why? Because you want to cry yourself to sleep? Or because you hate me?"

"Why would I hate you?" She rolled to face him and gasped. Her gaze traveled down his body, and he remembered he was only in his boxer briefs.

Her gaze had an effect on him he couldn't hide, but he wasn't there for his dick. He was there for Lacey. "Your mother hates me."

"My father never did. He always told me you're a good man."

"I'm not feeling like it right now," Austin murmured.

"What?"

"Nothing." Austin shook his head. "Will you sleep with me in here? If I lie with you again?"

"I..." She nibbled her lip and nodded once. "Maybe."

Austin didn't need more than that. He slid under the blankets with her and curled himself around her body. He knew as he did it he was going to regret it, but he needed her as much as she seemed to need him. The best sleep he'd gotten in days was when he held her. The selfish asshole he was wanted more of that.

Lacey's body stiffened for a minute, then relaxed against him. Her breathing evened out in minutes, and she fell asleep with Austin's arm around her stomach, holding her to his body.

He wasn't so lucky with his erection leading the charge to get closer and wake her up, but eventually, Austin followed her into sleep.

LACEY WAS ALONE when she woke up. The sheets behind her were cool. But she felt better than she had in days.

When Austin walked into her room, she wanted to send him away. She tried. But when he wrapped himself around her and his warmth sank into her body, everything inside her quieted.

After spending however many hours in his arms, she finally felt like she was well-rested. Like she could function on all cylinders instead of floating through the days and aching to do something that would knock her out at night. Who knew that something would be Austin Ward holding her?

Lacey rolled over and out of bed, opening the bedroom door to hurry across the hallway to the bathroom. She heard the soft voices of the men protecting her, but she couldn't make out what they were saying.

After her bathroom stop, she went to find them and, if she was lucky, coffee.

"Morning," Walker said before she made it into the kitchen. "Sleep okay?"

Lacey's gaze slid to Austin as she nodded. "I did. Thank you."

"Good. Coffee?" Walker nodded to the pot behind him.

"Yes. Definitely." Lacey made her way to it and poured herself a cup. She added powdered creamer and two spoonfuls of sugar, then took a sip.

"Quiche will be out soon," Walker said.

"Quiche?"

Walker grinned. "Frozen, but it's pretty good."

Lacey's stomach rumbled. "Sounds good."

Austin got up from his seat at the small table and offered the chair to Lacey.

She thanked him and sat, enjoying the warmth of the chair he vacated.

Austin refilled his coffee mug, adding the same creamer and sugar as Lacey, then leaned against the counter to drink it. "Montgomery is coming this morning. He has some news for us."

"He does?" Lacey wasn't sure if *news* was good or bad.

Austin nodded. "He didn't tell us what it was, just that he would be here in about an hour."

Lacey nodded, grateful she wasn't the only one being kept in the dark.

"Hopefully, his news will tell us you guys are safe," Walker said.

"Is that possible?" Lacey asked.

Walker shrugged. "Anything is possible."

"Someone tried to kill me yesterday. Us. One of us? We don't know. What's the likelihood they're going to give up?"

"When Montgomery gets here, we'll know the answer to that question." Walker got up to check the oven, grabbing the mitts on the counter and removing the quiche. He set it on the stovetop and sat down again.

Lacey didn't like waiting, but she also understood the two men in the room with her didn't have the answers they all needed.

Walker finished his coffee, then cut the quiche for them. They ate in relative silence, the sounds of their breakfast the most prevalent ones.

After their breakfast, Austin excused himself to shower, and Walker headed outside to check the perimeter of the house. Lacey settled on the couch and tried to be calm. She might be going home. But was that the best? She never thought she'd want to be trapped in a safe house.

Walker came back inside with Montgomery, the two of

them talking as they walked in. "It's definitely for the best," Montgomery said.

"What's for the best?" Lacey asked.

"Where's Austin?" Montgomery asked.

"In the shower, I think," Lacey said, pointing to the closed bathroom door.

"Let's wait until he can join us," Montgomery said.

Lacey scowled. She was ready to understand what the hell was going on.

"I get it," Montgomery told her. "I know you want answers."

"Then why don't you give me answers?"

Montgomery chuckled. "I will. But my job right now is to make sure you're both safe."

"And you don't think we are," Lacey breathed.

Montgomery shook his head as the bathroom door opened. He looked up, eyebrows raised.

"Give me a sec," Austin said from the hallway.

Lacey kept her gaze on Montgomery instead of turning to look at Austin. Fresh from the shower. Warm skin, damp hair.

Damp panties. Lacey had to control herself. Not looking at him was a first step.

The three of them waited for Austin, which thankfully only took a few seconds. He stood to the side, not taking a seat next to her on the couch, and nodded for Montgomery to share his news.

"Someone was watching your house," Montgomery said to Austin. "Showed up after you were home from the hospital. Didn't stay long, but they were definitely watching your house."

"So they're after me," Austin said.

"That's what we believe. But the same vehicle was at the funeral. Zeke saw it, and we were able to find footage of the vehicle following Lacey to your house." Montgomery glanced at Lacey when he dropped that bomb.

"They followed me?" she breathed.

Montgomery nodded. "Yeah. Our assumption is it's the person who killed your father. Likely tying up loose ends with Austin. Probably didn't know he was alive. Even more likely, didn't know he was at the safe house that night."

"Do we have proof of who sent them there?" Austin asked.

Lacey looked at him, wondering what he was talking about.

"No. We're going to get a visit today."

"I want to be there," Austin demanded.

"Not an option," Montgomery said.

"Make it an option."

"I want to be there, too," Lacey said.

All three men turned to her.

"No," they said at the same time.

"Whoever you're talking about killed my father. I want to know why." Lacey's lip wobbled, and she clamped it in her teeth.

"Lacey," Montgomery started.

"Okay," Austin said at the same time.

"What?" Montgomery and Walker said.

Austin met her gaze. "She's broken. She's not sleeping. She's been trapped here, and she was trapped with me yesterday. She needs the same answers the rest of us need. Let her get them. He won't be able to get to her."

"But it'll put a target on her," Montgomery argued.

Austin snorted. "Yeah, because yesterday didn't already?"

Montgomery shook his head, running a hand over it.

Walker glared at Austin, not speaking.

"Please, Montgomery. I went to Austin yesterday for answers. My mother... She can't handle this. I can't either. He was my favorite person in the world. He was..." She gripped her locket. "I need to know why."

Montgomery looked at her, the pain in his eyes enough to give Lacey a tiny bit of hope. "You don't get to speak."

"Okay."

"You do exactly what we say."

She nodded.

"Don't make me regret this."

"I won't. I promise."

Montgomery sighed heavily. "I already do. This is a horrible idea."

"We all want to know how he did it. We need to understand. That safe house wasn't known to anyone. He not only found it, but he executed the witness who was going to make sure he never got out. There's a hole somewhere." Austin's fists clenched.

"We don't have a hole," Montgomery growled.

"Someone fucked up. We need to know who and how. And he's the only one who can tell us."

Montgomery nodded, pulling out his phone. "I need to make a call."

Lacey watched him walk out the door, wondering if he was going to leave without them.

"Why don't you take a quick shower?" Walker suggested. "Check the drawers for clean clothes. You can wear whatever you want."

Lacey knew they were trying to get rid of her. She didn't want to be left out of whatever they were planning, but she didn't want to go out in the clothes she slept in.

Lacey took the fastest shower of her life and was back in the living room within ten minutes. The three men were talking quietly, and none of them looked happy.

"What's going on?"

They exchanged glances before Austin met hers. "There

was a hearing this morning. With the witness dead, the man she was supposed to testify against is getting released. Today."

"The man who killed my father is going to walk free?" Lacey shrieked.

The men all winced.

Austin nodded. "Yeah. The good news is it'll be easier to talk to him. The bad news is, we don't know who will be with him."

"How in the hell is this even possible? He killed people! He killed my father. How does he get to go free?" Lacey collapsed onto the couch.

"He won't get away with it," Austin promised her.

"You can't say that. It sounds like he's already gotten away with it."

"The police will find the evidence they need to put him away again. But right now, we need to go. If you still want to," Montgomery said.

Lacey wiped her tears and stood. "Let's go."

EIGHT

Austin was not a good passenger. He hated not being in control. Samuel knew that about him and understood, letting Austin drive whenever they were together.

Walker? He didn't give a shit. Said with Austin's shoulder, he shouldn't be driving and to shut up and get in.

Austin had a few choice words for his teammate, but he chose to swallow them. His shoulder fucking hurt. One injury shouldn't sideline him, but sleeping in one position all night made him stiff. In more ways that one.

It was worth it to know Lacey slept, though. She settled when he pulled her into his arms and held her. So did he, if he was being honest. Better than usual.

The look Walker gave Austin when he left Lacey's room early that morning said he didn't approve, but he kept his comments to himself. It was the best Austin could hope for. And part of the reason Austin didn't argue about driving, or share his thoughts on where Walker could go for telling him to get in the SUV.

"Something's going on," Walker said, slowing the vehicle.

They were headed toward Peter Howard's office. Montgomery said that was where he was expected to be. Hannah was an employee of Howard Enterprises for three years. She held four different positions, and the last one was as Peter Howard's personal assistant for a year. The documents she provided when she blew the whistle on his illegal activity were ones she came across when she was working directly for him.

The man was a workaholic and a real piece of shit. His wife had been by his side for every single hearing and advocated for his release, telling every news outlet she could speak to that her husband was a good man and didn't do the things Hannah accused him of.

Austin didn't really care either way. It wasn't his job to prove the man was guilty of money laundering and embezzlement. All that mattered to Austin was keeping the witness safe. But since he failed to do that, and lost his partner in the process, he was out for blood. Peter Howard's blood.

Austin's fists tightened as the SUV crept closer to the building that housed Howard Enterprises. A swarm of police cards blocked their progress as they drew closer to the building. The vehicles ahead of them turned down side streets and swung U-turns in the middle of the road.

Walker kept going.

They reached the barricade stopping them from moving any closer to the building and saw a black SUV engulfed in flames.

"What the fuck?" Walker whispered. He turned off the SUV and got out, leaving Austin and Lacey to follow.

Lacey was out before Austin could decide if it was a good idea. He scrambled to follow her, sticking to her side as they approached the police barricade.

"What happened?" Walker asked the cop blocking traffic.

"Car accident. We need everyone to keep moving, sir," the officer said.

"We have a meeting. Any way to get into the building?" Walker asked.

The officer shook his head. "Not at the moment. You're going to need to reschedule."

"Dammit." Walker turned to Austin and Lacey. "Guess we're not getting answers from Peter Howard today."

"Uh, apologies, but Mr. Howard was in the SUV," the officer said.

"What?" Austin barked. "How the fuck does that happen?"

The officer gave him a funny look.

"Who's in charge?" Austin demanded.

The officer looked Austin up and down.

Austin puffed his chest and tried to look as menacing as possible. He didn't have a badge or an ID that would tell the officer he was anyone important, but if he looked like he belonged, most people didn't question him.

"Our Captain is on his way. You can speak to him when he arrives. Please wait near your vehicle, though. This area needs to be clear." The officer ignored them to direct a vehicle onto the side street.

"Call Montgomery," Austin said.

"He's already on the phone with Marcus. Marcus is going to find us when he gets here." Walker pocketed his phone and looked around.

"He's dead?" Lacey asked.

Austin had almost forgotten she was there. He could feel her presence, but he pushed it out of his mind. Lacey was a distraction he couldn't afford. "Yeah."

"We'll get answers," Walker told her.

Lacey exhaled a mirthless breath. "No, we won't. He had my father killed, and now he's dead. Or he's making it look like he's dead. Either way, he's not going to pay for what he did."

"If he's dead, someone wanted him to pay. Someone went after him."

"The officer said it was a car accident."

Austin shook his head. "Car accidents don't usually end with an explosion. This wasn't an accident."

"Someone killed him?" Lacey asked.

Austin nodded. "That would be my guess."

Lacey ran her hands up and down her arms. She looked around like she was expecting someone to jump out of the crowd on onlookers and confess.

Austin nearly laughed at the thought. It would make things so much easier if it worked that way, but in his experience, the guilty ones were the ones who felt no remorse for their actions. The ones who were happy to sit back and let law enforcement chase them, knowing even if they were caught, they'd get away with it.

Like Peter Howard.

Austin wanted his pound of flesh from the man. His death was too easy, too neat. The man should have to face what he did, and the people he destroyed. But he was dead. If the officer was right.

A police siren whooped behind them, and they stepped to the side. The car parked and Captain Marcus Patrick climbed out. He nodded to the officer directing traffic that made it to the barricade, then approached Austin, Lacey, and Walker.

"Heard you were on the way to see Mr. Howard," Marcus said.

Walker nodded. "Since he was lucky enough to be set free this morning, we wanted to catch him before he had a chance to secure all his connections and get protected."

"Looks like you're not the only one," Marcus said. He turned to Lacey. "I'm sorry about the loss of your father. He was a great man."

"Thank you," Lacey whispered.

"Did you three happen to see anything?" Marcus asked, his cop face in place.

Walker shook his head. "It happened before we got here. We didn't know we were coming to this until we were here and the officer said Howard's in the vehicle."

Marcus's brows went up. "He shouldn't have told you that, but I know you three weren't involved."

"Thanks, Marcus."

"We still need to investigate, though."

"He was a bad man. His death is a blessing," Lacey said.

"I don't disagree, but we have to make sure whoever did this pays for it," Marcus told her.

"What about him paying for killing my father?"

Marcus rolled his lips in. "That's still under investigation, too. If he was involved, we will have no choice but to close the case. But we're not sure of that, especially after this accident."

"How can you say that?" Lacey gasped.

Marcus glanced at Austin and Walker. "If this was intentional, it's likely someone didn't want him out of jail. Which could mean they wanted him to take the fall for everything, and him getting released was bad for them, for some reason."

"I don't want him out of jail. I want him to pay for what he did to my father," Lacey hissed.

"I know. And I understand. And if you weren't with these two, I'd be asking if you could prove you weren't involved in this, but—"

"She's been with us since yesterday," Austin growled at the police captain.

"I'm aware. Montgomery already told me. But someone wanted this to happen, and I need to start figuring out who." Marcus shook hands with the three of them, then turned and approached the officer they spoke to earlier.

"Let's get out of here," Walker said.

"Why? We need to know what happened," Lacey argued.

Walker put his arm around her shoulders and guided her to the SUV. Austin resisted the urge to punch his friend for touching her. She was his.

Shit.

No.

She wasn't his. She couldn't be his. She wasn't allowed to be his.

Walker spoke quietly to Lacey, and Austin followed behind them, wishing he could hear the words Walker said.

Walker opened the door for Lacey to get in the SUV, then turned to Austin. "I'm not sure about her being alone. Or going back to her mother's. I want to head to the office and see what Montgomery wants to do."

"I thought she wasn't in danger," Austin said, his throat closing with fear. He couldn't lose her.

"She's not, but she's also not herself. She's going to have a hard time processing everything. She shouldn't be alone."

"Are you angling for the job?" Austin spat.

Walker's eye twitched. He crossed his arms and rocked back on his heels, assessing Austin. "I'm not after her."

Austin let out a breath. His fists eased. He hated he was so easy to read. "I wasn't saying you were."

"Maybe not, but you were about to piss all around her and mark your territory. Have been since yesterday. You have to treat her like any other job."

"She's not, and you fucking know it."

Walker stepped into Austin's face. "What I know is you need to keep your shit in check. Do you really think Montgomery's going to tell you to go for it with her? Do you think Samuel would be okay with you sniffing around his princess? Her mother already lost her shit when she found out you were trapped together. You need to stay away from her. She's not in a place where she can make smart choices."

"And you think I'm going to take advantage of that?"

Walker assessed Austin closely. "Are you?"

"Fuck you, Walker. You don't know a damn thing about me. Or about Lacey. She's beautiful and smart and capable of thinking for herself."

"I agree. But not right now. Not when she's so broken over her father that she doesn't know which way is up. What did she say to you when she showed up at your house? You're ignoring everyone's calls, but she ends up in your panic room? How did that happen?"

Austin's rage boiled. He rushed Walker, intent on knocking his teeth down his throat.

Walker sidestepped Austin's attempt, caught him by the back of his shirt, and slammed him into the side of the SUV. "Don't you dare come at me again. I'm not the one you're mad at, and I'm not going to be your punching bag."

"Screw you."

Walker released Austin and stepped back. "None of this is on you, Austin. Stop beating yourself up about it. Montgomery already told you that."

"Yeah, well, Samuel's still dead. And I was the one who was supposed to be watching his back."

"We've all lost people," Walker said, his gaze drifting away. Haunted. "We all have people we were supposed to be watching over. We can't change the past."

"Doesn't mean I shouldn't have done better."

"Better." Walker laughed without humor. "We all should do better. Different. Smarter. Faster. It never changes. There's always a choice we could have made that would have changed everything. But living with those choices is inevitable."

"He should be here. He has a family. People who counted on him." Austin's guilt forced the words out.

Walker shrugged. "It's not the way it went down. We can second guess everything, but at the end of the day, we have to live with the things we've done."

Austin looked at Walker. Really looked at the man. Walker was steady, solid, emotionless. But there was a hell of a lot of emotion in him at the moment. Despair. Doubt. Regret.

Then Walker shook his head, and the look cleared. He was back to the ruthless asshole Austin had known since he joined Rose Protection Agency. "Let's go."

Austin stood there while Walker stalked around the vehicle. He didn't know what just happened, but it didn't matter. He'd figure out Walker later. Right now, he needed to make sure Lacey was safe.

LACEY FOLLOWED Walker and Austin into the Rose Protection Agency offices. She'd been there a handful of times with her father, but it had been years.

"Lacey! How are you?" Berkeley Russell hurried from behind her desk as they walked in. Berkeley was a few years older than Lacey and knew her father well as the office manager for the company.

Lacey always liked Berkeley. "Hey. I'm... I don't know how I am."

"Stupid question." Berkeley hugged Lacey and held her arms. "Can I get you anything?"

Lacey shook her head and looked over at Austin. Walker disappeared through the door to the back, but Austin waited for Lacey. She focused on Berkeley again. "I think I'm okay. They said no one was really after me, so I can go. But I want answers. Of course, now that's not possible." Lacey let out a half-sob, and Berkeley folded her into her arms.

"Oh, I'm so sorry. We all loved your father. He was so kind. He always stopped by my desk to see how I was doing and to catch up. So many people are going to miss him."

Lacey sniffed and nodded. "Yeah. That's how he was. He really cared about people, you know? Like it actually mattered to him. I remember him telling me when it was your birthday last year. He was so mad no one got you anything. He ripped Montgomery a new one and went out and got your cake and a card and made all of them sign it."

Berkeley stared at Lacey like she was crazy, mouth hanging and eyes wide. "I never knew that. He didn't tell me. I thought..." Berkeley shook her head. "He was special."

"Yeah, he was."

Berkeley held Lacey for another minute, then released her. "If you need anything at all, please let me know. I don't have the skills of these guys, but I can drink a bottle of wine better than they can. And watch sappy movies and not judge you for crying."

Lacey chuckled. "Thanks. I might take you up on that."

"Good. I hope you do."

Austin cleared his throat, and Lacey looked over at him. He nodded toward the security door. "We should go in."

Lacey nodded. "Thanks, Berkeley."

"Any time."

Lacey smiled and followed Austin. It was good to know she wasn't the only one who would miss her father. He was a good man, special in so many ways. And the man who ordered his death needed to pay for it.

Lacey followed Austin through the short hallway that led to their open bullpen type area. Austin's desk was next to her father's, both in the middle of the foray. He didn't go to his desk but continued around the outside ring to the offices in the back.

Montgomery was waiting for them when they walked in. "Marcus already filled me in. Said first guess is there was no accident, but it was staged to look like it was. There are three bodies inside the SUV, believed to be Peter Howard and two guards."

"So, it's over?" Lacey asked.

Montgomery shook his head. "No. They will confirm the identities, then an investigation will happen."

"I want to be involved. I can't walk away from this. I need to know what happened to my father and why. I deserve that much." Lacey fought the tears filling her eyes. For the second time in one day, she was arguing with her father's boss to get answers about his death, and losing the fight with her emotions. She hated that she cried when she was mad, and it didn't help that she was overcome with grief constantly since Zeke walked into the library and said her father was dead.

"We don't know what is going to happen. We aren't going to be leading the investigation. Our job is to protect people, not do police work," Montgomery said.

"Seriously? You're really going to sit there and tell me none of you care about my father? None of you want to know what happened to him? Why he was murdered? Why all of this happened? He trusted you! He gave his life for you. And all you're going to do is sit back and let the police handle it?"

"That's not what I said," Montgomery growled.

"Watch it," Austin barked.

Montgomery slid Austin a look, but Austin didn't back down. He'd positioned himself between Lacey and Montgomery, fists clenched and shoulders back. He was ready to fight.

For her.

"Someone came after the two of you. We believe they were watching Austin. But that was before Howard was released. Either he was behind the attack on your father, and the attack on the two of you, or whoever killed him was." Montgomery glared at Austin as he spoke, even though his words were addressing Lacey.

"What does that mean?"

Montgomery slid his gaze past Austin to Lacey. "It means we don't know what's going on. But we're going to find out."

NINE

Austin left Montgomery's office with even more anger fueling him. They knew nothing. They needed answers, and instead of having more, they had less. Lacey was still in danger, but maybe not. Peter Howard was to blame for Samuel's death, but maybe not.

What the hell good was their team if they couldn't get answers?

Austin went to his desk, the one opposite Samuel's desk, and resisted the urge to swipe everything off it. He wanted to throw something. Hit something. Fucking do something.

But he couldn't because he was recovering from surgery. And being shot. And letting his partner down.

"What's Lacey doing here?" Lance Kilgore was another teammate and Austin's closest friend after Samuel. Lance was quiet and distant, but he was reliable. A former Army Ranger, Lance was deadly and smart, with a brutal side when needed.

"We still don't know what the fuck is going on," Austin told him.

"With what?"

"With all the shit about Samuel's death. Someone showing up at my house. If Lacey's in danger or not. Too many fucking questions and not enough answers."

"Montgomery's going to protect her?" Lance asked.

"We're staying together. He won't let me take care of myself. Thinks I can't do it," Austin grumbled.

Lance nodded to Austin's shoulder. "Looks like he's not wrong. What the hell are you going to do if someone takes a swing? You can't even drive."

"I can protect myself."

"Okay, fine, but you can't protect the princess."

"Fuck you," Austin growled.

"You can get pissed all you want, but if she's in danger, you need to stay away from her. Samuel just died. She looks like a wounded bird. And the last thing a wounded bird needs is a predator."

"I'm not a fucking predator."

Lance snorted. "Sure. And I didn't see the way you looked at her."

"I didn't... She's Samuel's daughter. She's off-limits."

"Yeah, she is," Lance said, his voice full of steel. "She's his world. You know that better than the rest of us. Fucking around with her, especially now, is a bad idea. Cut her loose. Let Montgomery watch her. Fuck, I'll do it."

Austin wanted to punch his former friend, knock Lance's ass out right there in front of all of them. He was in Lance's face so fast he almost missed the smirk that ran across his damn face. "Stay the fuck away from her."

"Or what? You're going to hit me?"

"I might. She's not yours. She'll never be yours."

"She's not yours, either."

"I know!" The room around them stopped, and Austin lowered his voice. "I know. But I let Samuel down. I'm not going to let Lacey down. She's..." Austin swallowed past the fear gripping his throat. She had to be okay. He had to make sure she was okay. Then he would leave town and do what Valerie asked. Never see Lacey again.

"You're not good enough for her. None of us are. Samuel wanted the world for her. And Montgomery said Valerie told you to stay away. Why do you think this is a good idea?"

"Because it's my fault he's dead."

"The fuck it is."

Austin shook his head. "It is. We all know it is. I was his partner." Austin growled the word. "I was supposed to keep him safe. And instead, he died alone, without me there, protecting our witness by himself."

"You couldn't have done anything different."

"I don't know, since I don't remember what happened. What I do know is I'm here, and Samuel isn't. He's the one who had people counting on him. A wife, a daughter with her whole damn life ahead of her, a fucking dog. What do I have? A house with a panic room so I can lock out the outside world when it comes for me." Austin cut off his words, drawing a shaky breath. "I wouldn't have been missed. So, I owe that family my life to make sure she survives this."

Lance drew a breath, hands on his hips as he glared at Austin. "You're wrong, Austin. You would have been missed. Just like Samuel will be. You might not feel like you have anyone, but you do. You have us, and when Valerie gets past her grief, she'll realize she was wrong to blame you for what happened."

"Valerie said a whole lot more than that. She doesn't want me in their lives. She never liked me. Said the only reason I was ever included was because of Samuel."

Lance shook his head. "She's wrong. And that woman in there is proof of it." Lance nodded toward Montgomery's office.

Austin followed his gaze and found Lacey watching him. She looked away as soon as she saw Austin looking at her.

"She's deep in her grief."

"And you're the one she keeps looking for."

"Maybe she's looking at Samuel's desk."

Lance shook his head. "You believe what you want, but you're wrong. What's the first rule of this job?"

"Don't fuck the client."

"Okay, the second rule?"

Austin sighed. "When you imprint on someone, you're up."

"You imprinted on her. She trusts you. She wants you with her. Which tells me she doesn't blame you for her father's death. If she did, she'd hate you, not want you close."

"Then why'd you tell me to stay away?"

Lance smirked. "To see how deep you were."

"What?"

"You're in love with her. I saw the same look on Zeke's face when Nina came back. The same anger and defense and all of it."

Austin wanted to argue and tell Lance he was wrong, but he couldn't force the words out. His mouth opened, then closed, then opened again, but nothing came out.

"Let's go," Montgomery said from right behind Austin.

Lance smirked. "Where are you headed, boss?"

Austin turned and saw Lacey with Montgomery. Her gaze met his, and he felt like he'd been shot. Again. Her brown eyes were wide with red circles around them. She toyed with the locket around her neck, nibbling her lower lip.

Austin wanted to do the same. To taste her and tease her and tempt her. To know what it was like to have a woman like Lacey want him. But Lacey was too good for him. She'd never be his. She deserved better than him, more than him.

He tore his gaze from hers, knowing Lance was right.

Yeah, he loved her. He wanted a future with her. But Austin was all wrong for her. No one was good enough for Lacey, but Austin was worse than not good enough. He needed to give her space, keep his distance. He loved her enough to know it was best for her.

"Lacey insisted she's safe with Austin. Since we have no answers, we're putting the two of them in a hotel, and the rest of us are going to get some fucking answers."

"A hotel? How cozy," Lance said.

Austin wanted to argue, to tell Montgomery that was a bad idea, but he snapped his mouth shut when he saw the look on Lacey's face. A plea. A desperate longing. A need he never thought he'd see from her.

His cock swelled at the look. She didn't mean it the way he took it, he was sure of that, but he couldn't convince his dick of that.

Austin nodded, agreeing without words. Montgomery gestured for Lacey to go ahead of him, then followed her.

"Keep it in your pants," Lance whispered as Austin walked past him.

Austin choked on a strangled laugh and nodded. Definitely the plan.

KIMBERLY HOWARD STARED at the sleeping form of her sister in the hospital bed. Her hands shook. She was cold. The whole thing was surreal, like it wasn't really happening to her. To Nicole.

A knock on the door had Kimberly turning to see which doctor was going to give which bullshit assessment of Nicole's choice to take her life. All Kimberly wanted to do was see her sister's eyes again. To know Nicole was going to be okay. She didn't care about the diagnosis. Just about her sister.

But the man who walked into the private room at the hospital was not wearing a white coat. He was wearing a police uniform.

"Mrs. Howard? Could I have a word?"

"Um, I suppose so. What can I do for you, officer?"

He extended his hand and offered her a smile that was more sad than friendly. "I'm Captain Marcus Patrick, Mrs. Howard. I'm afraid I have some sad news to share with you."

"Sadder than my baby sister tried to kill herself last night and hasn't woken up yet?" Kimberly's breath shuddered through her. She squeezed her eyes closed at the tears welling up, but it was no use. They were going to fall anyway.

"I apologize, but your husband is dead."

"You must be confused. My husband is fine. He has a security team, and the man is damn near indestructible."

"Well, that may be, but he is definitely dead. Peter Howard? That's your husband, right?"

"What? He's really dead?" Kimberly sank to a chair, burying her head in her hands so the officer didn't see her smile. She was shaking with relief. With joy. Feelings she wasn't allowed to have when she was notified her husband was dead.

"He is, Mrs. Howard. I'm very sorry for your loss."

"What... what happened?" Kimberly brought her thoughts back to her sister lying a few feet away in a hospital bed and was able to dig up some grief, showing the look to the captain.

"There was an accident, but we believe there's more to it than that."

"I don't understand." She didn't. The less she knew, the better. Plausible deniability was a beautiful thing.

"The SUV your husband was riding in hit another vehicle

this morning. A few hours ago. Did you know he was being released from prison today?"

Kimberly laughed mirthlessly. "I've been a little preoccupied. He said something the last time we spoke, but I don't even know if I know what day today is."

"It's Friday."

Kimberly nodded like the information was valuable to her.

Captain Patrick looked at her for a long moment. Studying her. Evaluating her. He was a police officer, and from what she knew, a good one. She needed to convince him she was hearing about Peter's death for the first time from him.

She was, but she'd had a little warning it might happen. A warning she'd been too scared to hope would become the truth until the officer confirmed it. She wanted to do a dance, but she'd wait to do it on the son-of-a-bitch's grave.

"You said there was an accident?"

"Yes. His SUV hit another vehicle, or was hit by, we're not sure yet. But when it happened, there was an explosion."

"Explosion?" That was news. She fought a grin. Very thorough job.

"Yes. The entire vehicle was engulfed in flames in seconds. All three men were trapped. It happened too quickly for them to have a chance to get out. Or for anyone to help them."

"Oh, no. That's horrible. Do you know who the two men with him were?"

"Not yet. Do you know who they might be?"

Kimberly shrugged. "My guess would be his security team. He had two men working for him for the last few years. Jacob Vaughan and Frank Alexander."

Captain Patrick wrote something on his notepad. "Thank you for those names. We'll confirm them."

"Is there anything else?"

"Yes, if you don't mind. When was the last time you spoke to your husband?"

"Um... You said it's Friday?"

"Yes."

"Then Wednesday, I think. He called to say his lawyer was petitioning the court for his release since the woman who accused him of those horrible things was finally gone."

"He used those words? She was finally gone?"

Kimberly shrugged. "I believe so. Why?"

"You can understand why her death and the death of one of the men guarding her are under investigation. Your husband was the primary suspect."

Kimberly laughed. "Of course he was. But my husband is... was a good man."

"Are you sure about that, Mrs. Howard?"

"What are you implying, Captain?"

"He seemed to have quite a few enemies."

Kimberly crossed her arms, posing as the indignant wife. She'd played that role so well over the last year that even her husband believed it. "He's wealthy and powerful. People have a tendency to not like others who have all the things they want."

"And you think it was jealousy that led someone to murder your husband?"

"Well, I certainly wouldn't know what someone was thinking that led them to the conclusion that killing another person was a good idea."

"What happened to your sister, Mrs. Howard?"

Kimberly looked at Nicole, then positioned herself between Nicole and the captain. "I don't know why that's relevant."

"Maybe it's not, but it's strange you spoke to your husband on Wednesday, your sister attempted suicide on Thursday, and your husband is dead on Friday."

"Bad luck, I suppose."

"Is it? Or is something else going on?"

"Are you asking me if I was involved in my husband's death? Or are you implying I had something to do with my sister's suicide?"

"You tell me, Mrs. Howard."

"I love my sister, and I would never do anything to hurt her. I have been at her side since she was brought here, Captain. I haven't left for any reason. You can check with the staff. And I'm sure there are cameras around here."

"What about your husband? Would you do anything to hurt him?"

"How could I have been involved in my husband's death when I have been here since my sister was brought in?"

Captain Patrick shrugged, not looking at all like he believed her.

Smart man, but Kimberly couldn't have that. "From day one, I've told everyone who would listen that my husband was innocent. I stood by him. I fought for his release, even stepping up to make sure his company survived. My father wasn't the businessman my husband is, was. My husband provided a good life for me, and my sister when she moved in with us. I did everything I could to make sure my husband could step back into the life we had before he was accused of stealing from the company he built, to make sure it was thriving when he was released. And I knew he would be released because he was innocent. I always knew he was innocent. Why would I kill him if I knew he was innocent?"

"That is a very good question, Mrs. Howard."

Kimberly narrowed her eyes. "I loved my husband. I was looking forward to him being exonerated and being a free man again. I would have been there when he got home if I hadn't been here with my sister."

"Your husband wasn't going home when he was killed."

"Excuse me? What do you mean?"

"He appeared to have been on his way to his office.

Seemed he wanted to get a start on something right away. Any idea what that could have been?"

Kimberly shook her head slowly. She was thrilled she hadn't known any details. It made selling her innocence to the police much easier.

"Well, I should get back to work on finding your husband's killer. I am sorry for your loss, Mrs. Howard."

"Thank you, Captain."

Captain Patrick shook Kimberly's hand again, but this time, he held on for a second longer. "May I ask why your sister tried to commit suicide?"

Kimberly gasped. "I... She was depressed. Has been under treatment for years. Therapists, medication. Depression is a horrible illness that is easy to hide in plain sight. She fought it for a long time, but she finally got too tired to keep fighting against her own demons."

"I'm very sorry for that. I have heard amazing things about this place. I am sure they are doing everything possible for her."

"Yes, they are."

"That's good." Captain Patrick headed for the door, then stopped. "Mrs. Howard?"

"Hmm?"

"Please stay in town."

"Excuse me?"

"Don't leave town. Just in case we have more questions for you."

"So I am a suspect?"

"Not yet."

"Then I guess I'll need to notify my lawyer."

Captain Patrick smiled like he was hoping she would say that. "I'll be in touch. I hope your sister improves quickly and gets the help she needs."

"She will."

Captain Patrick nodded, then let himself out of the room.

Kimberly exhaled when the door closed behind him. Then she smiled.

Peter was gone for good, and even if the cops did piece it all together, the most important piece was done.

Her husband was dead.

TEN

Lacey had never been in a hotel as nice as the one Montgomery put them in. The suite had two bedrooms with private bathrooms, a living room and kitchen, and a balcony that overlooked Niagara Falls. It was fancy and elegant and so much better than the safe house they'd spent the previous night in. It smelled like bleach with a hint of lemon, and had red roses in a large vase on the kitchen island.

"Some of your things have been put in the bedrooms," Montgomery said. "We went to your places and collected stuff, so you'd feel more comfortable." His cheeks went red when he looked at Lacey. "Berkeley went to your place. She said she'd know what you would need."

"What if we didn't agree to this?" Lacey asked.

"That wasn't an option," Austin answered for Montgomery.

Montgomery nodded. "Once we found out Peter Howard was released, we started making plans to move the two of you. We've used this hotel before. They have top of the line security and a great staff. The woman in charge knows you two are under our protection and is going to make sure her staff is keeping an eye out for any concerns."

"Okay," Lacey said.

"Eve?" Austin asked.

Montgomery nodded.

Lacey wanted to ask who Eve was and why Austin knew her name. Jealousy bubbled up inside her. She had no claim over Austin. No right to ask about the women he knew. But all of a sudden, the red roses made sense. She wasn't just a colleague. Eve was someone who Austin knew, and who wanted Austin to remember her.

"Now what?" Lacey asked, needing to change the subject.

"Now we figure out what the hell is going on and make sure you're safe. There's an SUV in the garage if you need something, but we will have someone available to you at all times. You shouldn't need the vehicle, but if you do, Lacey's driving." Montgomery glared at Austin as he dropped that one.

Austin growled but didn't argue.

Montgomery handed Lacey the keys. "Don't let him drive. Doctor's orders."

Lacey nodded.

"Kitchen is stocked, you can order room service, whatever you need. We're going to figure all this out and make sure you're both safe." Montgomery nodded at Lacey, then slid a look toward Austin.

"Thanks, Montgomery." Lacey had a thought before he left. "What about my mom?"

"Kirk and Stephanie are staying with her until she's okay. We're going to make sure she's safe, too."

"Thank you," Lacey said.

"You can call her. Or anyone else. Your phone is safe to use."

"Okay." Lacey wasn't sure she wanted to tell her mother

where she was or who she was with, but she probably should check in. Let her know she was safe. Mostly.

"You need anything, you call us."

Lacey nodded again.

Montgomery waved, then let himself out of the room, the door closing behind him with a loud click.

Austin went to the door and flipped the deadbolt, then flipped the latch.

Lacey watched, unsure of what to say. She couldn't remember ever being alone with Austin, besides in his panic room and there was more on her mind than being alone with him. Every other time she'd seen him, her dad was there. Or his team. Or someone. Someone who could lead the conversation and keep Lacey from feeling like the awkward woman she was.

"You're not afraid of heights, are you?" Austin asked.

Lacey shook her head. "No. I'm fine."

Austin nodded. Guess he was just as uncomfortable.

"I'm going to... take a shower. If you don't mind."

Austin shook his head. "No. Make yourself comfortable. There's no telling how long we'll be here."

"You think we'll be here a while?" Lacey asked, her voice tipping toward a screech.

"I don't know. I think that asshole dying this morning changed things."

"What do you mean?"

Austin looked at her as if deciding how much to share.

Lacey raised her brows, hoping her curiosity was enough to convince him to tell her the truth.

"Peter Howard was supposed to be on trial the day after... the day after your father died. The prosecution was going to have the woman we were protecting testify on the first day so she could go into witness protection. They wanted to start out with her testimony because it was the most damning, and then everyone who followed her was going to build on what she said, supporting her account. When she was killed, his attorneys were quick to request his release. Montgomery said it was almost like they knew they would have a reason to file the paperwork. Like they were prepared."

"Meaning he was the one who killed her and my father."

Austin nodded. "That's what we believe. When someone came after us, it was only logical they were trying to take me out since I was there and could have been a witness. But with him dead..."

"There's someone else making decisions. Someone who wanted him silenced."

"Yeah."

"And until we know who that is, we're stuck here?"

Austin shrugged. "The assumption is still that I was the target. You could go home, Princess."

The nickname caught her off-guard. He said it before to piss her off. To get her to leave his house. This time was different. She grabbed her locket and rubbed her thumb over the smooth back of the book. If her dad was there, he would know what she should do. What was the best move. But he wasn't there.

The pain took hold again. Lacey tried to swallow past her tight throat. She chewed the inside of her lip. "I'm going to shower," she breathed, needing space from Austin and his confusing behavior.

He didn't reply, and she hurried to the bedroom, hoping it was the right one.

Lacey closed the door and flipped the lock. She leaned her back against it, then let her tears fall. She slapped her hand over her mouth before she let out a sob and pushed away from the door.

Pants, shirts, and a light sweater hung in the closet. Her most comfortable clothes were folded on the shelves. Three pairs of shoes sat on the floor. There was a dresser in the bedroom, and she opened the drawers to find panties, bras, socks, and pajamas.

The clothes Lacey was wearing didn't belong to her. They were fine for the day, but she didn't feel like herself. She wanted her own clothes, her own things.

She grabbed clothes that would be comfortable to sit around the hotel in, debating on a bra but deciding it was necessary when she was living with Austin. She carried everything to the bathroom and turned on the shower. She left the borrowed clothes on the floor and stepped under the hot water.

The shower was big enough for three or four people. Lacey used all the shower heads, playing with the controls until water shot out from the walls, rained down on her from above, and pelted her back in a soothing pattern. She wanted to stay in the shower forever, forget the outside world and pretend everything was fine.

As the water massaged her body, she let out the fear and anger she'd been feeling, giving in to the pain and crying out all her tears into the water. She washed her hair and her body, enjoying the soothing scents of the hotel supplied products, then accepted she couldn't hide from Austin forever.

Lacey got dressed, then explored the rest of her room. A few books were in the nightstand, some favorites that always made her feel good to read them. Her phone charger was plugged in, ready for her to feel like home. Lacey checked for any messages, then plugged her phone in, deciding she didn't want the outside world to invade.

She carried one of the books to the door and debated. What would Austin think of her reading a romance novel?

Did she care?

Lacey decided it didn't matter. Austin made his lack of interest pretty damn clear. She's slept in his arms twice, and twice he snuck out, or tried, when she was still asleep. He wasn't interested in her. He was just being nice. Getting lost in a story about a man who couldn't resist the woman he loved was better than wishing things were different with Austin.

Lacey's stomach rumbled when she opened the bedroom door and smelled whatever Austin was cooking. She followed her nose back to the kitchen, taking a seat at the island as Austin turned to her.

"I figured I'd make something for us to eat. Are you hungry?"

Lacey nodded. "Starving. Didn't realize until now."

"It happens. Help yourself." Austin carried a bowl away from the stove, nodding for Lacey to go in.

Lacey slid off her stool and grabbed the bowl he left on the counter for her. She filled it up with pasta, chicken, and vegetables. She added a sprinkle of cheese to the top, then followed Austin to the living room, taking a seat in the chair to the side.

Austin glanced her way, then focused on the TV. "Have you seen this?"

Lacey looked up at the TV, finding a documentary she'd been hoping to catch. "No. I wanted to, but I kept missing it."

Austin nodded. "Your dad mentioned you enjoy them. I haven't seen this one either. Are you up for it?"

"He told you that?"

Austin chuckled. "He talked about you all the time. I remember telling him about a documentary I watched years ago about color psychology, and he told me I sounded like you."

"I saw that, too. It was fascinating."

"I agree. He wasn't as entertained as I was, though. Always asked why in the hell—"

"I wanted to have someone else tell me how to think," Lacey finished with Austin.

Austin chuckled. "Yep. Got the same argument, huh?"

"All the time. I'd tell him I wasn't letting them tell me how to think, I was learning about the beautiful and amazing things out there in the world. That a lifetime wasn't long enough to learn all there was to learn, but if I listened to people who spent their life understanding one thing, I could learn a little bit about a lot and be a more well-rounded person."

Austin nodded as she spoke. "That's exactly it. Why would we not want to learn about things? Why would we want to be stuck in our own little space in the world when there are so many amazing things out there? Can you imagine what's possible? The discoveries we haven't made. The science that exists if we're willing to look for it. Cures for diseases and illnesses, resources that are renewable, technology that can change the world."

"Yep. That's how I feel, too. We have all the answers, we just don't always know the questions."

Austin smiled, a genuine smile that lit Lacey up from the inside. "Absolutely."

Lacey sucked in a breath, his one word slamming hard into her. She'd never known someone who felt the same way she did about so many things. Who understood her without having to get to know her.

Her father loved Austin like a son. Said he was family. Lacey always thought it was because they worked closely together, knew each other so well, but maybe it was because Austin was so similar to her.

She never saw the side of Austin her father knew. He was her dad's gorgeous partner, not someone Lacey thought would ever look at her. A secret fantasy. But he was looking at her. He was seeing her. And it didn't seem like he was seeing her for the first time.

He knew her. And he wasn't running scared.

RELAXING with Lacey was unlike anything Austin had ever experienced. She was intelligent and added to the show they were watching, plus she was funny and sarcastic and so damn cute.

If he wasn't already in love with her, he would have fallen hard right then and there.

"I can't believe you've never seen this. And you call yourself a fan," Lacey chastised him with a cluck of her tongue and a shake of her head.

Austin chuckled. She'd relaxed since her shower, her face lighting up with delight as they talked. She was still just as beautiful as she'd always been, but without her guard up, she was even more stunning. He loved a woman who could jump in and joke with him.

"Yeah, yeah. I've been out saving the world and shit," he said.

Her laughter faded as the memory of why they were there drifted back in.

Austin could have kicked himself for his offhand comment. It was something he always told Samuel when questioned why he wasn't dating more. Why he hadn't settled down? Why he wasn't looking for more out of his life?

The answer to all of Samuel's questions was the woman sitting across from Austin on the couch. He dated more than his share when he was younger, sleeping his way through every town he landed in with the military. He never wanted to settle down and risk his own temper becoming like his father's. The military taught Austin to direct his anger at a target. Life taught his father the same, but Austin was his father's favorite target.

When Austin left the military at twenty-six, he followed

his old sergeant to Rose Protection Agency. Teddy's word got Austin a spot on the team. Austin met Samuel and the others, finding he liked the work they did even more than the military service. The stability of being in one place was a change, one that would have made relationships easier, if he wanted one. But Austin had no interest in a steady relationship at the time That changed over time, and the longer he stayed in Niagara Falls, the more he wanted to stay. The more he wanted what Samuel and Teddy and some of the other guys had.

But the only one Austin wanted any of that with was the one woman he couldn't have. So he stuffed those dreams away and did his job.

"I still remember the first time we met," Austin said, hoping to pull Lacey back from her darkness. "Your dad invited me over for dinner. He said your mom wanted to meet his new partner. I was young and cocky and thought I was hot shit. Your dad... He told me the wrong day. Wanted to fuck with me a little. Start me off on the wrong foot."

"Sounds like him," she said with a small laugh.

"When I showed up, you were just getting out of your car. You'd been at school, I think. You had a stack of books in your arms, and you were not paying attention to anything around you."

"Oh, no. What did I do?"

Austin shook his head, smiling at the memory. "Nothing. You were just so lost in thought you didn't realize I was there. I parked behind you and watched you walk toward the door. I was mesmerized by you."

She snorted. "I'm sure. The dorky girl lost in her own world."

"You were beautiful," he breathed.

She sucked in a breath.

"The light hit your hair and made you look like you were glowing. I thought I was at the wrong house because you looked younger than I thought you'd be. Samuel told me about his brilliant daughter who was studying to be a librarian, and I had this vision in my mind of a woman close to my age, but you were twenty-one or twenty-two when we met."

"Twenty-one. I remember that day. I'd finished up a big assignment for school. It was my last project for my undergrad, and I was coming home to crash. I'd been at the library almost nonstop for months, and all I wanted to do was sleep. And then you showed up."

Austin laughed. "You were not happy when you opened the door right after you'd closed it and I was standing there. You told me I had the wrong house, and that you weren't buying whatever I was selling."

"I thought you were a solicitor!"

"I think that would have been better. Then you could have actually made me leave. Instead, your dad heard me and walked up, laughing his ass off that I'd caught them at home. He planned to be gone by the time I got there."

"That's right. My mom was in a dress. They were going out. She was so mad you were early."

Austin grinned. "I was trying to make a good impression. Instead, I pissed her off and got him in trouble."

Lacey snorted. "You did. But I think it was a good night."

"Yeah, it was." Austin knew she was thinking about the takeout he and Samuel picked up and brought back for everyone to enjoy. He was thinking about watching her all night and wishing someone so sweet would give him the time of day. Instead, she yawned the entire night and went to bed before he even left, barely paying him any attention.

The next day was the first time Samuel told Austin his princess was off-limits. Definitely not the last.

They settled into silence, both lost in their memories. Austin hadn't had time to process the loss of his partner, and sharing the story with Lacey brought a wave of sadness. He choked out, "Excuse me," and left the room.

In his bathroom, he squeezed his eyes shut. Men weren't supposed to cry. His father beat that into him. Men should be tough. Crying was for babies.

Austin couldn't remember the last time he let tears fall, but as he thought about Samuel dying alone, a bullet likely killing him before he knew what happened, more tears welled up and demanded to be let out.

Austin hung his head and let it out. Lacey needed to know he was strong for her, that she could count on him. Samuel was her father, not his, and he couldn't let his emotions overshadow hers.

After a few minutes, Austin controlled himself and stopped the tears. He splashed cold water on his face and used the bathroom. He went back to the living room and found Lacey sound asleep.

He grinned, chuckling to himself that she'd passed out so quickly. He settled back onto his spot on the couch, grabbing the remote and tuning the volume down on the TV so it wouldn't wake her up. He flipped through the mediocre offerings before choosing a show about manufacturing.

The show lulled Austin to sleep, and before he knew it, a cry woke him up. He sat up fast, searching the hotel room blindly, struggling to put the pieces into place before the cry came again.

Lacey.

ELEVEN

Austin's heart pounded at the agony in her voice. He wanted to take all her pain away. Forever.

Lacey cried out again, still asleep. Her arm swung wildly and connected with his thigh. She kicked a foot out, barely missing the solid coffee table a few feet from the couch.

"Lacey," Austin called, hoping his voice would pull her out of her dream. "Lacey, wake up."

She stilled for a second, then flung her arms again. One hit the side of the couch, the other bounced off the cushions on the back. She was going to hurt herself if she kept flailing like she was.

"Lacey, come on, sweetheart, wake up." Austin moved closer to her, catching one of her hands before she punched him.

She fought him, struggling to free her hand. "No!"

"Lacey, wake up. You're having a dream."

She kept fighting him, punching and kicking, shouting.

Austin was going to hurt both of them if he didn't stop her wild movements. The only thing he could think of was to lie on top of her. Pin her down and stop her movements.

She fought him, but he didn't let her buck him off. He brought his hand to her face and realized her cheeks were soaked with tears.

"Aw, Princess. Wake up, Lacey. Come on, sweetheart. Wake up for me."

Her eyes flipped open, panic in them before they landed on him. "What... What are you doing on top of me?"

"You were having a nightmare. We both fell asleep on the couch, and I woke up when you cried out."

She shifted, her body coming into contact with his erection. She let out a gasp.

"Sorry." Austin eased off her, giving her space.

"It's fine. I know it's not personal."

"What... What does that mean?"

"It's a biological thing. I was... It's fine."

"You think... I don't even know what to say."

"It's fine." She stood and moved around the other side of the couch, away from him. "I'm going to get some sleep."

"Lacey."

"Good night, Austin." She raced to her bedroom and closed the door before he could say anything else.

Like *what the fuck?*

Austin shook his head and tried to put it out of his mind. She thought he was hard because he just woke up instead of because he was pressed against her curves with his hands on her softness. She thought it had nothing to do with her.

Correcting her would have only led to disaster. Lacey MacNeil did not want him. Letting her go was the best option.

Austin went through the suite and made sure everything was good for the night. The door was still locked, the balcony secure, and everything inside hadn't been touched while they slept. He turned off the TV and the lights in the living room, closing the curtains. With all the lights off, the space was dark. Too dark. Austin turned on a light over the kitchen island.

He went to his room, closing the door before he decided to open it again. He wanted to hear Lacey when she got up, or if she needed anything during the night.

He hurried through his bathroom routine, debating checking on her before he went to bed. He eased out of his room, standing at her door and listening for any noises from her side.

He was about to turn when a soft sob broke through the silence. A sniffle followed, and Austin closed his eyes and knocked.

"Lacey. Are you okay?"

"I'm fine," she said through the door, her voice a watery muffle.

"You're not okay. Can I come in?"

"You don't need to keep saving me, Austin. I know it's not part of the job."

"What are you talking about?"

He was standing close to the door, his ear nearly pressed to it, and was surprised when the door whipped open and revealed her.

Thick, creamy thighs were exposed below lace-edged shorts. A full, soft belly was encased in soft blue fabric. Breasts hung free beneath the tank, two taut nipples pressing against the blue. Wild, brown hair hung around her shoulders, teasing the tops of her breasts.

Two arms blocked his view, crossing over her chest.

He cleared his throat and took a step back. "I'm sorry."

"I'm talking about you comforting me when I'm crying. It's not part of the job, Austin. My dad..." She sucked in a breath, those breasts lifting once more. "My dad always said you were protection, not comfort. It wasn't a part of the job to make whoever you're protecting feel better. You don't have to keep trying to make me feel better."

"You shouldn't be alone when you're upset, Lacey."

She laughed. "I already told you I'm always alone. I'm used to it, Austin. It's not ever going to change."

"Yeah, well, when I'm here, you don't have to be alone."

"Stop," she said, halting his progress. "Just... stop, Austin. I know this is some misplaced guilt or something. You're not my boyfriend. You're my dad's partner. I know you don't want to be here."

"No, I don't. I want your dad to be alive. I want him back to telling me to stay away from you. I want to see you laugh and smile and roll your eyes at something he did. I want to go back to my place and imagine you looking at me the way your mother looked at him. But none of that's happening anymore."

"Why would he tell you to stay away from me?"

Austin closed his eyes, realizing what he confessed to. "Never mind. I shouldn't speak when I'm so exhausted. I'll leave you alone." He turned to go.

"Tell me," she whispered.

Austin couldn't face her when he said it, so he told his room the truth. "Because he always caught me looking at you. Said you were sweet and innocent and needed to be protected."

Her soft gasp went straight to his dick. "Why were you looking at me?"

"Because you're gorgeous."

She snorted. "Hardly."

Austin turned to face her, letting the desire he felt for her lift to the surface. "Oh Lacey, you have no idea. You hide yourself behind oversized clothes, but I don't care. You're beautiful, and you're far too good for me. Your father knew it. That's why he always told me to stay away from you."

She shook her head and moved toward him. "You're lying. You don't want me. No one wants me. I don't know why you're saying all this, Austin, but—"

He cut her words off with a kiss, charging toward her and sealing his lips over hers before she could continue to insult him with her disagreement.

One hand speared through her hair, the other landed on her side, his fingers finding the soft skin at the gap between her tank and her shorts. His tongue pried her lips apart, and she sighed.

She fucking sighed.

A soft mewl came from her, a cry like she still didn't believe he was kissing her.

He slid his hand around to her back, teasing her flesh as he got his first taste of her. He brought her body into contact with his, letting her feel the effect she had on him.

She gasped and jumped back.

"Fuck. I'm sorry. I shouldn't have touched you. I... Fuck. I'll get someone else to stay with you. I'll call right now so you know you're safe."

"Is this real?" she whispered.

"What? Is what real?"

"Are you real? Are you..." She swallowed roughly. "Men don't want me, Austin. I'm not desirable or attractive or sexy. I'm invisible. I'm forgettable."

"You are none of those things. Not to me. You're beautiful. You're smart. You are kind and sweet and way too damn good for me."

"I... No one's ever said those things to me."

"You deserve to be told that every day, Lacey. To know how amazing you are."

"My dad was the only one who ever saw me. Not in a creepy way, but he knew me. He always said I'd meet someone who made me so happy I'd forget all about the pain I'd been through."

"What pain?" Austin growled.

"It doesn't matter," Lacey said, shaking her head. "He's... He was my hero. He was the only one who ever made me think there might be someone out there for me."

"He knew you better than anyone else."

"Yeah." She nodded, chewing on her lip. "I don't know how to live without him." She covered her mouth with her hand, her whole body shaking with her sob.

"Lacey, can I hold you? Please? You can say no, but I don't want you alone. Not because you can't handle it. Not because I feel guilty. Because I want you to know I'm here. I want to be here for you."

"Okay," she whispered.

Austin stepped up to her and pulled her into his arms. He kissed her hairline and held her for a long minute.

"Let's lie down, Lacey. You can sleep."

"You don't want... I mean, of course not, but I thought..."

"You thought what?"

"Nothing."

"Please tell me, beautiful."

"I figured you'd want sex or something."

Austin sucked in a breath, releasing it slowly. "If I'm ever lucky enough to have sex with you, it's not going to be because you're crying. It's not going to be because I'm comforting you. It's going to be because you can't resist my charms."

She chuckled.

"I'm not worthy of you, Lacey. I never will be. But I'm not going to take advantage of you when you're upset. That's not who I am."

"I didn't mean—"

"It's okay. I know. Let's get some sleep. Let me hold you so you can rest, Lacey. Okay?"

She looked up at him and nodded.

Austin followed her to her bed, feeling something click into place when she wrapped her arm around his middle and settled her head on his good shoulder. He kissed the top of her head and held her close to his side.

Her breathing slowed almost immediately, sleep claiming her just as quickly as it had before. Austin held her tight and closed his eyes. He made a promise to Samuel that he would protect her. He would make sure she was safe. And then he'd let her go so she could live the life he always knew she'd have. With a man worthy of her and a family she dreamed of.

He just hated he wouldn't be the one to share that life with her. But she deserved better. He'd keep his word and let her have it.

LACEY WOKE to the sound of a crash. She sat up straight in her bed, her heart pounding as she searched for reality.

Hotel. Dad gone. Austin.

She looked at the empty bed next to her. For three nights Austin had been sharing her bed, holding her as she slept, and disappearing before she woke.

She listened for sounds of Austin, explanations of the crash that woke her, and silently swung her feet from the bed. She tiptoed to the door, hoping the noise was Austin and not someone else. That they were still safe.

Her ears rang with the silence of the hotel room. Her door was open, just enough to squeeze through, and she stepped out of the room.

There was a light on in Austin's bedroom. Maybe the bathroom? Lacey crept closer, hoping to see what was going on without alerting anyone to her presence.

"Dammit," Austin hissed as Lacey drew closer to the bathroom.

She peeked around the doorframe, and her breath caught in her throat. Austin was standing in front of the oversized bathroom mirror, shirtless, trying to change the bandage on his shoulder. The angry scar she saw the day they were in the panic room was less angry, but still not completely healed.

"Can I help?" Lacey asked, her voice morning rough.

Austin met her gaze in the mirror. "I didn't mean to wake you."

"It's okay." Lacey stepped into the bathroom and spotted the reason for her racing heart. The reason that wasn't Austin. His shaving kit was splayed on the floor, items strewn all over the bathroom behind him.

"I had it too close to the edge and knocked it over. I should have been watching." Austin's tone read regret.

"You're injured. And all you've been doing is taking care of me. You should have asked me to help you with this."

Austin shook his head. "It's fine."

"Let me help you." Lacey moved toward him, taking the bandage from his hand.

Austin glared at the mirror, his gaze lingering on Lacey and making her shiver.

She ignored his attitude and less than friendly look and focused on her task. She was absolutely not enjoying the feel of his warm, soft skin. Or the way his heat soaked into her body being so close to him. She'd slept in the same bed as him for three nights, but he was always dressed, a tee blocking her ability to feel his bare skin next to hers.

She hadn't been able to appreciate his body when they'd been trapped in his panic room, not really. She'd been too wrapped up in her father's death and the overall panic of the situation they were in. She'd noticed it, for sure, but without someone outside the room with a gun ready to kill both of them, she could appreciate it a lot more now.

Lacey taped the gauze over his wound and reluctantly stepped back. She only got half a step away before his hand snatched hers.

"I'm sorry."

She shook her head and forced a smile. "Nothing to apologize for."

"I should be out there finding out what happened to your father. Or I should just know. I should be doing something. But I'm stuck here and fucking useless." He inhaled a rough breath and slammed his eyes closed. "I let it get to me this morning. I won't let it happen again."

"You don't have to be perfect all the time, Austin."

He snorted. "I'm never perfect. Not like you, Princess."

She gasped at the nickname. He kept using it. Sometimes with affection, sometimes with a sneer. It was messing with her head. Messing with everything.

"I'm sorry. That was…"

"It's fine," she breathed, stepping away and regaining her hand from his grasp. She moved out of the bathroom and through his bedroom, needing space from him. She needed to get the hell out of the hotel. To get some fresh air and some clarity and some space from Austin.

She went to the kitchen without thinking about anything other than a need for coffee. She started the pot, grabbing two mugs from the cabinet above the coffeepot. It was domestic, being there with Austin. But it wasn't real. He said he was stuck. He didn't have a choice. He wasn't there because he wanted to be with her. He was there because his boss wouldn't let him do anything else.

She wasn't under the same restrictions. She could leave.

As she waited for the coffee to brew, she debated what to say to Montgomery. She agreed to stay with Austin, but it had been three days. No one had come after them, and all of Montgomery's thoughts on who was after them pointed to Austin, not her.

She had to go back to her life. To work, see her mother, begin to heal. Playing house with Austin was not helping her.

Austin came into the kitchen as the coffee finished. He accepted the mug she handed him before she poured her own.

Lacey turned to face him. She swallowed the tightness in her throat. She didn't like disappointing people, but it was time to move on. "I'm going to call Montgomery and go home."

Austin set his mug on the counter with a heavy thud. "What? Why? You can't do that. You could be in danger."

Lacey shook her head. "No one cares about me. I'm not important. And I need to go back to work. Start to move on with my life."

"Is this about me getting angry? Are you afraid of me?" Austin's voice was low, almost a whisper. His gaze was locked on the counter, not meeting hers.

"Of course not, but you've made it clear you don't want to be here. If I leave, you can, too. I know you're only here because of me. If I weren't a part of this, you'd be home."

"Montgomery put me here, too," Austin growled.

"Yeah, to watch me. I get it. I'm a pain. I'm not wanted. So I'm going to go."

"Lacey—"

"It's okay, Austin. I know this has been less than fun for you. I know you're ready to do something besides babysitting me. It's time." She turned and walked away, closing the door to her room so she could pack without him trying to convince her she was wrong about leaving.

It was time to go. She needed to go. She couldn't pretend any longer. No matter how much fun it was to imagine what a life with Austin Ward would be like.

TWELVE

Austin stared at her bedroom door and resisted the urge to burst in and change her mind. She was determined to leave, and there was nothing he could say or do to convince her otherwise.

Not without crossing a whole bunch of lines.

He'd already crossed a few of them when he held her every night. When he pulled her into his arms and pretended she belonged to him. He imagined more than once what their lives would be like together, but she didn't want that. After he kissed her that first night, he hadn't done it again. She pretended it hadn't happened, moving on with things like they were just friends who shared a bed at night. Platonically, if that were possible.

And now, she was ready to go.

So was he, but fuck. He didn't want it to be like that. Not when there was still a threat out there. Maybe Montgomery...

Austin tapped the screen to call his boss before he could finish the thought.

"Rose."

"Lacey wants to leave. She's sick of being cooped up with me."

"Okay. We don't think she's in any real danger. We said she could go home before. She wanted to stick around and find out what's going on."

"You're just going to let her walk around? Go back to her life? Pretend someone didn't try to kill her a few days ago?"

"What do you want me to do, Ward? Hold her hostage? Tell her she can't leave until we figure out everything, even when we have no evidence to suggest she's a target?" Montgomery growled. "She's grieving. Her father died. She needs closure, and sometimes people need to go back to their lives in order to move forward."

"I fucking know!" Austin exhaled roughly. He glanced toward Lacey's room, then closed his eyes. "She's not... We can't let anything happen to her."

"If I had any reason to believe she was in danger, I'd tell you it's not an option for her to leave. We've been looking. For days, we've been looking. We don't have answers, but we don't have anything to confirm she's being targeted. She'll be fine."

"What if she's not?" Austin barked.

"What are you really worried about, Ward?"

Austin blew out a breath and shook his head. "Nothing, sir. Nothing at all."

Montgomery's sigh said he didn't like that answer. "Lacey has the keys for the SUV in the lot under the hotel. I'll get in touch with Eve and have her escort the two of you down to it. Think Lacey can drive you two here and we can go through everything before she goes back to her world?"

"Yeah," Austin said, knowing it was his last chance to convince Lacey she could be in danger. "Yeah, we'll do it."

"Okay. I'll reach out to Eve. I'll let you know when to expect a knock."

"Thanks," Austin said, feeling slightly better.

"Hey Ward?"

"Yeah?"

"Don't fucking swear at me again."

"Yes, sir." Austin breathed. He hung up the phone and closed his eyes. Montgomery was a good boss. A great boss. But Austin knew that also meant he deserved more respect. Montgomery took a chance on Austin, thanks to a good word from Teddy, but Austin proved he was a valuable part of the team.

Until he wasn't.

Lacey's bedroom door opened and the woman Austin had gotten to know over the last week was gone. Back were the oversized clothes and downcast eyes, hiding in her own shadow and taking up as little space as possible.

She wheeled a small suitcase behind her, standing it up in front of the door to her room. "I'm going to call for a ride. My friend can pick me up."

"No!" Austin shouted.

Lacey jumped at his word.

"I mean, I talked to Montgomery. He wants us both to go to the office. If you don't mind driving."

"I forgot about the SUV."

"Eve will be up here soon to walk down with us. If you don't mind waiting for me to pack."

"Why are you leaving? I thought you were in danger."

"I'll figure something out. Just... wait. Please?"

She nodded.

Austin rushed to the room he'd used to shower and change, thankful he never unpacked everything. He tossed his clothes into a bag, shoveled the stuff off the bathroom counter into his shaving kit, and unplugged his charger just as his phone buzzed with a text from Montgomery.

Eve is on her way up.

Copy. Thanks.

Austin pocketed his phone and carried his things to the small hallway with Lacey's. She stood to the side, staring at her phone and toying with her locket.

"Eve is almost here. Then we can go."

"Okay," she whispered, pocketing her phone and stepping out of the way.

Austin moved past her to the living room. The suite had been a good place for them to lie low for a few days. He hadn't missed the chance to get to know Lacey MacNeil in a way he was never allowed to before. To know she was funny and emotional and such a good person she made him feel bad for the thoughts he had about her.

Thoughts he absolutely had to keep to himself going forward.

"I'm—"

Her sentence was cut off by a sharp knock on the door.

Austin moved past Lacey, putting himself between her and the door as he checked the peephole. He smiled when he saw Eve on the other side of the door.

Austin unlocked the door and swung it open, smirking at the small Black woman shaking her head at him. "Hello, Eve."

"Austin Ward. Always getting yourself in trouble."

Austin snorted. "You know me."

"I do. That's why you're here. So far, everything has been quiet, but I hear you're heading out."

Austin nodded. "Yeah. Thanks, Eve."

Eve looked past Austin to Lacey and smiled kindly at her. "Hi, Lacey. I knew your father. I'm so sorry for your loss."

Lacey sucked in a sharp breath. "Thank you. I'm sorry, I don't think I know you."

"There's a reason for that. I'm Eve Barnes. I run security here. If you knew who I was, it meant I wasn't doing my job.

But I've been watching your hallway since you two moved in, and all the access points here. Making sure you're both safe."

"Thank you?" Lacey said, the end rising like a question.

Eve chuckled. "Your father was a kind man. I was sorry to miss his service. Please give your mother my condolences."

"You know my mother?" Lacey blurted.

Eve nodded. "We've met a few times. Your father talked about her constantly. And you. He was quick to tell anyone who asked that he was a lucky man and had the two best girls on earth as his."

Lacey's smile wobbled. She clutched her hands in front of her and sucked in a shaky breath. "Thank you."

Eve nodded to the keys Austin held out for Lacey. "I've been told you're driving this one around and to see the two of you downstairs."

Lacey accepted the keys and nodded. "Thank you."

"SUV is parked in the employee lot underneath the building. Spot C6. Can I help with your luggage?" Eve asked, reaching for Austin's bag without waiting for agreement.

"I can take mine," Lacey said, reaching for the handle of her suitcase.

"Looks like we're set. I'll make a run through the room before I let housekeeping in to make sure nothing was left behind. Are you two ready to go?" Eve asked.

Lacey nodded and followed Eve out of the room, leaving Austin to trail behind the two women, his hands uselessly empty.

Eve charmed Lacey, as she did everyone she met, on the elevator ride down to the ground floor. Eve was smart and cutthroat, when she needed to be, but she kept that side of her hidden from most people. Rose Protection Agency used The Davidson Hotel for years when they needed something not quite as protected as a safe house but more secure than a standard hotel. Eve was excellent at her job, and she ran a great crew of employees who worked to keep the guests safe.

Eve led the way to the SUV, nodding to it before Lacey unlocked it. Lacey hit a button to lift the tailgate, and the women loaded the luggage into the trunk. Eve hugged Lacey warmly, then turned to Austin.

"Be careful. Both of you." Eve shook hands with Austin.

"No hug for me?"

Eve snorted. "We're colleagues. Lacey's my new friend."

Austin shook his head. "Thanks for your help, Eve."

"Any time. Tell Montgomery I'll be in touch later."

Austin nodded, wondering what that was about, and climbed into the passenger seat while Lacey settled behind the wheel.

"She's nice," Lacey said tightly.

"Yeah. She's a real badass, too."

"Eve?" Lacey was surprised by that news.

"Don't let the smile fool you. She'd just as quickly knock you out as help you out, depending on who you were."

"I can't imagine her as someone to be afraid of."

"That's part of why she's so good. She looks like someone you should underestimate, but I promise you, she's not. She's trained with us a few times. Brought her team to a few things we've done. She's knocked both me and your father on our asses more than once."

"Wow. That's impressive." Lacey backed out of the parking spot and turned to leave the parking lot.

Austin waited for her to get out onto a city street before he got his bearings. "You know where to go?"

Lacey nodded. "I'm good."

Austin leaned back in his seat and watched the sights go by. People were out in droves, enjoying the sights of Niagara Falls and the warm spring weather.

Lacey swerved, the sudden movement making Austin's shoulder hurt.

"You okay?"

Lacey nodded, her gaze on the rearview mirror. "Yeah."

"What's wrong?"

"The vehicle behind me is getting really close. They almost rear-ended me."

Austin looked back, trying to see what was going on. The driver swerved, like they were going to come up next to them.

Lacey slowed down to let them pass her. A red light ahead had the oncoming traffic stopped.

The window lowered, and the barrel of a gun appeared.

"Gun! Lacey, go."

"What?" The window exploded. Lacey screamed.

"Are you okay? Lacey, drive! Can you drive?"

She screamed again. "What do I do?"

"Hit the gas, Lace. Go. Now!"

The SUV lurched as she pressed her foot down hard on the gas. They jumped ahead of the SUV shooting at them, racing toward the red light.

She slowed down again.

"Lacey, you have to go."

"It's a red light!"

"They're going to kill us! Go!"

Lacey pressed the gas again, blowing on the horn as she approached the intersection. She sped right through, narrowly missing one vehicle but hitting the front bumper of another.

"Oh my God, I hit her car." She slowed again.

"Lacey, go! We'll send help, but you have to go."

She hit the gas again, and Austin checked the mirror. The SUV that had been shooting at them was stuck behind the accident, but it wouldn't hold them for long. They had to get to safety. Now.

"What if someone's hurt?"

"If you're dead, you can't help them, and that's what would have happened. You need to get us to the office now. As fast as you can, Lacey. Keep going. Don't stop."

Lacey nodded, her jaw set and her gaze locked on the road.

Austin called Montgomery.

"You almost here?"

"Someone's shooting at us."

"What?" Montgomery barked.

"We're on the way. Two minutes. But you need to call Marcus. Blew through the intersection at Fortieth and Pine, hit a car. They were right on us, already got a shot off. Driver's window shattered."

"Shattered? It's supposed to be bulletproof."

"Yeah, well, those bullets didn't get the damn memo. Ninety seconds."

"We're ready. Have her pull up to the door."

"Pull up to the door," Austin told Lacey. "Don't park in a spot. Get as close as you can. They're waiting for us."

Lacey nodded, not speaking.

"Get her first," Austin told Montgomery.

"Copy."

"Almost there, Lace. Thirty seconds," Austin said. Silence met his words. "I see you."

Lacey turned into the parking lot and went straight toward the building. The team was outside, forming a perimeter for them to pull into. Lacey brought the vehicle to a stop in front of them, scrambling to get out so fast she didn't even put the SUV in park.

Austin yanked the parking brake on, thankful it was where he could reach it, as Lacey collapsed into Lance's arms. Lance wrapped an arm around her and led her to the door, glancing back at Austin before he disappeared with Lacey.

"Let's go," Montgomery said, opening Austin's door.

Austin shook off the hand offered to him and got himself out of the SUV. "Bags are in the back. Eve saw us off, carried our stuff. No clue when we picked up a tail, but check on her."

"On it," Zeke said, moving ahead of Austin into the building.

They moved as a unit, the doors opening ahead of Austin as he and Lacey were guided to the back of the building. Where whoever was shooting at them couldn't get to them.

"WHAT THE FUCK HAPPENED?" Kimberly hissed into her phone.

"I don't know."

"Well, that wasn't good. Why don't we have a handle on what is going on right now?"

"Because they're better than we thought."

"We can't let something like that happen again."

"Understood."

"Where are they?"

"Ward and MacNeil's daughter are back at Rose offices. There's no way anyone's getting in there."

"They have to leave eventually," Kimberly said.

"I'll be waiting when they do."

"Good. This needs to be over. All of it."

"It will be soon. I promise you."

A sound outside the door had Kimberly looking up. "I need to go." She hung up without waiting for an answer.

The door swung open, and Nicole shuffled in with a nurse right behind her. Nicole's green eyes were muddy with the meds they were keeping her on, even though Kimberly asked every day for Nicole to be taken off of them.

The nurse helped Nicole get settled in the bed again. The hospital was a good one. Private and personal, but still a medical facility, which meant Kimberly couldn't just tell them to fuck off and leave.

"I'll be back in an hour with some dinner," the nurse said before leaving Nicole and Kimberly alone.

Kimberly was by her sister's side before the door closed. "Are you okay?"

Nicole shook her head, her throat working to swallow. "I don't want to stay here. When can we go?"

"I don't know. They're worried about you. I am, too."

"I should have told you the truth. I should have come to you the first time," Nicole whispered.

Kimberly hugged her sister tight. "I don't blame you. I wish you'd been able to, but I understand why you didn't. I was so wrapped up in everything else, but I should have been paying more attention to you. To what was going on."

"None of it is your fault."

"I let daddy tell me what to do. I knew Peter was an asshole, but I didn't know... I didn't know he would hurt you."

"It's over now. He's not going to hurt me again."

"No one is. I'm going to make sure of it."

"I love you, Kimmy."

"I love you, Nicki."

Kimberly held her sister until the meds did their job and Nicole fell asleep. Kimberly laid Nicole on the bed and cried silent tears for the innocence stolen from her sister.

Kimberly hated that Nicole had been abused, but for it to happen under Kimberly's roof, for her own husband to have been the one who hurt her sister...

Death wasn't anywhere near enough punishment for the piece of shit.

But death was better than risking he got away with his crimes again.

He'd never get away with anything again.

She made sure of that.

THIRTEEN

Lacey's hands shook as she accepted the bottle of water from Lance. She squeezed a fist and released it, trading the bottle to the other hand and repeating the move. It didn't help.

"You doing okay?" Lance asked.

Lacey shook her head. No sense lying to the man. He could see she wasn't. "I'm not like you guys. I'm not used to getting shot at."

"You got here safely. That's the most important part."

"Yeah, but I hit someone. A car. They were driving through the intersection, and Austin told me to go. I saw the woman's face right before I hit her. She knew there was nothing she could do." Lacey closed her eyes. "I'll never get her expression out of my head."

"The police are taking care of her and her son."

"Her son! She had a kid in the car!" Lacey was on the verge of a breakdown before. Fighting it was out of the question now.

She reached her hand forward to set the water bottle on the table in front of her and missed. The bottle tilted on the edge, then tipped over and plunked onto the floor. The water sloshed inside the closed bottle, sending it rolling a foot.

Lacey sank to the couch behind her. Cold washed over her. She trembled, her hands turning to ice as she saw the woman's face and realized why her fear was so palpable.

She had a kid in the car. A son Lacey didn't see, which meant he was small enough to be in the backseat. And Lacey hit their car.

"Lacey, there was nothing you could have done. You would have been killed if you hadn't driven through that red light." Lance's tone was placating, but Lacey knew it wasn't revealing the whole truth.

"It doesn't matter. I still hit someone. I ran a red light and someone could have gotten hurt. Or killed. Oh, God, tell me I didn't kill anyone." Panic seized her.

Lance shook his head. "No. We haven't heard anything about any fatalities."

"But they were injured. Weren't they?"

Lance did not have a poker face.

"How bad?" Lacey whispered.

"Bumps and bruises," Montgomery said, joining them without Lacey noticing. "The little boy was in a car seat, so he was fine. The car was spun around, but all other traffic through the intersection was able to stop, so they weren't hit a second time. They'll be fine."

"Are you sure?" Lacey gasped.

"Yeah. Marcus has already been to see them. He explained what was going on and got a statement from the mother. She said you looked terrified and hoped you're okay."

Lacey exhaled a laugh. "She's too kind. I hit her, and she's worried about me?"

"She said her husband works for a collision shop and he's told her about some nasty accidents. She knows how lucky she and her son were."

Lacey swallowed and nodded. "I'm glad they're going to be okay. I just... Who was shooting at us?"

"Eve pulled security from the hotel. There was nothing on their side."

"Which means what?" Lacey asked, feeling like she was missing pieces. Lots of pieces.

"It means whoever came after you was not waiting for you at the hotel. It was either chance they saw you or they were waiting a little farther away."

"What's the likelihood it's chance?" Lacey asked.

"Basically zero."

"So someone knew we were going to be leaving the hotel and coming here and waited on our path back to try to kill us. Or one of us."

Montgomery nodded.

"What the hell is going on?" Lacey cried.

Montgomery jerked his head toward the door for Lance to leave, then took a seat next to Lacey. "We don't know."

Lacey laughed mirthlessly. "You're supposed to make me feel better, Montgomery. You should have answers and be able to give me something."

"I know. And I wish I could, but the truth is we don't know. I won't insult you with lies or empty promises. What I will say is I'm very grateful you were with Austin today. I know being sidelined is making him mad, but if he'd been alone or driving, I don't think you and I would be having the same conversation right now."

The cold was back, washing over Lacey like she'd been shoved into a deep freezer with the door slammed shut behind her. She shivered.

"Whoever is behind all of this seems to want silence."

"So they think we know something."

"That would be my guess."

"I don't need more guesses. Who knew we were coming here today?"

"Me and Austin, and you."

"What about Eve?"

Montgomery shook his head. "She didn't know where you were going, only that you were leaving. And I trust her."

"How do you know you can trust her?"

"Because we were in the services together. She's as solid as they come. And..." Montgomery trailed off.

"And?"

"She's a friend. She's someone we rely on. Have for a long time. I have no reason to believe she would ever betray us."

"Then who told these people we would be out there?"

Montgomery shook his head. "Again, I don't have answers."

"Then how do you know they're not going to just walk in here and put a gun to my head?"

Montgomery grabbed Lacey's hand. "This place is secure, Lacey. As secure as anywhere else could possibly be. We have security on it, and outside. No one will get within fifty feet of the door with a weapon without us knowing."

Lacey nodded but she didn't feel any more comforted than before he told her that. She wasn't safe. None of them were. "I can't do this, Montgomery. I can't live like this."

"I know, Lacey. I know. Your father was good at his job, but he never wanted you to know the details of how things work around here. He wanted to protect you, make sure you didn't see the ugly we deal with every day. No one should know about this world we live in."

"Why do you do it?" Lacey whispered.

Montgomery rubbed his forearm, right over a rose tattoo. "My sister. When she disappeared, I was lost. She was my only family. My mother... My mother swallowed a bottle of pills. My father was... He was a piece of shit. Nina was sweet and kind and innocent. We thought someone took her, and it killed me that no one found her. That she was out there and had no one to protect her. Zeke and I decided we didn't want anyone else's sister to feel like she had nowhere to turn. We started out just the two of us, helping the police and keeping people safe. Over time, and once my father died and I had money, we grew. Hired more people, protected more people."

"Is it worth it?"

Montgomery looked at Lacey, his gaze locked on hers. The edge of his mouth lifted slightly. "Most of the time."

"The bad guys are always going to be out there."

"Yeah."

"If you stop fighting to protect people from them, doesn't that make you just as bad as they are?"

A laugh puffed out of him. "Your dad said something similar once. Right after Nina came back. I was... I'd stopped looking for her. I thought she was dead. I was beating myself up for having missed everything, for her being right here in our city and never knowing it. Your dad told me we can't save everyone. That the ones we lose are always going to be the hardest ones. We do what we do because of the ones we save, but the ones we don't save are the ones that stick with us. For every one we lose, there are dozens more that we save. But that one makes us keep coming back. Because we want to make it safe for everyone to stand up to people doing the wrong thing."

Lacey smiled. "He was a pretty amazing man."

Montgomery put a hand on her knee and squeezed. "He was. And none of us are ever going to forget him. We never wanted one of our own to be one of the ones we lost."

Lacey nodded. "Yeah."

"Lacey, I want you and Austin to stay in some kind of protective custody."

She started to argue, but Montgomery held up his hand.

"I know you don't want that. I get it. I know it's not a long-term plan. Or a solution. But I also know if either of you is killed because we let you choose and you were too stubborn to listen, I'll never forgive myself."

Lacey closed her eyes. She pictured her mom, the grief that swallowed her since they found out her father died. Would she survive if Lacey was killed? Did it matter? Because Lacey didn't want to die. She had a lot of life ahead of her. Even if that life was alone.

"Okay," she whispered.

"You'll do it?" Montgomery asked.

Lacey nodded. "Yeah. I don't want to end up dead, and I don't want to put my mother through planning another funeral. It would break her."

"None of us want anymore funerals."

Lacey nodded. "Are we going back to the hotel?"

"We can talk about that and decide. If it's either that or a safe house, what—?"

"Hotel," Lacey blurted before he finished his question.

Montgomery stood, not commenting on her interruption. "I'll talk to Austin, see what he's open to."

"Do you think the hotel is still safe?" Lacey whispered.

"I do. There are always risks, but a hotel means we can go in and out without drawing a lot of attention. With a safe house, you never know if someone's watching."

"Will Austin and I stay together?" Lacey asked, toying with the edge of her shorts.

"That's up to you," Montgomery said slowly. "Are you opposed to that?"

"No! No. Austin was great. He's fine. I... I know him well and trust him. He'd never let anything happen to me."

"None of us would, Lacey. We'll figure out what makes sense and go from there."

"Thanks, Montgomery."

He nodded, then let himself out of the office.

Lacey grabbed the abandoned water bottle from the floor. Her hands didn't shake as badly anymore. She twisted off the top and took a sip. How was this her life?

AUSTIN SAT in the conference room with Captain Patrick, getting grilled about the chase and shooting that sent one woman and her two-year-old son to the hospital with minor injuries. Thankfully, they were both going to be fine, but Austin was to blame for the accident. Even if he wasn't behind the wheel, it was his fault.

"You saw the gun," Captain Patrick stated, confirming, not asking.

"Yes. Lacey said a vehicle behind her almost rear-ended her, and they came around to the side, so she slowed down. When she did, they got next to us, and I saw the gun. I told her to go. I told her we'd die if she slowed down. She went through that light because of me."

"Let's get one thing clear. She did what you said because someone was shooting at you. Neither of you is to blame for this."

"Yeah, well, it sounds like no one knows who actually is to blame, so until we have answers, I'll believe what I believe." Austin's glare at the police captain wasn't really at him, even though his department hadn't found the answers either. No one knew what the fuck was going on, and it meant for the second time in less than a week, Lacey was in danger.

Austin didn't give a fuck about his own risk. He would tear the damn world to pieces if anything happened to Lacey.

He adjusted his arm, trying to hide his wince when his

healing wound tugged and his shoulder reminded him it had been shot and surgically repaired just nine days ago.

"Do you need something?" Captain Patrick asked, nodding to Austin's shoulder.

"I'll be fine. I just need this to all be over. Valerie lost her husband. She can't lose her daughter, too."

"What about you? You lost Samuel. He was your partner for seven years."

Austin didn't appreciate the way the police captain saw through him. "I want whoever killed him to suffer. To lose everything that matters to them. To rot in a prison forever with no chance to see daylight again. But we both know that's not going to happen. If someone does find whoever did this, they're not going to have any remorse. People don't attack a safe house, track down the only survivor, and try to kill innocent people, and then feel bad about it."

Captain Patrick smirked, nodding in agreement. "Not in my experience, no. But that's a lawyer thing. My job is to catch them."

"How's that working for you?" Austin growled.

Captain Patrick breathed a mirthless laugh. "Next time you're going to get shot at, make sure there are cameras around."

Austin chuckled. "I'll keep that in mind."

"You do that." Captain Patrick looked up just before there was a knock on the glass door. He waved whoever it was to enter. "I think we're good."

"Any suspects yet?" Montgomery asked.

Captain Patrick shook his head. "Obviously, we're working on the belief it's tied to Peter Howard, but since he's dead, he's obviously not behind this attack. I told Austin to make sure next time there are cameras around."

Montgomery snorted. "Yeah. Good advice. I'll walk you out. Ward, don't go anywhere."

Austin nodded, knowing he was going to get a lecture from his boss, and be sent right back into some kind of protection, likely with one of the team watching out for him instead of just staying at The Davidson Hotel under Eve's guard.

Fuck.

The last time Austin wasn't the one running into danger was when he was living in it. His father was a mean son-of-a-bitch and not afraid to go after Austin whenever he felt like it. Austin tried to fight back once, but his dad was bigger and stronger, and meaner. Austin ended up in the hospital for a week, his dad claiming they were in an accident on a friend's property. The looks Austin got from the nurses said none of them believed the lie, but none of them did anything about it either.

Austin worked his ass off to stay out of his father's way after that, joining every school team and activity possible to spend as many hours away from home as possible. He enlisted in the Army the day he turned eighteen and never looked back.

Fifteen years of running into the fight had him wanting to ignore the pain in his shoulder and get out there and do what he did best. Even though he knew that was a bad idea. Sitting out of the fight reminded him of being stuck in his childhood home, pretending to be invisible so he didn't invoke his father's wrath.

His stomach turned with the memories. Sneaking in late at night when his father was already passed out and wouldn't come after him. Getting up early and leaving when his father was in the shower so he didn't have to face the man. Bulking up with football, wrestling, and rugby. Running with the track and cross-country teams so he knew he could get away. Hiding outside kickboxing and karate studios to pick up any moves he could without actually paying for lessons his dad would never approve or support.

The only reason Austin didn't end up exactly like his

father was the Army recruiter who showed up his senior year. Austin went to the college information night with no intention of going to college but every intention of spending a few hours away from home. The Army recruiter, Steven, took one look at Austin and the fading bruises on his face and said the Army would give him skills to protect himself and others.

That was all it took for Austin to make the decision. He spent the rest of the night asking questions and would have signed up that day if he was old enough. Steven gave Austin his contact information and offered to go with Austin on his birthday to sign up.

It saved his life. Sent him on a path that meant Austin was helping people instead of repeating patterns from his father. Steven pulled strings and got Austin onto a team with Teddy after his basic training was over.

The glass door to the conference room opened and Teddy stepped in. Austin breathed a laugh, not surprised his former sergeant knew Austin needed him. "You okay?"

Austin shook his head. "I will be if she is."

Teddy took a seat next to Austin. "She's shaken up, but she'll be okay. Thanks to you."

"I'm not so sure about that."

"You told her what to do. You got her out of there."

"I should have been driving," Austin growled.

"Do you remember when we got caught in between those abandoned buildings in the middle of town?"

Austin nodded. "I remember." They were pinned down, enemies on both ends of their path, and alone.

"Did you also know I got a concussion the day before? Argued that I was fine and insisted I go out?"

"You what?" Austin knew something was off with Teddy that day, but he thought it was something back home.

"You asked me three times before we went out there if I was okay. I was trying to prove I was fine, and I almost got all of us killed." Teddy hung his head. "None of us like to stand down. We want to be in it. The best thing you can do for her is to listen. To heal up so you can get back out there and take care of the fuckers who killed Samuel."

Austin closed his eyes, the pain hitting him square in the chest again. He didn't think he'd ever hear those words and not feel like the wind was knocked out of him.

Teddy was Austin's mentor, the first man who made him feel like he was capable. He was a friend of Steven's and took Austin under his wing from day one. When Teddy retired, Austin felt lost in the Army and didn't take long to follow Teddy's footsteps and put in his paperwork to leave. Teddy made Rose Protection Agency possible for Austin, and had him paired up with Samuel. In the seven years since, Austin found his way and felt like he could do anything.

But hearing his mentor tell him to rest and heal, and knowing it was advice Teddy hadn't been able to follow, told Austin it wasn't a punishment. He wasn't being pushed aside because he couldn't handle it or because they didn't trust him. He was being benched so he could handle more. One day.

"Okay," Austin breathed. "I'll do whatever I have to do."

"Good. Because I'm your new protection detail."

Austin snorted a laugh and shook his head. "You just wanted an easy job."

"Fuck yeah, I did. Nice to know I'll have one."

Austin smiled for the first time all day.

FOURTEEN

It had been three days since someone tried to kill them, and Lacey still hadn't stopped jumping at every noise. She had nightmares about the window shattering from the impact. She woke up in a panic every night.

And the worst part was she knew if Austin was in bed with her, she would sleep. But with Teddy in the hotel suite with them, Austin kept his distance from her.

She felt less alone when she was in her own apartment with no one else around.

"I'm staying home tonight," Teddy said at dinner, not meeting Lacey's gaze.

"Is that safe? For us?" She looked between the two men, who were both staring at their plates.

Teddy nodded and looked up at her. "Montgomery is going to have people posted in the hotel. Eve is working overnight and will be watching the monitors, and they're going to have someone watching the entrances."

"What are you not telling me?"

Austin smirked at Teddy. "Told you."

Teddy sighed heavily.

"What is going on?" Lacey wanted answers.

"Austin said you would know there was more to this. We think if I leave, we'll know if someone is watching us. Might follow me, might not, but likely we'll draw someone out."

"So you're leaving to see if we're still being watched?" Lacey wasn't sure she agreed with that plan.

"We have no answers. Peter Howard is dead. His wife hasn't left her sister's side and answered every question asked, but the police can't tie her to anything. She doesn't appear to be involved in any of his activity. His security team, the ones who weren't in the SUV with him, have disappeared. We aren't getting anywhere. We need to do something to draw out whoever is behind all of this."

"Whoever killed my father," Lacey said.

"And tried to kill you," Austin said.

Lacey looked at Austin. "Do you agree with this?"

Austin nodded. "We need answers, Lacey. We need to know what the hell is going on."

Lacey looked at Teddy. "What if they come after you?"

"We have a plan. I won't be on my own. We have vehicles ready to follow me out and stationed throughout the city on my path to the office. We aren't going to let them get away again."

Lacey exhaled and nodded. "I guess I don't really have a vote on this, do I?"

"You always have a vote," Austin said.

Lacey looked at him. He looked as exhausted as she felt, like he wasn't sleeping any better than she was. He'd been moving better and was no longer covering his incision with bandages. He was healing, but he still wasn't sleeping.

"If you don't agree with this, we'll come up with another plan," Austin said. "But we all want answers. We all want you to be able to go back to your life and know you're safe."

Lacey swallowed at the look in his eyes. Like he cared. Like he couldn't stand the thought of anything happening to her.

She wanted to crawl onto his lap and let him hold her. Let him take all her fears away.

But they didn't have that relationship. They didn't have any relationship. Her father held them together, and her mother refused to continue that bond. After all this was over, Lacey wouldn't see Austin again. He would go back to his job, and she would go back to her life, and they wouldn't intersect again.

Both men were watching her, and Lacey realized they were waiting for her to agree with their plan. She nodded, returning to her dinner before she blurted out something she shouldn't.

Like *what about you*? Or *why do you care if I'm safe*? Or *do you feel this, too*?

Nothing good could come from asking those questions.

Teddy finished his dinner quickly, then went to the room he and Austin had been sharing and packed his bags. Lacey was still pushing food around on her plate when Teddy made his way to the door.

"I'll let you both know what happens. Hopefully, this is all over soon. Be safe." Teddy shook hands with Austin and gave Lacey a smile.

She smiled back, feeling both better and worse with his news. She should want it to be over. She did want it to be over. But she was going to miss Austin. She wasn't ready to say goodbye to him forever.

Teddy and Austin exchanged some quiet words, then Teddy let himself out. Austin locked the door behind Teddy and leaned against it for a minute before he turned back to Lacey.

His face was pinched tight. His steps were unsure.

He didn't want to be alone with her.

Lacey felt like such an idiot. She'd been telling herself he cared, but he was just being nice. She wasn't important to him. He wasn't missing sharing a bed with her. He wanted to be away from her.

He was probably the one who asked Teddy to stay with them. He requested a third party so Lacey would keep her distance.

She couldn't believe she'd read everything so wrong. When he said he liked her, when he talked about how much he wanted her, it was just a tactic to get her to relax. He never made a move after the one time he kissed her. Never touched her or kissed her or anything besides sharing a bed for a few nights.

Her cheeks warmed with acceptance. It wasn't the first time she thought a man cared about her and found out just how wrong she was. Wouldn't be the last.

Lacey stood and carried her plate to the kitchen, scraping the food she couldn't choke down into the trash. She put it in the dishwasher, then busied herself putting away the leftovers they had.

Austin watched her quietly, his posture awkward.

"I'm going to take a shower and go to bed early," Lacey said without looking at Austin.

"You are?"

Lacey nodded, going the long way around the island to avoid passing next to Austin. "I'm tired."

"There's a documentary on tonight about fears and the biological response we have to them. I thought... we could watch it."

Lacey hesitated. She'd seen the ads for the show and wanted to see it. It was new. Before she realized how Austin felt about being alone with her, she'd hoped to watch it with him. "I... um..."

"If you don't want to see it, that's okay. I'll be watching if you decide to join me," Austin said, giving her an out.

She didn't want him to give her an out. She wanted to curl up next to him and find out what his fears were. She wanted to crawl into bed with him. She wanted to find out if he meant all the things he said the week before.

She got her answer to that last one, though. And that answer told her everything she needed to know about him. He was off-limits.

"I'll think about it," she said, going around him to get to her room. "Thanks."

Austin nodded but didn't turn to look at her.

She closed her door and drew a full breath. She had to keep her distance from him. He didn't want her, and she wouldn't make things more awkward between them.

She tossed her clothes into the pile in the corner of the bathroom and turned on the shower. The water was warm and soothing on her body. Lacey ducked her head under the spray and exhaled a long breath. She was tense and tired and teetering on the edge. She had to do something to alleviate at least one of those things.

She debated with herself for a few seconds, then slid her hand between her thighs. She hadn't had an orgasm since before her father died. That was why she was unable to keep her attraction to Austin under wraps. A quick orgasm would help.

Her core was already slick, the slippery moisture easy to spread over her clit. She pumped a finger inside, wishing she'd been able to pack her own stuff and include her favorite vibrator. She would have to make do with her fingers, and a few images of Austin.

She slicked her fingers over her clit, the feeling intense and perfect. She spread her thighs wider and grabbed for the safety bar with her free hand to make sure she didn't fall. She leaned forward, her core tightening as she rubbed her clit, the pressure sending tendrils of pleasure through her body.

"Yes," she breathed, rocking her hips to add to the pleasure. She rubbed faster, the friction and the pressure just what she needed to race toward her orgasm.

Faster, more, harder. Her hand gripped the safety bar tight as pleasure washed over her and her orgasm snapped free. A moan slipped out before she could clamp her lips shut, but she couldn't care as she came hard against her fingers.

Her knees fought to ease, but she held herself upright, her fingers toying with her sensitive flesh before she eased them away. She leaned against the wall for a minute, allowing the hot water to wash over her back as her breathing slowed and she trembled with pleasure.

It didn't solve any of her problems, but if she was lucky, she would be able to sit on the couch next to Austin without wishing he would kiss her, or do more to her.

He didn't want that.

AUSTIN FROZE when he heard Lacey's moan through the walls. His dick was already hard with the image of her in the shower, but that moan was not one of pain. It was a pleasure moan.

She was taking care of herself in the shower. On the other side of the wall from where he stood. Dick hard and heavy in his pants.

Fuck, he wanted to go in and watch her. Taste her. Touch her and love her and fill her up.

He was so lost in his thoughts of Lacey coming that he didn't notice the shower turned off until her bedroom door opened.

He hid behind the countertop so she didn't see the effect she had on him.

Her gaze went from the dark TV to him, and her brows shot up. "I thought you were going to watch the show."

"Yeah." His voice came out rough, desire lacing his tone. He cleared his throat. "I was just cleaning up and waiting for a text from Teddy."

She nodded and nibbled her lip.

"How was your shower?"

Her gaze snapped to his.

He froze, watching the flush climb her neck and settle on her cheeks. He wasn't wrong about what he heard. His dick throbbed, the need to come backing up in his throat. He was going to blow in his pants if he didn't get a hold of himself. Either literally or figuratively.

"It was good," she said after a second. She ducked her head and went to the couch, pulling a blanket from the side to cover her bare legs.

Bare legs and another pair of tiny shorts. A heavy sweatshirt covered her top half, but he could tell by the way her breasts rested she wasn't wearing a bra.

Not helping his hard cock. But totally helping his imagination.

Austin moved to join her, settling on the other end of the couch and angling away from her. He grabbed a pillow and covered his lap. He cued up the documentary and told himself they were just two friends watching a show. Nothing was going to happen between them. He would not cross that line.

The documentary started, and Austin watched Lacey out of the corner of his eye. She was beautiful. Her curvy figure made him want to sink into her softness. Her hair dried in loose waves that teased the tops of her covered breasts. He wondered if it brushed against her nipples when she made herself come in the shower. If she liked having her nipples played with. If she liked to come fast and hard or if she dragged it out slowly. If she—

She snorted at something they said on the TV.

Austin dragged his gaze to the show and wondered what it was that she found funny. The narrator said something about autophobia, the fear of being alone.

"Some believe it's a fictional phobia, but research has shown it's becoming more common. The fear is more than just not having anyone near you, but being completely alone. No human contact with the desire for it. Some people have said they feel this way even in crowded spaces, like residents of large cities who don't know anyone. But research has shown it's more prevalent in people who live in isolation, whether intentional or not."

"You don't agree?" Austin asked.

Lacey chuckled again. "I think everyone has a fear of being alone. Maybe not something as far as a clinical fear, but we're pack creatures. We need people. We like having people around us. When we don't have others around, we can quickly go from okay to not."

"It can also depend on who is around, though. If you don't have anyone around that you can actually count on, is that any better?"

Lacey looked over at him, her expression one of surprise. "I know what you mean."

The sadness in her tone sliced through him and left him reliving the loss he felt when he heard Samuel was dead. It would have been less painful to have died with his partner, but knowing the man he counted on for years was no longer there left a hole inside Austin he wasn't sure would ever be filled. "When your dad... I don't know if I can keep doing my job."

Lacey's brows tugged together. She tilted her head. "Why would you stop?"

"When I woke up in the hospital, no one would tell me what happened. I demanded they take me to your dad, but they wouldn't. I didn't know why, and that..." Austin pointed to the TV. "That's how I felt. Alone. I thought Samuel blamed me. I thought he was mad at me, refusing to see me for some reason. It never occurred to me that he would be... That something happened to him. I don't know if I can go back and do this anymore."

"People count on you."

Austin breathed a mirthless laugh. "No one counts on me. I'm doing my job. I should have been the one who died. I have no one. No one would have cared if it had been me instead of Samuel. It should have been me instead of Samuel."

"I would have cared," Lacey whispered.

Austin's surprised gaze snapped to hers. "Lacey."

"I care about you, Austin. I know I'm just Samuel's daughter to you, but I care. You've been a part of our family for years. I... I didn't want to lose my father, but I wouldn't have wanted to lose you, either."

"You would have gotten over me dying. I'm no one. I'm alone, Lacey. I'm always going to be alone."

"You don't have to be. You can walk into any room, and you'd have women throwing themselves at you. You are everything any woman would want."

"Not every woman," Austin said, his gaze locked on her.

She gasped. "Austin."

"It's fine. I... I'm... I know I'm not good enough for you. That you have bigger dreams and goals than someone like me. You're too sweet, too perfect. Teddy... Once they know you're safe, you can go back to your life, and I'll stay out of it."

"Why are you saying these things?" Her voice wobbled.

"Because if I'd been better, your dad would be here. You and I wouldn't be stuck in this hotel with people shooting at us every time we leave. You deserve better than me, just like your dad did, Lacey."

"You were the best partner my father ever had. He told me. He sang your praises every chance he got. I know you never would have let anything happen to him on purpose. You might not remember, you might not know, but I know, Austin. I know you. I know my father's death was not your fault. Because you would have traded your life for his if you had the chance. You are a good man, Austin Ward, and you need to stop saying you're not."

"Lacey."

"No. Fuck that, Austin." Tears streamed down her cheeks. She reached for his hand and leaned toward him. "You don't get to blame yourself for my dad dying. You don't get to run away and say no one cares about you. You don't get to do any of it. He would want you to continue. He would want you to live your life. He would have given his for you, just like you would have given yours for him. He loved you like family. Don't you dare let his death stop you from living."

Austin surged toward her, his lips crashing down on hers before he had a chance to think through what he was doing.

He tried to pull back, to put space between them again, but she moaned that same sound he heard from the shower, and he couldn't do it. His hand went to her hair and breath rushed past his cheek.

She parted her lips and pulled him on top of her. She was soft and warm. Her nails scraped the back of his neck and sent sparks down his spine.

He pressed his cock against her hip, letting her feel the effect she had on him. He ached to be inside her.

She tugged at his shirt, scratching her nails down his chest, then pulling his shirt all the way off. Her eyes dilated, the brown disappearing. She licked her lips, then pulled him to her again.

Lacey MacNeil was even more tempting than Austin ever thought she was. He eased a hand beneath her sweatshirt, and she broke their kiss to whip it off, revealing her bare breasts to him.

Austin cupped one and brought it to his lips. She moaned and pushed it into his mouth, reaching for his cock at the same time.

"Lace, I won't be able to go slow if you touch me."

"Who said anything about slow?"

Austin growled. "Fuck."

Her hand dove into his shorts and wrapped around his cock. She stroked him with urgency, and he stopped thinking. Stopped fighting. Stopped everything except getting closer to her.

Austin shoved his shorts down, letting his cock free. He surged against her hand, gasping at the feel of her hand on him.

She pushed at her shorts, not releasing his dick. She kept stroking, his resistance fading with each pump of her firm grip.

"I don't have a condom, Lacey."

"I'm on the pill. I'm clean. Please, Austin."

"Fuck. I'm... I'm clean, too, but are you sure about this?"

She laid on the couch and spread her thighs, pulling him toward her. "I'm sure."

He wanted to slow down. To take his time with her. To taste every inch of her body and make her crazy with need.

But she hooked a heel around his thigh and pulled him to her body. His cock took over with one feel of her slick channel. He surged into her, her body stretching to accept him.

"Fuck," Austin whispered. He'd never had sex without a condom, and the feel of Lacey's warm and wet body sucking him in was the best thing he'd ever experienced in his life. He tried to catalogue every sound she made, every move of her body, everything.

Her core tightened around him, and he slammed into her. She gasped and lifted her hips to meet his. He lost it.

He pounded into her, tilting her hips back to hit deep

inside. She moaned again, the sound a vice around his balls. He lowered his thumb to her clit and rubbed over it.

"Austin!" she cried, the pulsing of her body telling him what he already knew. She was primed and ready, sensitive from her shower activity. A few strokes, and she came hard, whimpering and moaning as she let go.

"Fuck, Lacey." He slammed deep into her, the pulsing of her body as she came dragging him with her. He grunted and shook, his orgasm taking what was left of his strength and sanity.

He could die happy now. Inside Lacey MacNeil. Life didn't get better.

FIFTEEN

LACEY WAS NOT GOING TO EXPECT MORE FROM HIM. She couldn't. She knew what happened. She knew what it meant. She wasn't going to let her poor sappy heart dictate anything. She had a memory that would last her a lifetime, a memory of Austin calling her name as he lost himself and came inside her.

That was all she could take with her. All the other men she'd been with were one and done. They had her, then they left her. Austin would be the same. It didn't matter how Lacey felt. She had to keep her emotions in check.

Austin kissed the side of her neck, and dammit, she nearly gave in to her heart and sighed at the sweetness of the move. He didn't mean it like that. He was trying to be nice. Trying to get her to let go of him.

Their lives were as tangled as their limbs, and Austin was being nice. Lacey had to let him go.

She released her arms from around his back, giving him the freedom to roll off her and clean up. He kissed her neck once more, then trailed his lips to her mouth and kissed her soundly, his tongue probing her lips until she relented and accepted his teasing tongue.

He groaned, his dick twitching inside her.

Her core clenched, eager for another round she knew would never come. She couldn't ask for it. She wouldn't. She couldn't bear the look on his face when he had to turn her down, or worse, when he agreed and then regretted it.

She pushed at his shoulders, breaking the kiss and whispering, "I need to use the bathroom."

Austin kissed her nose, then moved off her, his cock slipping from her body and releasing the fluid that filled her.

She rolled off the couch, trying to keep from making a mess, and squeezed her thighs together as she hurried to the bathroom in her room. She closed the door and sat down, letting the emotions flood her for a minute. Just one minute.

She relived the way he kissed her and touched her and filled her. She smiled at the roughness, like he couldn't wait to be inside her. She wouldn't taint the memories by asking him for more. It was a one-time thing, and that's all it would ever be.

Lacey washed her hands and opened the door, wishing she'd grabbed clothes before she ran from the living room, and stopped when she saw Austin on her bed. Naked.

"Hey," he said, his eyes lighting up when she stepped out of the bathroom.

"What are you doing here?"

He looked around the room. "I was going to sleep in here with you. Maybe get my hands on you again. Unless..." He stood and ran a hand through his hair. "Sorry. I shouldn't have assumed."

"Assumed what?"

"That this was okay." He walked to the door. "Did you feel like I forced you, Lacey? Because I never meant to pressure you. Lock the door behind me. I won't touch you again. I'll stay away."

"This is a new one," she muttered, hating that tears filled her eyes.

"New what?" he asked.

"It doesn't matter. I... You don't have to make me feel like it's my fault. I know this is just because I'm the only woman around. But you didn't have to get ugly about it and make me feel like this." She swiped the tears from her cheek and crossed her arms, wishing she at least had clothes on.

"You think..." He breathed a laugh. "You think that was because you're here? That I slept with you because I'm so desperate for sex that I was willing to fuck whoever happened to be in the room?"

"We're friends, Austin. I thought we were. Don't insult me by telling me this was more than that."

He huffed. "But you can insult me by saying the only reason I'd have sex with you is because I'm so horny that I can't keep it in my pants for a week? You think that little of me?"

"I'm no one's dream girl, Austin. I'm the substitute. I'm the good enough for one night girl. I'm used to that role. I kissed you back. I was completely fine with this being once. You trying to make me feel like I'm some cold fish who flips and says I was forced to sleep with you is just mean."

"I wasn't..." He deflated, his shoulders rolling forward as his eyes closed. "You have no idea how fucking sexy you are. How much I've wanted you for years. You really honestly believe I just fucked you because you're here? Or are you lying to yourself because it's easier than admitting you liked it, Lacey?"

She flinched at his crass words. She didn't want to think of what they did as fucking. "I'm not sexy. Men don't come back for more from me. I... I liked it. But that's not enough. It doesn't matter how I feel. It matters that you feel some twisted sense of responsibility and it's crossed into something more."

Austin moved closer to her, one step at a time. "There's nothing twisted about the way I feel about you. And any man who can't see what he's missing out on by not coming back for more with you is a fool. You're gorgeous, Lacey. You're... God, you make me so crazy. Your father warned me to stay away from you because I'm not good enough for you, and I've tried. Fuck, I've tried. But you're the only woman I've wanted for years, Lacey. Years. This... This isn't some casual, forced proximity thing for me. If that's all it was for you, I'll leave you alone, but I'm not walking out of here because I want to. I'm doing it because you want me to."

He turned and walked away, leaving Lacey to watch him leave. He made it to the door before she got up the courage to speak. "Wait."

He stopped but didn't turn around.

"Are you telling me the truth?"

"Yes."

"About everything?"

"Yes."

"You really want me?"

"So much it hurts, Lacey."

"Will you... will you stay with me?"

"If that's what you want."

"Is it what you want?"

"More than you know."

Lacey drew a shaky breath. "Please stay with me, Austin."

"Okay." He turned and came back to her, his cock leading the way. "I'm not sure I'll be able to keep my hands to myself if you're naked all night."

Lacey pulled back the blanket on the bed and slid between the cool sheets, completely naked.

Austin groaned and crawled in next to her, reaching for

her immediately. He pulled her into his arms and kissed her forehead. His dick settled between her thighs. His arms held her tight. "Get some sleep, Lacey."

She nodded, sure she wouldn't sleep with him so close, but before she knew it, she was fading.

AUSTIN WAFFLED between wanting to fall asleep with her in his arms and wanting to stay awake and remember every sound she made in sleep. Her slumber had him fading, her soft snores lulling him to a restful sleep that was only aided by the powerful orgasm he shared with her.

A sound woke Austin, soft and intimate against his ear. He rarely slept deep, a leftover habit from a lifetime of danger, so the noise startled him as much as it aroused him.

His cock was up before he was, throbbing against the soft warmth in his arms. His eyes flickered open and found Lacey still asleep, her mouth parted and a look of pleasure on her face. One he now recognized after being treated to that look just a few hours earlier.

Her earlier argument about him being done with her so quickly had him hesitating before he let his hands roam free on her beautiful body.

Her curves were soft, pliant under his fingers. She was full and lush and womanly. He'd never been particular about a woman's size, finding all women beautiful in their own ways. But when he met Lacey, he knew her size was the perfect one.

She gasped in her sleep, pressing her breasts against his chest, then hooking her thigh around his hip.

Austin's erection notched between her open thighs, rubbing against her body. He slid one hand down her back to squeeze her thick backside, wanting to touch every inch of her. Wanting to show her he wasn't done with her by a long shot.

"Austin," she breathed. Her eyes popped open, catching his gaze.

"Hey, beautiful."

"What..." She moaned and shifted, rubbing herself against his erection. "Oh, God." She moved again, trying to get away from him, but he tightened his grip on her ass.

"Don't."

"I'm all over you."

"It's pretty much a team thing at the moment."

She breathed a laugh, and it was the sweetest sound he'd ever heard.

"You don't see me trying to get out of here, Lacey. I'm right here with you."

"Please."

"Please what, Lacey? What do you want me to do to you?"

"Inside me. Please."

"You want to feel my cock again? You want all my cum to drip from you like it's been all night?"

"Yeah... yes."

Austin pressed into her, her dreams making it an easy move. They laid side-by-side, her leg thrown over his hip. He couldn't get a hand between them, and he couldn't thrust far, but he was content with slow. With taking his time and feeling every ridge of her channel before he filled her up again.

"You don't have to..."

"I don't have to what, Lace?"

"Slow. You can go fast."

"Is that what you want? You want fast? You want me to take you hard like I did last night? Because I was thinking slow feels pretty fucking fantastic."

"Yeah," she whispered. "Yeah, it does."

"Then I think I'll stick with slow for now." He shifted on the bed, barely thrusting into her with each shallow stroke. Her body pulsed around him, and the feel of being inside her without a condom made it harder for him to hold back.

The one and only good piece of advice his father ever gave him was to always wear a condom. The son-of-a-bitch usually delivered the advice when he was complaining about Austin's existence, but it was good advice. He wasn't a virgin, but feeling the inside of a woman for the first time made him feel like he was. And that woman being Lacey... She was already special, but it made her even more special.

She moaned softly, her eyes closing. Her face twisted in something that looked like frustration. She groaned.

Austin could have stayed inside her all night without coming, but he wanted it to be good for her, too. And the look on her face said it was missing the mark. He rolled them, bringing her on top of him.

She immediately pushed up, exposing her breasts. "I'll crush you."

"Not a chance." Austin's hands went to her breasts like magnets. He plumped them up and brushed his thumbs over her nipples.

She moaned.

"Good?"

"Yeah."

"Did you play with them in the shower yesterday?"

Her eyes flew open. Her hips stopped rocking. "What... You..."

"I wanted to join you. To see what made you feel good. Will you tell me, Lacey? Show me?"

"I... That's private."

"Okay. I won't push. But I hope you'll tell me if you don't like something."

She nibbled her lip.

Austin surged up, snapping her out of her trance. He needed her to forget thinking and feel again.

"I like... Rub my clit."

He abandoned one breast and brought his thumb to her clit. The nub was plump and swollen. One brush of his thumb had her crying out and her hips rocking.

She was a goddess, riding him, her thick curves on display for him to enjoy. The patch of hair between her thighs hid his thumb from view, but when she lifted her hips, he could see himself disappear inside her. His cock glistened with her juices.

Her head was thrown back, her dark hair dancing down her back as she mindlessly rocked herself over him. Her lips parted in pleasure, her mouth open with her soft gasps and moans.

He slid his hand between them as she lifted her hips and captured the moisture easing from her body, bringing it back to her clit. He swirled around the sensitive nub, watching her muscles tense and ripple. He wanted to know what she liked, and her body told him the story. Her clit was the key, with direct pressure making her cry out. Whenever he circled it, she gasped and tensed. And when he pinched it, she leaned back, exposing it to his fingers as she bounced on his thighs.

"Oh, yes," she whispered.

Austin grunted, taking his job seriously. She was going to scream his name, and he wasn't going to stop until she did. He pinched and rubbed, tugging the little button as she thrashed above him, all concern gone as she chased the orgasm he was serving up to her.

Her core pulsed around his cock, and he surged into her, taking care of all her pleasure zones. She moaned when he hit her just right inside. He did it again, and the scream he'd been waiting for came.

"Austin. Oh, fuck. Austin. Yes. Please. Austin!"

She came as she cried his name, her body drawing him in and locking tight around his erection as he emptied himself into her. "Lacey. Fuck. Princess."

She collapsed onto him, her body falling forward as she heaved for her breath. He held her, his arms banding around her before she could even think about getting up.

She trembled as she sucked in breath after breath. When she tried to roll off him, he didn't let her. "What are you doing?"

"Look at me, Lacey."

She lifted enough to meet his gaze.

He brushed the hair back from her face so she wasn't hidden from him at all. "I am still not done with you, so before you get more ideas about how I am, I want you to know I'm not. If you are, I will stay away, but I am not done."

She nibbled her lip and nodded.

He leaned up to kiss her softly, then released her so she could go to the bathroom and clean up.

Austin smiled. Lacey MacNeil screamed his name. He was wrong before. Life did get better. And he wanted to know how much better he could make it.

LACEY RUBBED her thighs together as she poured her coffee the next morning. She'd never been sore after sex before. Not even after her first time. She wasn't used to it, but she'd also never had sex four times in one night.

Austin was a very attentive and eager lover. She snickered at the thought. He was her lover. She'd never been with a man enough times to consider him that. She liked the word, though. The thought of a man who'd been inside her more than once.

He kissed her shoulder and nipped her earlobe. "What are you laughing about over here?"

"Just thinking about you as my lover."

"I'll happily accept that title."

She turned in his arms and studied him. "You will? What about everyone else? The rest of your team?"

"I'll deal with them," Austin said.

She wasn't sure what he meant by that. Would he lie to them and keep her as his secret, or would he defend her to them? Would he have to explain why he wanted to be with her?

"What are you thinking?" he asked, kissing her neck.

She pasted on a smile and shook her head. It was temporary. They were temporary. Fighting about it wasn't going to change that, it would just end things even sooner. "Just wondering what we're going to do today."

Austin raised an eyebrow and smirked. "I have quite a few ideas."

She laughed. "We can't just spend all day in bed."

"I was thinking we could spend it on the couch, the kitchen island, in the shower." He waggled his eyebrows and slid his hand beneath the shirt she wore, cupping her breast and tugging on her nipple. "I'd be willing to try the bed again, too, but we have all day. We can get creative."

Lacey wanted to resist him, but who was she kidding? Austin Ward, the man she'd wanted for years, was practically begging her to have sex with him. She'd be insane to refuse.

"I can be very creative," Lacey said. She reached between them and cupped his erection. "I watched this documentary about pleasure once."

He groaned and pulled her lips to his. He plundered her

mouth with his tongue and fucked her hand. When he pulled back, his lips were wet, and his cock was dripping on her hand. "We're going to try all of it. Every last minute of that. Until you beg me to stop."

"Deal."

SIXTEEN

AUSTIN NEVER LAUGHED DURING SEX. OR CRAVED more even in the middle of it. He was always ready to move on as soon as he was done, sometimes before. But he'd never been with Lacey MacNeil. Two-and-a-half weeks with her was nowhere near enough. He watched her over the rim of his coffee mug, wondering how soon he could slide into her again.

She looked up at him, a smile teasing the corners of her delectable mouth. "What?"

He shook his head. "Just thinking about all the things I haven't done with you yet."

"Like what?" she asked, setting her mug on the counter. She was in one of his shirts, a tee she insisted would be too small for her but actually hugged her curves and made his mouth water. The dark blue was a disappointment because he couldn't see through the fabric, but he knew what beauty lie beneath.

"You keep pushing me off when I try to taste you."

Her cheeks turned red. She picked up her mug again, hiding behind the ceramic that did nothing to hide her from him.

"Do you not enjoy that, or you just don't want me to do it?"

She nibbled her lip, her mug simply a block. "I've never done it."

"You've never..." Austin's dick swelled at her quiet confession. "Fuck, Lacey." He set his mug on the counter with a hard clang, his knees going weak at the thought of being the first and only person to settle between her legs and lick her until she let go. She was eager to come whenever he teased her clit, but licking it...

"I haven't had... relationships," she continued, still avoiding his gaze. "I've had sex, but it's always been just once. You're the first person..."

"I'm the first person what, Lacey?"

A knock on the door had Austin moving in front of Lacey, putting himself between her and whoever was banging on the door at eight in the morning.

Her soft gasp said she was as startled by the early visitor as he was. And just as happy about it. She gripped his bicep, her fingers tightening on his uninjured arm to the point of pain.

Austin left his gun in the bedroom and mentally calculated if he could get to it before whoever was at the door made it inside. He started to move toward the room, also toward the door, when there was another knock.

"Check your phone, asshole, and let me in."

Austin breathed easier when he realized it was Lance outside the hotel suite. He turned to Lacey. "It's Lance. Go put some clothes on while I let him in."

She nodded, still trembling and not moving.

"Come on, sweetheart. If we don't answer, he'll break down the door." Austin eased her off the stool and held her hips until she managed to support her weight.

Lacey stayed behind him as they moved toward the door to the suite. She jumped when Lance knocked again.

"I'm coming!" Austin shouted so Lance would quit the banging. When they made it to the bedroom door, Austin turned back to Lacey. "We're going to finish that conversation we were having. Just as soon as I can get rid of him."

Lacey nibbled her lip and nodded, then closed the bedroom door so she was a little more presentable in front of others.

Austin waited a few seconds for his erection to fade enough to open the door to his friend and teammate. He hadn't thought to grab a shirt before Lacey went into the bedroom, and his sweatpants did not hide... anything.

Lance knocked again, and Austin yanked the door open. "What the fuck?"

Lance pushed his way inside with Walker right behind him. Walker paused to scan Austin head-to-toe, then met his gaze with a raised eyebrow. He looked past Austin to the unused bedroom with the bed made and few things inside.

There was no hiding that Austin was not using the second bedroom. Or hiding the fact that Austin was shirtless in a hotel room alone with a woman he was sharing a bedroom with. A woman who was so off-limits none of them would dare touch her.

"Do I need to do something about this?" Walker asked in a low, threatening tone.

"Mind your own fucking business," Austin growled at the older man. He respected Walker, but Walker didn't get a vote. The only votes went to Austin and Lacey.

Walker's brows went up. "We don't blame you for Samuel, but you fuck with Lacey and there's no forgiving that."

"Again, Walker, mind your—"

"I heard you the first time," Walker interrupted. "She's a good girl, Austin. Don't hurt her."

"I have no intention of hurting her. Ever."

Walker looked closely at Austin, sighing at whatever it was he saw. "Fuck."

"What—?"

"Hey Walker," Lacey said, opening the bedroom door right behind him. She stepped forward, a smile on her face and her own oversized clothes hiding her curves.

Austin's mouth still watered as he looked at her.

"Hey Lacey. How are you? This guy taking care of you?" Walker jerked his head toward Austin and stepped forward to pull Lacey into a hug.

Austin growled, wanting to rip Walker's hands off his woman. He would, too, if Walker didn't step back as quickly as he did, shooting Austin a glare in the process.

"He's keeping my mind off everything going on. Are you here with news?" Lacey turned toward the kitchen with Walker, leading him away from the bedroom.

Austin took advantage of the distraction and snuck into the bedroom to grab a shirt. He spotted the one Lacey had been wearing on the bed and yanked it over his head. It smelled like her, like them, and he almost took it off so he didn't have to fight an erection all day, but he decided he didn't care. He wanted to wear the shirt that was still warm from her body.

Lacey was pouring coffee for Walker and Lance when Austin joined them in the kitchen. Lance had a muffin half-eaten in his hand and a fork in the fruit bowl.

"Do you have manners?" Austin asked.

Lance took a bite of his muffin and shook his head.

Austin rolled his eyes and grabbed his forgotten mug. He took a sip, wincing at the lukewarm coffee. He swallowed it anyway, then set his mug in the dishwasher and moved next to Lacey.

"Why are you guys here?" Austin asked, looking from one teammate to the other.

"There's been some new information," Walker said, his gaze landing on the countertop.

"What information?" Austin asked.

"Eve called," Lance said, capturing Austin's attention.

"Someone's here?"

Lacey gasped.

Austin put his arm around her waist and pulled her closer to him. She stiffened for a second, her gaze sliding to his teammates before she wrapped an arm around his middle.

Walker and Lance didn't miss the move, both of them going brows up at Austin.

"Talk," Austin barked.

"Someone's been watching the hotel. Come inside a few times, wandered around, then left. No one's gotten any information, as far as we know. But an employee didn't show up for work this morning," Lance explained.

"Doesn't that happen at every hotel?" Lacey asked.

"Yeah, but this employee has never not called in. Patrol is on the way to his house right now, and Montgomery asked us to come here. Just in case." Walker left out half the truth, the truth Austin could read between the lines.

Someone was likely coming. And they weren't coming alone.

"How long do we have?" Austin asked.

"No way of knowing. If they find the guy home in bed with a hangover, we're panicking for no reason. If not..." Lance trailed off with a shrug.

Lacey's grip on Austin tightened, and he turned to her, cupping her jaw and not caring about his teammates seeing him do it.

"Go pack. Put everything that's here in your bag. Just in case. We can unpack later if we find out we can stay. If not, it's better to be ready to go."

Lacey nodded, the move jerky. She held his tee in her fists, not releasing him.

"Want me to go with you?"

She nodded again, but the panic in her gaze didn't recede.

"Let's go."

Austin led the way, making sure he was between her and the door the entire time. They turned into the bedroom together, then he blocked the exit just in case someone came through the suite door.

Lacey grabbed her suitcase from the closet and tossed it on the unmade bed. Austin had big plans for tossing her on the bed, but his plans would have to wait until they knew they were safe.

Lacey threw clothes in the bag without folding anything or being neat about it. He wasn't sure what was normal for her, but he guessed she was someone who liked things neat and orderly. She was a librarian for crying out loud. Disorganized would mean chaos.

But panic made her hands shake. Her movements were all jilted and stiff. She disappeared into the bathroom, and he heard something hit the floor.

"You okay?" Austin asked, rushing to the door to check on her.

She shook her head, bending to grab the deodorant on the floor.

Austin took her hands in his and brought them to his lips. "I'm sorry you're in the middle of all of this."

"I just... I wish I understood what was going on. Why all this is happening."

"We will figure it out and make sure you're safe again, Lacey. I promise you."

She nodded, a small smile lifting her lips before a phone rang loudly in the other room. Her smile vanished, panic filling her gaze once more.

"Let's finish up," Austin said, grabbing the rest of her things from the bathroom and carrying them to the open bag on the bed. He grabbed his own duffle and shoved clothes in without thought or care. It didn't matter. They couldn't leave anything behind, but he wasn't going to be the reason someone got to them.

Got to Lacey.

Walker stopped at the bedroom door and scanned the room. "We need to move."

Lance was ahead of him, watching the hallway through the peephole in the door.

"Two minutes," Walker said. "Max."

"Less would be better," Lance added, glancing at them before focusing on the door.

"Time to go, sweetheart," Austin said, shoving his feet into the sneakers he left near the door. He slung his bag over his good shoulder and grabbed her suitcase, then her hand.

"I... I don't know if I can do this," Lacey whispered.

"We won't let anything happen to you. Trust me, Princess."

She sucked in a breath and grabbed her necklace. She nodded, her throat working to swallow, then let him lead her out into the hallway.

Lance led the way, gun raised on the way to the stairs at the end of the hallway. He looked into the stairwell, then opened the door for Austin to follow, with Lacey right behind. Austin held her hand to stop her while Walker followed last through the door. It closed with a soft click, then Lance took the lead again.

The four of them made their way down the stairs quietly but quickly. They were almost to the ground floor parking garage when the door at the top of the stairs opened.

Voices carried down the stairwell, angry voices.

They were coming.

Austin pushed Lacey ahead of him, hating that he was a bellhop instead of one of the men with guns. He had his gun, but he still wasn't back to full strength and his gun was for emergencies only.

He hoped they weren't about to be in an emergency.

Lance pushed the door at the garage level and kept going, not waiting for Austin to follow him out. The SUV was parked right at the door, and Lance opened the backdoor for Lacey. Austin followed her in as Walker rounded the hood and got behind the wheel.

Lance climbed in as Walker pulled away, a shout from behind them telling Austin just how close their escape was.

The ping of bullets against the back of the SUV had Lacey screaming. Austin ducked her head down, resting it on his tense lap. He turned to watch the men disappear in the distance, but knew that wasn't the end of it.

"Who the fuck were they?" Austin asked.

"Best guess is Howard Enterprises." Walker checked the mirrors and took a sharp right turn.

"He's dead. Who's calling the shots?"

"FBI thinks it's his wife. They believe she's the one who had him killed." Lance pointed for Walker to take the next left.

"Rough marriage," Austin said. "Where is she?"

"Her sister tried to kill herself. She's been by her side since before Howard was released from prison. Captain Patrick spoke to her. She has an alibi, but she would have had it done."

"Why?"

"Rumors were she was forced into marrying him and he made sure she knew she was his property. When he went to jail, she was believed to be innocent. Showed up for all his hearings before trial and would tell anyone who'd listen her husband was being framed," Lance explained.

"Was she on our radar? Was she behind the attack on Hannah?" Austin asked, glancing at Lacey. "On Samuel."

Lacey gasped.

"FBI says no," Walker said.

"How are they sure?"

"They have a guard in custody that helped Peter Howard. The guard said Howard had someone watching his family and threatened to kill his pregnant wife and two-year-old if he didn't pass along information to Howard's people." Walker took another sharp turn and pulled into the Rose Protection Agency lot.

"Won't they be looking for us here?" Austin asked.

"No other choice. Not enough notice to secure another location," Lance explained. "FBI and local cops were on us the whole time, so hopefully, they have some answers. Walker made sure to drive by as many cameras as possible without delaying our return."

Lacey's door opened, and she screamed before she saw Teddy right behind her.

"Let's go, kid," Teddy said, taking Lacey's hand and leading her out of the SUV.

Austin followed out his door, dragging their bags with him as the others protected them on their way inside the building.

Déja vu.

Fuck.

Austin wanted to throw something. To punch or kick something. He was having a perfectly wonderful time with Lacey at The Davidson Hotel, and instead of being able to continue playing house with her, they were back at square fucking one. No answers, another threat on their lives.

"What the fuck is going on?" Austin demanded when everyone stopped moving. "Why didn't we know about this until they were on the way to us?"

"Eve was late getting to work today. She didn't get any notification about the guy not showing up until she got there." Montgomery was the one who answered, crossing his arms and glaring at Austin.

"Are we sure she's not a part of this? Pretty damn convenient she was late and everything went to hell." Austin matched his boss's stance, ignoring the tug in his shoulder when he crossed his arms.

"Eve is not involved. The employee who didn't show up was found dead in his apartment. Our working theory is he told whoever shot at you a few weeks ago that you were leaving. He worked closely with Eve and had access to the same information as her, knew her schedule and that she'd be late. He was no longer useful to them, so they killed him and made their move when it was likely to go undiscovered as long as possible."

"Doesn't mean she's not involved," Austin growled.

"Eve was here. Interviewing for a job. She wasn't out there sharing intel," Montgomery declared.

"Interviewing..." Austin's gaze went to Lacey, the understanding hitting her at the same time it hit Austin. "You're replacing Samuel."

Montgomery slid a look toward Lacey, then a glare toward Austin. "What we need to figure out right now is who was after you and why. We still believe it's the wife. If she was behind Howard's death, she's hiding something."

"But why is she coming after these two?" Walker asked. "If she killed her husband, and he killed Hannah and Samuel, what does she care about them?"

"Revenge?" Montgomery asked. "It's the only thing we can think of. But it doesn't matter. She found a way to get information. Until we can prove it's her and get her into custody, the risk is out there."

"So now what? We had them in a safe place, but it wasn't safe enough. Are we talking around the clock monitoring? Safe house? Witness protection?" Lance asked.

"We don't know yet. For today, they're staying here. Once the police and FBI have more information, we'll figure it out," Montgomery said.

"So we just sit here? Hide? Act like this is normal and everything's great?" Austin barked.

"No. You work. You help us figure this out. Because even though you don't remember shit, you're the only witness. We need you to get us some answers."

Austin looked at his boss. Well, fuck.

SEVENTEEN

Lacey sat at Austin's desk while Montgomery and Teddy grilled Austin about the night her father was killed. The pained look on his face said either he remembered something or hated that he didn't. She wasn't sure which she preferred.

"You doing okay?" Lance asked, offering her a bottle of water.

She forced a smile for him and nodded. "As good as I can be. Thanks."

Lance nodded. "No problem. He's a good guy."

"I know." Lance took her comment as an invitation to sit next to her. An invitation Lacey didn't realize she extended, but she wasn't going to tell him to leave either.

"Your dad was pretty damn amazing," Lance said. "I really enjoyed working with him."

Lacey nodded, hating the way she teared up at hearing her dad spoken of in past tense. "Yeah. He was the only person who ever believed in me. Didn't want me to change everything about who I am."

Lance chuckled. "He was like that with all of us. Said everyone has a gift and we just have to figure out what it is."

Lacey grinned. "What's your gift?"

Lance snorted. "Hell if I know. Pushing others away?"

Lacey nodded. "Sounds to me like keeping your distance from people who don't matter. When you meet people who do, I don't think you're pushing them away."

"What makes you say that?"

Lacey gestured between them. "You're sitting here with me. Telling me about my father. Keeping me company instead of ignoring me. You love this team as much as my father did, and you're working hard to figure out what happened to him. There's probably other people in your world that you don't push away."

Lance looked past Lacey's face, and a flush crept up his neck.

Lacey didn't call him on it, but she couldn't stop her grin, either.

"I don't have friends. These guys are my family, but outside here, I'm pretty closed off."

"Maybe you don't always have to be. Who were you thinking about?"

Lance shook his head, then chuckled. "You're more like your father than you know."

"I take that as a compliment."

"It was meant to be one." Lance stood, moving to the side of his chair and watching behind Lacey. He jerked his head, then nodded to Lacey and moved away.

She looked behind her and found Austin standing a few feet away. "Hey."

His shoulders relaxed, and his face transformed from a scowl to a smile. "Hey."

She raised her brows, asking if he was going to join her.

He took the seat Lance vacated and sighed as he sat.

"That bad?"

Austin shook his head. "I can't remember anything. It's just gone. They want me to talk to a hypnotist or a therapist or both. Someone who can access suppressed memories."

"That sounds reasonable. I've read good things about that sort of treatment."

"I guess."

"What worries you?"

He looked up at her, surprise flashing across his face before he smiled. "I should have known."

"Known what?"

"That you could read my mind."

She snorted. "Please don't ever assume that. I'm notoriously bad at reading minds. Especially of men."

"I don't want you doing anything with other men," Austin growled softly.

She shook her head. "Don't change the subject. What are you worried about?"

His shoulders lifted again, creeping toward his ears. "What if my memories aren't suppressed? What if I don't remember because I was out cold?"

Lacey reached for his hand and held it between both of hers. "Then you know. Then you can stop beating yourself up about what happened."

"But I should have had his back. I should have been with him." His words were punctuated with anger and disappointment.

"You can't change what happened, Austin. You can't bring him back. I want to know what happened, too. I want whoever did this to pay for it. But it won't change that he's gone."

"I just... What if there was something I could have done?" Anguish filled his gaze.

"There wasn't."

"What? How could you know that?"

She breathed a laugh. "Because I know you. If there was anything you could have done, you would have done it. You would have saved my dad and the witness if it was at all possible. I know that as well as I know my dad would have done the same for you."

Austin closed his eyes and drew a deep breath. As he let go, his entire body relaxed. "He was the closest thing I've ever had to family."

"I know."

"I'm so damn sorry I didn't protect him."

She pulled him into her arms and held him awkwardly on the rolling chairs they were perched on. His hands clutched at her back, pulling her as close as they could get.

"I wish I'd died instead of him."

Lacey jerked out of his arms so fast he almost fell off his chair. "Don't you dare say that," she growled. "Don't you ever say something like that."

"He had your mom and you. He had a full life. I don't have anything. Anyone."

Tears leaked from her eyes. "Don't minimize his death by saying you wish you'd taken his place. He died doing what he loved to do. He died trying to protect someone. You don't get to act like you don't have something to live for."

"Lace—"

"No. You saying that cheapens his death. It says it wasn't worth something. You're wrong. We don't get to know why he died and you didn't, but saying it should have been different isn't better. I will miss my father forever, and it hurts so bad that he's gone, but you don't get to tell me you wish you'd died instead. Don't. Just don't." She drew a shaky breath. Her hands gripped the armrests so tight her knuckles hurt. Her entire body was tense with fear at losing Austin, too. She couldn't choose between him and her father. She wouldn't.

But she never had to choose. The choice was made for her, and she had to live with it.

"I'm sorry," he whispered. "I'm so damn sorry, Lace. You're right. I wish he was still here, but I can't change it. But I do have to find out what happened. I have to stop anyone else from feeling the way I do."

Lacey reached for his hand. He grabbed onto her, then yanked her from her seat and onto his lap. He pressed his nose into her hair, and she let out the breath she'd been holding.

"Thank you."

She nodded and held him, needing the connection as much as it seemed he did.

A throat cleared behind them, and Lacey looked up into the scowling face of her dad's boss. "Hi Montgomery."

"Lacey. Do you want someone to take you to a safe house? We can make arrangements for your protection... separately."

"Did my mother ask you to do that?" Lacey asked, not getting up even as Austin's hands released her.

Montgomery's quick avoidance of eye contact told Lacey the answer.

"I'm twenty-eight years old, Montgomery. I've been a legal adult for a decade. She doesn't get to dictate my life. I'm perfectly safe here, and I'd like the opportunity to stay with Austin after this. Unless he's the one requesting separate accommodations." She looked at Austin as he shook his head.

"No. We didn't talk about that. I had no idea he was going to try to take you away." Austin glared up at his boss.

Montgomery sighed heavily. "Valerie isn't going to like this. She's been on me every day to separate the two of you. Said—"

"I'm aware of what my mother's said. She said it to me, too. But she's in pain. She doesn't know what she's saying. She's lashing out at anyone and everyone. I'm surprised she hasn't laid the blame at your feet for putting my father in that position."

Montgomery's silence spoke volumes.

Lacey pursed her lips. "My mother doesn't know what I need. And I expect you to treat me like someone who can think for herself."

Montgomery nodded and slipped away.

Austin squeezed her hip. "I've never seen anyone stand up to him like that. Besides his sister, but that's different. Are you sure this is what you want?"

Lacey smiled down at the man who held her heart. He wasn't asking about anything beyond the conversation they just had, but it was all the same to Lacey. Wanting to stay with Austin now and wanting a future with Austin later were no different. "Yes."

AUSTIN SAT across from the memory therapist and tried to let her voice quiet the thoughts racing through his head. He had little hope Bridget would be able to get anything out of his mind, but that only made it worse. If he believed it wouldn't work, it wouldn't work. He had to be open to the idea.

He needed to know, too. He couldn't live with himself if there was something he could have done and didn't do it. Didn't save Samuel. And Hannah.

"Can you see the room, Austin?" the therapist asked. Her voice was quiet, soothing, calm.

Grating. Irritating. Annoying.

Austin took another breath and let it out slowly. It wasn't the woman's fault he'd suppressed so many damn memories he was afraid of what she might pull out of him if he let her really try. He was a treasure trove of shit, and he had to keep it all locked away. It was the only way he could handle it. The only way he could function.

He pictured the safe house where they'd been staying. He'd been by the kitchen peninsula during his last memory. "I'm there."

"Okay, good. Can you describe the room to me? What do you feel? See? Touch? Taste maybe?"

Taste? Did the woman think he was licking the cabinets? He'd rather lick Lacey.

Fuck!

He had to stop thinking about her.

He drew another breath, his eyes aching to open. He didn't like not being able to see who was near him. His father would sneak up on him and smack him, then laugh like it was even funnier to hit him when he wasn't expecting it.

Fucker.

Austin groaned, frustrated with himself. He dragged his focus back to the room. The peninsula. Crouching behind it.

His hands full of Lacey. Cupping her thick backside under his tee and dragging her toward him.

"Austin?"

Dammit. Austin clenched his hands. Wrong kitchen. He sighed and flopped back on the couch, giving in to the desire to open his eyes. "This isn't working."

"Do you want to take a break?"

"Yeah." He got up and walked out of the office. The lights in the rest of the space were bright, a sharp contrast to the dim lighting where he'd been. His head ached with the sudden intrusion of light.

He stalked to the bathroom, pushing his way inside and sending up a prayer that no one else was in there. With twenty men in one office, it was rare the bathroom was empty.

He washed his hands and splashed water on his face. He wanted to remember what happened to Samuel. He really did.

But he didn't want to remember everything else in his life. All the other shit he'd worked hard to ignore.

Yeah, he probably should deal with it. Had been told that for years by teammates and required counselors. Austin agreed and moved on.

But burying it all was getting harder and harder. Since losing Samuel, Austin had no family. He didn't have the man who convinced him he wasn't a worthless piece of garbage, as his father frequently declared.

Samuel was gone, and Austin knew keeping those old words of his father's at bay was only going to get harder. They'd already been ringing in his ears when he was with Lacey. In the quiet moments when she was asleep. When everything else was still. When it was just Austin and the dangerous memories.

Bringing them all up would be bad.

So he fought them.

Voices outside the bathroom brought Austin back to the moment. He dried his hands and moved toward the door. It opened just before he got there, letting Walker and Lance in.

"You okay?" Lance asked.

Austin shook his head and continued out the door. Lance was even more reluctant to share his past than Austin. And Walker was the King of Quiet. Austin had been working with the two of them for seven years and still knew next to nothing about where they came from, what their families were like, and if they had any plans for a future beyond Rose Protection Agency.

They knew as little about him, so he never felt the need to push for more, but as he walked away, Austin knew that wasn't who Samuel was. It wasn't who Lacey was. They were good and open and kind and wanted everyone to feel seen.

Austin veered toward Lacey instead of going back to the therapist in the dark office. He needed a minute with her, a minute to remind himself why this was worth it. She was looking at a picture on Samuel's desk when Austin walked up.

"That was after one of my first cases," Austin said.

Lacey smiled up at him. "Yeah? What was the case?"

Austin moved closer and sat on the edge of the desk. "We had a teenager who witnessed a murder. She snuck out of her house to go visit her girlfriend. Their parents didn't know they were dating. The girls hadn't come out yet, so they were meeting in secret to figure out how they felt."

"That had to be tough on them."

Austin nodded. "Yeah. I can't imagine what they went through. Kate, the one we were protecting, she said when she first met Gabby, it was like something clicked in her mind. She always felt awkward because she wasn't boy crazy like her friends. She was indifferent to the boys in school. But when Gabby moved to town, Kate knew why she'd never responded to boys."

"Wow."

"She was funny about it. Her parents were always supportive, but she wasn't sure what they thought about being gay, so she hid it from everyone. The night she snuck out, the girls met at a park not far from where they lived. They were there for an hour, and both decided they needed to go home. Gabby went one way, and Kate went the other."

"Oh no."

Austin forced a smile. "They both survived. But Kate walked right toward an execution. She heard shouting and hid. She was behind a group of bushes and watched as a man was beaten, then shot."

"How old was she?"

"Fifteen."

"I can't even imagine. How scary for her."

Austin nodded, remembering the same thought. "She was brave, though. She waited to make sure the men were gone, then she went home and woke up her parents. She told them the whole story and what she saw. They called the police and reported it. They found the body right where she said."

"I'm kind of surprised they believed her."

"They didn't entirely. They had to prove she wasn't responsible."

"A fifteen-year-old?" Lacey barked.

Austin shrugged. "She ended up knowing the man who was killed. She didn't recognize him with his face beaten, but he was a teacher at her school. He was selling drugs to students on campus."

"Oh my God."

"It was ugly. The whole thing was just... Gabby's family ended up moving away because of the whole situation. Gabby wasn't a witness, but her family thought she could be used against Kate and never looked back. Kate was sad to lose her first love, but she was a brilliant and brave kid." Austin looked at the picture again. "Your dad and I took that picture after the trial ended. Kate's testimony put away two men who flipped on their employer and helped to bring down the entire organization."

"Is that Kate?" Lacey asked.

Austin smiled as he looked at the picture. "She went to college for criminal justice and is going to be an FBI agent. She's considering military service first, but her goal is to join the FBI."

"Wow. She sounds pretty amazing."

Austin nodded. "She was. She is. She..." A flash hit him.

"Are you okay?" Lacey asked.

"Yeah. I just remembered something."

"What did you remember?"

"Your dad. When we were trying to get to the shelter at the back... Our witness was hurt. She couldn't walk on her own. My shoulder." He reached up and touched it. "Your dad was going to take us both, but I told him to get her to safety. Take her first."

"And that's what he did?"

Austin squeezed his eyes shut, willing the memory to stick.

"Go. Get her out of here."

"I'm not leaving you," Samuel growled.

"You have no choice. I'll draw their fire so you can get to the back. She's the one that matters."

"You matter, Austin. You've always mattered."

"I'll be right behind you." Austin pushed away from the peninsula, the pain in his shoulder making his stomach flip again. "Go, Samuel. They're not going to stop."

"You should take her."

Austin shook his head. "I can't carry her. You have to go."

"You better be on my ass."

Austin chuckled. "That's where you taught me to be."

"Don't forget it."

"Head out, old man. I'll see you in a minute."

Samuel went to the back door. He looked out, then picked Hannah up, carrying her over his shoulders. His steps were unsteady, favoring his left side. He would be fine. He had to be fine.

Bullets pelted the walls and the peninsula Austin hid behind. It was coming from everywhere. Too much. Too close.

He looked back, but Samuel and Hannah were gone. The door left open for Austin to follow. He took two steps, then...

EIGHTEEN

Lacey watched Austin with a mix of horror and anticipation. Nothing he said would change that her father was dead, but maybe it would bring her some peace to know what happened.

Austin's shoulders fell. His face twisted in pain.

Lacey stopped breathing, waiting for him to say something. To tell her what he was seeing in his mind.

He blinked his eyes open, looking around the room as if surprised to see he was there. He looked down and reached for her hand when he saw her. "I..."

"What did you see?"

"He was supposed to go, to get Hannah out. I was going to follow him. Something happened. Something... It all went dark again."

"Do you think you saw more?"

Austin shook his head. He looked so defeated. Shoulders hunched, the weight of the world on his body.

All Lacey wanted to do was hold him and tell him it would be okay, but would it? Would he ever be okay? Would she?

She lost her father. She lost her favorite person in the

world. She knew her world would never be the same. The way Austin spoke of her dad, she believed he would carry the same pain for the rest of his life, too.

"I'm so fucking sorry, Lacey. I should have been out there with him. I don't know... I don't know why I didn't follow him."

"It's okay. It sounds like you were pretty bad off." She wanted to sound normal, to feel normal. She didn't blame him. She knew the work they did was dangerous, but even knowing that was different from hearing about it. His story about Kate and what the teenager went through was a reminder that the people they protected were in real danger. They were brave, but the people who made Rose Protection Agency work were even braver. They walked into work every single day knowing they might not ever leave.

Her father paid that price. And Lacey knew he did it without a second thought. He would have been there if he could. He would have given his life for Austin, or any of the others. He gave it trying to stop a woman from being killed. She was killed anyway, but maybe her dad did something that saved Austin. Even if he didn't, he was a hero. He always would be.

"I... I'm sorry, Lacey. I really thought... I don't know. I should have been with him. I should have gone with him. I can't... do this." Austin stood and looked down at her. He shook his head in anguish. "We never should have done this. I'm sorry. I just... Your father told me to stay away from you. I need to respect that." He turned and walked away. Stalked away.

His feet pounded against the floor, the sound echoing in her ears and her heart.

He wasn't coming back. She knew that as well as she knew he wasn't to blame for what happened to her father, but it didn't matter. Austin blamed himself.

"Is everything okay?" Brodie Douglas asked, appearing next to Lacey. Brodie was not one of the guys she knew well, but he was one of the few who always seemed to be smiling or ready with a joke. Seeing a serious look on his face threw Lacey off.

She shook her head. "He remembered something. He said he was supposed to follow my dad, but everything went dark again. He doesn't know why or what happened. He said it's his fault."

"It's grief. Don't blame him."

"I don't," Lacey insisted.

Brodie caught her gaze and held it. His eyes roamed her face before he nodded. "He loved your dad. We all did. Him not being here is going to be impossible."

"Yeah. I feel the same."

Brodie nodded and squeezed her shoulder. "Did he say anything else? About what he remembered?"

Lacey shook her head. "No. But he's not coming back."

Brodie looked at where Austin went. His face pinched. "What do you mean?"

"He's done. With me. With us."

"How do you know that?"

"He just told me." Lacey wanted to cry. To scream about how unfair it was. Her father was her favorite person ever, and he wasn't there. He didn't know how Austin was with her. He didn't know how loved Austin made her feel. "I should go."

"You can't. You were just attacked again."

"Maybe, but I can't force myself into his space. Not when he doesn't want to be around me."

"He said that?"

"He said my father asked him to stay away from me, and he's going to respect that."

"Let me talk to him." Brodie was off the desk and following Austin before Lacey could argue.

She didn't want to be the wounded woman who sent a friend to chase after the guy she was crushing on. High school was too damn long ago for her to act like that. It wasn't her, and she didn't want that. "Brodie!"

He stopped, turning back to her and realizing the entire room had gone still. He returned to her side. "Yeah?"

"Let him go."

"Lacey—"

"You told me not to blame him, but that means you can't either. He's hurting, just like I am. We all are. And if being with me is one too many things for him to handle, that's his choice. I'm not going to demand he stays with me. I can take care of myself."

"Montgomery's not going to let you go back to your apartment."

"I know. But he'll assign me someone else. Or I can go to my parents' house... my mom's house. Kirk and Stephanie are staying with my mom, right?"

Brodie looked like he wanted to do anything besides admit that, but he nodded.

"Then I can go there. Kirk is already there, and I'll be fine. Can you give me a ride?" She stood and gathered the things she had with her. She didn't love the idea of going back to stay with her mother, but it would mean being somewhere that was sort of like home. She could do laundry, cook and eat like normal, and she'd give Austin the space he needed from her.

"I need to talk to Montgomery."

Lacey nodded. "Okay."

Brodie hesitated, then shook his head and walked away.

Lacey watched as he went to Montgomery's office and knocked. Montgomery waved Brodie in and stood at attention while Brodie spoke. When Montgomery looked out through the glass walls and met her gaze, Lacey nodded.

Montgomery's arms dropped to his sides. His sigh was not

a welcome one. He didn't like her idea anymore than Brodie did, but he wasn't charging out of his office to tell her she was crazy. He was talking it over with Brodie.

When Montgomery made a call, Lacey knew he was calling Kirk, asking if it was okay to send Lacey home, and she felt a victorious jolt.

Followed immediately by a sad realization that her temporary fling with Austin was over. She'd have her memories, but she wouldn't make new ones. Austin was done with her.

Brodie came back and grabbed her suitcase. "Looks like I'll be joining you."

"What?"

"Kirk said everything's been quiet, but he wants to make sure he doesn't miss anything with you, your mom, and Stephanie all there. He asked for me to stay, too."

"I didn't mean to drag you into all this, Brodie."

Brodie chuckled. "It's our job, Lacey. It's all good. I'm just not sure how Austin will take it."

"Austin won't care."

Brodie looked like he was going to argue with her, but Lacey turned and walked away. She didn't want to hear it. Austin said he was done, and she had to accept that. Too many times in her past she refused to hear those words and only ended up more hurt when she did. She wasn't going to do it again.

Austin Ward was done with her, so she was leaving with her broken heart and a tiny shred of pride.

AUSTIN HADN'T BEEN able to exercise in four weeks. Since he was shot, the doctors told him to take it easy. Besides his aerobic activity with Lacey, he hadn't done anything to alleviate the pent-up energy coursing through him.

It was taking a toll.

He hit the button to speed up the treadmill in the gym, ignoring the tug on his shoulder with every step he took toward the absolute nothing he was running toward.

Sweat dripped in his eyes and slid down his shirt. He needed the punishment. Samuel and Hannah would be alive if he'd followed them like he said he would. The shooters wouldn't have snuck up behind Samuel if Austin had been watching his back. They wouldn't have been able to put a bullet in his head.

But Austin let his partner down. And then spent the last few weeks screwing his daughter. After being told to stay away from Lacey for years.

Austin deserved whatever punishment was coming. Montgomery would definitely accept his resignation once he heard what Austin remembered.

"What the fuck is wrong with you?" Montgomery barked, slamming his way into the gym. The door hit the wall so hard it creaked. Montgomery took two steps inside, enough for the door to close behind him, then crossed his arms over his chest and glared at Austin.

"I needed to get out some energy."

"And that involved telling Lacey MacNeil she was bothering you?"

"I didn't say those words."

"Then what the fuck did you say that had her asking to go to her mother's house?"

"She's gone?" The news had Austin's feet stuttering. He lost his balance, nearly going down. He grabbed the handles on the treadmill before he ate belt and hopped his feet to the side rails.

"She told Brodie you said you didn't want to be around

her. She was going to leave. He talked her into not being alone, and she agreed to go to her mother's house because Kirk's still there with Stephanie."

"Good. The farther she is from me, the better." Austin hit the stop button and waited until the belt quit spinning before he stepped down.

"What the fuck is wrong with you?" Montgomery asked.

"I fucked up, okay? I know it now. I remembered what happened. I remembered Samuel walking out of the house."

"You what? Bridget didn't say anything about that."

Austin shook his head. "It wasn't when I was in with her. I walked out and was talking to Lacey. She was looking at the photo on Samuel's desk of us with Kate. I told her about that case, and flashes of the night Samuel died came back."

"What did you remember?"

"Nothing helpful. We were under fire. Samuel was slow getting to us, and when he got there, Hannah was pretty bad. My shoulder was blown to shit. Samuel couldn't help both of us, and I told him to take Hannah to the shelter out back. He was going to come back for me, but I said I'd follow him."

"You were still inside," Montgomery said.

Austin nodded. "I know. I don't remember leaving the house. Samuel had Hannah, and they walked out. The door was open, but it goes dark again."

"You never followed him."

Austin shook his head. "Nope. I let him down. He walked out there alone and they both died."

Montgomery shook his head slowly. "You know you're not to blame for that."

"How the hell can you say that, boss? Samuel's dead. I was supposed to be there for him, and instead, I wasn't. There's nothing I can say that makes it okay. And Lacey..."

"She blames you?"

"No." Austin laughed mirthlessly. "No, she said she knows I would have done something if I could have."

"She's right."

"It doesn't change that he's gone. Whoever is after us is after me. She's innocent. She's never done anything wrong in her life. She's too good. She needs to stay far away from me or she's going to end up just like her father. You all do."

"You need to stop saying shit like that. We are a team. None of us are invincible. Shit happens. It sucks, and it hurts, but Samuel would never have blamed you."

"Valerie doesn't feel the same."

"Our loved ones can't be rational."

"You never blamed Zeke when your sister disappeared."

Montgomery snorted. "Yeah, I did."

"What? You said you never blamed him."

"I fucking lied. I was furious with him. I wanted nothing to do with him for a little while. Luckily, I went to training and couldn't see anyone for a few months. I had a lot of time to myself. A lot of time to realize I was blaming the man I thought of as my brother for something my sister did. Even though I didn't know she made the choice not to come back, I knew she made the choice to leave that night. We can't control other people, and Zeke wasn't to blame for Nina."

"Yeah, but—"

"When someone we love suffers, we want to blame everyone. The truth is the person we usually blame the most is ourself. I blamed Zeke, but I blamed myself for not seeing what Nina was going through. I felt like I should have convinced her I'd keep her safe. She ran because of my asshole father. She wasn't wrong to do that. He was... Well, you know what that's like."

Austin nodded, hating that Montgomery knew his past, but thankful he didn't judge him for it.

"Zeke was my only family left. If I blamed him and refused

to see that he was hurting as much as I was, I would have lost the man I thought of as my brother right after I lost my sister and my mother. I couldn't handle all of it."

"I still... I don't know if I can... Valerie hates me. I don't blame her for hating me. Even if I can ever not blame myself, Valerie will always hold me responsible for Samuel's death."

"Then it sounds like we need to find out who's actually to blame and bring them to justice."

"Do you think we can do that?"

"This team? Hell yeah."

"Then let's go. I need to know the rest. I need to find out what else happened that night. Is Bridget still here?"

Montgomery nodded. "She's waiting for you. Let's go see what else you remember."

LACEY WAS quiet on the drive to her mother's house. She appreciated Brodie giving her the silence she needed. She had a feeling her homecoming was going to be less than welcoming since the last time she saw her mother was weeks ago, during her father's funeral.

Before she went to see Austin.

Brodie pulled into the driveway of her childhood home and turned off the engine. He didn't rush to get out, and no one came out of the house to greet them.

Lacey stared at the house, wondering if she made the right choice going back there. Was she bringing danger to her mother? Or was she just running from Austin?

The second question didn't matter. Austin said he was done, and she wasn't going to stick around and make things uncomfortable. She had to trust Kirk and Brodie could keep them all safe.

"Are you ready?" Brodie asked after a minute.

Lacey sighed and nodded. "Let's get this over with."

Brodie grabbed her suitcase from the trunk while Lacey headed for the door. It opened before she got there, and Kirk welcomed her inside.

He hugged her tight. "How are you?"

She snorted.

"Yeah, I figured. I'm so sorry, kid. Your dad will never be replaced."

"No, he won't." Lacey was exhausted, tired to the point of collapse. She spent the last few weeks alternating between being scared and ravished, fearing for her life and wishing things would never change. It caught up to her all of a sudden, and she nearly fell over right there in the foyer.

"Whoa," Kirk said, catching Lacey before she fell.

She sank to the bottom stair, sitting and resting her head in her hands.

Brodie came in, catching sight of Lacey on the stairs, and put everything down. "What happened?"

"She just swayed and went down," Kirk said.

"When's the last time you ate?" Brodie asked.

Lacey shrugged. "I don't know. I'm just so tired. All of this is catching up to me, I think."

Brodie unwrapped a candy bar and shoved it at her. "Keep your blood sugar up. Eat that and you can go get some sleep."

A wet nose pressed in on Lacey, sniffing the candy car.

"Dogs can't have chocolate," she told the greedy beast trying to steal a bite.

"Come on, Cocoa," Kirk said to the chocolate lab. "Let's give her some space."

Cocoa whimpered and tried to stay by Lacey's side.

"He's okay," she said, taking a large bite of the candy. She reached for the dog with her other hand, knowing he was as lost as she was. Cocoa's favorite person in the world was her father, and without him, Cocoa had to be feeling the same gut wrenching pain Lacey was.

Kirk released Cocoa's collar, and the dog laid at Lacey's feet.

She finished the candy, then stood to go upstairs. She swayed again, and Brodie's arm came around her waist. It didn't feel as good as when Austin held her.

Brodie chuckled. "Sorry, Lace. Just don't want you to fall."

"Did I say that out loud?"

"It's okay. I understand." Brodie helped her up the stairs with the telltale sound of Cocoa following them.

Brodie guided her to her bedroom, once she told him which door was hers, then helped her to the bed. He removed her shoes as she stretched out on the bed.

"Cocoa," she called, patting the mattress. "Mom doesn't like you on the bed, but I need to snuggle."

Brodie laughed softly and backed out of the room. "Give us a call if you need anything. We'll be downstairs."

"Bye bye," Lacey said, wrapping her arms around the dog and letting sleep claim her completely.

NINETEEN

Talking to Bridget about the night Samuel died was not as productive as talking to Lacey had been. Austin knew he was the biggest part of the problem. He wasn't trying when he was with Lacey. He could just let go and let the memories come. With Bridget, he had to try.

"Do you need a break?" Bridget asked him after two hours of working on remembering the rest of that night.

"Probably," Austin agreed. "Maybe something to eat."

Bridget nodded and followed Austin out of the small conference room. Austin's gaze swung around the room, searching for Lacey, even though he knew she was gone. He wanted to make sure she was okay, though. He headed for his boss's office.

"How is Lacey?" Austin asked Montgomery.

"She's fine."

"That's all you're going to tell me?" Austin barked.

Montgomery raised one eyebrow at Austin's outburst and calmly set the folder he'd been studying on his desk. He crossed his arms and sat on the edge of the desk. "Do you want to try that again?"

"You let her leave by herself. She's not safe, boss. You know that. What if she never made it? What if someone ran her off the road or followed her? She shouldn't be alone."

"She's not alone, and from what I was told, you didn't want her around, so why do you care what happens?"

"She's not..." Austin trailed off.

Brodie.

Charming, smiling, good guy, Brodie.

Austin knew she was better off nowhere near him, but he didn't want to watch her with one of his teammates. Losing her was like losing something vital. Something he wasn't sure he could live without.

Did he want her to go?

No, but she needed to. Did he want her to go with one of his teammates? One of the single ones who had no problem getting a woman into his bed? Fuck no.

"If you didn't want her to leave with Brodie, why did you tell her you couldn't handle what was going on between the two of you?" Montgomery asked, his tone still calm and curious, with a smirk thrown in just to piss Austin off.

At least, that's what it did. "She's too good for me."

Montgomery snorted. "Are you really that full of yourself? Of course she is. But have you not been paying attention? That woman adores you. Has for years, if I had to guess. You'll never be good enough for her. But that didn't change the way she looked at you."

"It doesn't matter. It's better this way."

"Better for you, maybe. She's off licking her wounds and telling herself you don't want her." He laughed mirthlessly and shoved off the edge of his desk. "You know what? You're right. She is too good for you. Because anyone who's going to treat a woman like that doesn't deserve her. Good for her figuring it out and getting out before you completely ruined her."

Austin swallowed against the bile rising in his throat. He wanted to argue, but Montgomery was right. Everything Austin did proved that he wasn't worthy of her. Every damn thing.

"Did you remember anything else?" Montgomery asked, his voice harsh and bordering on cruel.

Austin shook his head. "No. I keep getting to where Samuel and Hannah walked outside, and then it's just dark. Bridget thinks I either lost consciousness or whatever I saw was so bad my brain is protecting me from reliving it."

"Are you done?"

"We're taking a break. I was..."

"Hoping I lied about Lacey leaving and that she was around so you could use her to remember her father's last moments," Montgomery spat.

Austin opened his mouth to tell his boss he was wrong, but he wasn't. That was what Austin was doing. He told himself Lacey was the magic bullet, and he wanted to talk to her and remember.

He was a selfish asshole.

He knew she wouldn't hang around when he rejected her. When he told her he was going to respect Samuel's warnings. She was smart. She got it. So she left. If she'd stayed...

He wished she'd stayed, but she was too smart for that. He was the dick who fucked her, loved her, and pushed her away.

Because he was to blame for her father's death. It didn't matter that someone else pulled the trigger. Austin should have been out there with Samuel and Hannah. Losing Lacey was his punishment for not saving Samuel.

"There's food in the conference room," Montgomery said, nodding his head toward the door and grabbing his file again.

Austin was dismissed.

He dragged himself to the conference room where the food was set up on the table. It wasn't unusual for them to have dinner or lunch delivered. They were all working on figuring out what happened to Samuel and bringing the sons-of-bitches who killed him to justice, and maintaining their existing jobs, so food was a necessity.

Austin grabbed a paper plate and two sections of the sub platter on the table. He shoved a bottle of water into his pocket and put two baby bags of chips on top of his sandwiches, then went to his desk.

He stared at the photo on Samuel's desk as he picked up one of the subs. Maybe he could remember what happened without dragging Lacey into it.

Austin tried. He really fucking tried. But nothing came back to him.

He finished his food and sucked down the bottle of water before going to find Bridget and hopefully get more answers.

Bridget was up front, talking to Berkeley. The two of them were laughing when Austin walked out. Their smiles felt contrary to how people should feel. It wasn't right. Samuel was dead.

That's how you felt with Lacey.

He scowled at the thought and knew it was true. He was able to forget about Samuel's death when he was spending time with Lacey. She made everything better. Everything easier.

She made him want to be worthy of her.

But he never would be.

"Austin?" Berkeley said, her voice loud.

Austin looked at her and realized both women had been trying to get his attention. "Yeah. Sorry."

"Are you okay?" Berkeley asked. She was halfway out of her seat.

Austin shook off her concern and took a step back. He looked at Bridget and said, "Whenever you're ready to try again, I'll be in the conference room."

"I'm right behind you," Bridget said.

Austin nodded and went toward the conference room. He sat down and rested his head in his hands, feeling worse than before he took a break. He wanted Lacey. To hold her in his arms and trust that all was right with the world.

He couldn't have that. He'd never have it again. He had to remember what happened to her father and give her that closure, then he could move on with his life and leave her to hers.

She'd find someone who deserved her. Someone who would worship her the way she should be worshipped. Someone Samuel and Valerie would approve of.

Someone nothing like him.

IT WAS dark outside when Lacey woke up. She didn't mean to crash so hard, but she was exhausted. Days of endless sex took more out of her than she realized. That and living in fear.

She stretched and rolled out of bed, nearly tripping over Cocoa when she forgot he was there. She bounced off the mattress and sank to the floor. She wrapped her arms around the dog and buried her face in his fur. She felt better after sleeping, but she was not excited about her choice to run home.

Lacey wondered if she could sneak out the window instead of having to go downstairs and face her mother, but she knew that wasn't a good idea. Not when there had been three attempts on her life in the last few weeks.

Lacey sighed and used the bed to push to her feet. She opened the bedroom door, drawing a deep breath and heading downstairs. Cocoa stuck to her side, taking each step with Lacey as she walked downstairs.

Voices in the kitchen preceded her, and when she heard Austin's name, Lacey stopped.

"Austin kept her safe, Val. You have to admit that." That had to be Stephanie.

"She never should have gone to see him," Valerie cried.

"She wanted the same answers you wanted. The answers we now have," Brodie said.

"It's all about money. Money," Valerie spat. "My husband was killed because someone was stealing money and that brave woman came forward with the truth. All of this for money."

Lacey sucked in a breath and burst into the kitchen. "Are you kidding me? That's what this was about? That's why Dad died?"

"Lacey." Brodie stood, facing her and looking like he was going to make a joke. Brodie always had a smile on his face, but Lacey was not in the mood.

She held up a hand. "Money? That's why all this happened? Why people are chasing me all over the city? Trying to kill Austin? Killed Dad? Money. Are you kidding me?"

"Lacey..." Valerie said, trying to go to her.

"No, Mom, you seem to have known this. This is all about money. Greedy assholes who couldn't work for what they had, who had to steal and kill for more."

"It's a lot more than that," Kirk said, drawing Lacey's attention.

"Then what is it? What else is it?" Lacey needed to know, needed to understand.

Kirk and Brodie exchanged a look, debating silently how much they were going to share.

"Tell me!" Lacey screamed.

"Lacey, come sit," Stephanie said, her voice calm in the midst of Lacey's crazy.

She wanted to argue. To yell. To fight. But more than that,

she wanted answers. So she listened to Stephanie and joined the women at the table.

"Peter Howard was embezzling money from the company he ran with his wife. The company, Howard Enterprises, was originally AMW Distributors. Kimberly Weston married Peter Howard, and eventually, her father sold AMW to Peter," Kirk explained.

"He was stealing money from his own company? That makes no sense," Lacey said.

"The evidence says he was stealing from AMW Distributors for years before the companies merged. Making his father-in-law's company less profitable so when he bought it, it was a cheaper sale. But he was greedy and didn't stop once he took over both," Brodie continued.

"Can't say I'm disappointed he's dead," Lacey murmured.

"Agree, but the real kicker is he obviously didn't kill himself. Street cameras and medical records confirmed he was one of the men in the SUV when it exploded. He didn't fake his own death, which means he was murdered." Kirk groaned like it was bad news.

"Remind me to feel bad for the man who had my father killed later," Lacey growled.

Valerie took Lacey's hand and squeezed. Tears ran down Valerie's cheeks, her eyes on the table.

Lacey held her mother's hand, grateful for the information and not a lecture, although she was sure that would come eventually.

"The witness who was killed with Samuel was Peter Howard's executive assistant. Hannah Savage came forward when she found incriminating evidence against her boss. She said there was a file left on her desk. She assumed Peter had left it by accident, and when she was cleaning up, she came across it. When she realized what it was, she dug into the files and found duplicated records. She called the authorities," Kirk explained.

Lacey knew that wasn't the end of it, but she was impressed with the woman who didn't hesitate to expose her boss.

"The FBI wanted to send her back in for more information, but she was let go. They decided to go forward with what they had, hoping they would be able to get more details once they had a warrant." Kirk's sigh said it didn't go as planned.

"I'm guessing that wasn't the way it went down," Lacey said.

Brodie sighed and shook his head. "All the records were doctored, the embezzlement covered up. The only proof of anything was what Hannah had. She was the star witness. The only real witness. Killing her... There was no case without Hannah, and Peter Howard knew it."

"So he killed her, and my father," Lacey said.

Valerie whimpered.

"Yeah."

"Then why is he dead?" Lacey asked.

Everyone exchanged glances.

Lacey was sick of the silence, of the secrets. "Tell me."

"Peter Howard... There were rumors of him being involved with Kimberly's sister, Nicole. She moved in with them when she was sixteen, after their father died," Brodie said, his words heavy with what he wasn't saying.

"He forced himself on her," Lacey said.

The men nodded. "That's what we believe," Kirk said. "There's no proof, no police reports or emergency room visits or anything that would say yes."

"Okay?" Lacey said.

"Nicole was institutionalized the day Peter was let out of jail. She tried to commit suicide." Brodie's somber tone was so unlike him that it caught Lacey off-guard.

"Did she... Was she the one...?"

Kirk shook his head. "The general belief is it was his wife, Kimberly. That she didn't know what was going on until then and didn't want her husband anywhere near her sister ever again. But there's no proof of that, so she's still out there. In the hospital with her sister."

"How old is Nicole?" Lacey asked.

"She's twenty," Brodie said.

"Four years," Lacey breathed. She closed her eyes and felt for the girl who was abused by her brother-in-law. Lacey knew what it was like to have no one want her, but to have someone who should have been protecting her taking advantage of her was... unimaginable.

"Yeah," Brodie whispered.

"I'm still missing something. If Peter killed my father, and Kimberly killed Peter, then who the hell is after Austin and me?" Lacey asked.

Everyone looked around, trading glances.

"We don't know," Kirk said.

KIMBERLY'S PHONE RANG, drawing her away from Nicole's bedside. The doctors had eased off some of the medications they'd forced on her initially, but she still spent most of her time sleeping.

"Yeah?" Kimberly said into the phone, her eyes locked on Nicole.

"MacNeil's daughter is back at home with her mother."

"And?"

"She doesn't know anything. They wouldn't have let her go if she had any information."

"She's still under protection," Kimberly said.

The man sighed. "Yes. They're keeping people at the house. But she's not being held in a separate location anymore."

"None of this should have happened. My sister is barely alive. She spent years..." Kimberly broke off her words, stifling a sob. It was her fault. Her fault for not seeing what was going on right under her nose.

"He's gone. He'll never touch her again."

"He never should have touched her in the first place."

"You can't blame yourself."

Kimberly clapped her hand over her mouth to stifle her sob. "I'll never forgive myself for what he did to her. For not seeing it. For not realizing that every time she asked to go with me on trips, it was because of what he did to her when I wasn't there. Or not seeing the way she withdrew over time. The way she hid in her room. I just... I should have seen it."

"You thought she was being a teenager." His sigh through the phone was more compassionate than she deserved.

"She's not a teenager now."

"And she's finally free of him."

"Yeah."

"What do you want me to do about the daughter?"

Kimberly turned back to look at her sister. All of this started when their father died. Nicole was safe when she didn't live with Kimberly and Peter. It wasn't Nicole's fault, and it wasn't MacNeil's daughter's fault.

"Leave her alone. If you haven't seen anyone watching her, we don't need to."

"You think they're only after Ward?"

"Peter surrounded himself with people who were willing to do whatever he said, and who were going to cover their tracks. If she's not a target for them, we don't need to watch her."

"Two of them are dead."

"Good. But we know there are more out there. The police do, too, even if they're only looking at me now."

"Have they been back to question you?"

"They've been here twice now, but hospital staff said they've been told to let the police know before they release Nicole."

"Not good."

"It's fine. We'll be gone long before anyone knows. Once this is over."

"You want me to go back to Ward?"

Kimberly sighed. "Yeah. Make sure he's safe. No one else needs to die because of my husband."

"What about you? Are you safe?"

"Yeah, I'm fine. No one will do anything to me in here."

"How's Nicole?"

Kimberly smiled. "Sleeping. But still alive."

"That's all that matters right now."

"Yeah."

"I'll let you go."

"Thanks. Keep me posted."

"I will. Good night, Kimberly."

"Good night, Devlin."

TWENTY

Austin hated the thought of going to a safe house. He didn't need someone to watch over him. Montgomery refused to let Austin go home, and after the shootout at his house and the destruction left behind, Austin knew that wasn't the place for him either.

Staying at the office sounded like a good idea. Right up until everyone left and Austin was wandering around alone and feeling like he was somewhere he shouldn't be. It was like being in school when it was closed. Every noise made him jump. He saw things that weren't there. And that was all before he thought about settling down to sleep in his boss's office.

How in the hell did people work at home and still sleep?

Austin padded to the bathroom for the hundredth time, for no other reason than it was a change of scenery. He splashed water on his face and dried it with a paper towel that scratched more than soothed.

Sleep was important, but every time he closed his eyes, he saw Samuel and Hannah walk out that back door. The look in Samuel's eyes, the determination.

Austin wanted to understand. He wanted to see the rest of the story. He needed to know what happened when Samuel walked out that door.

But it was all blank.

Austin went to the gym and wore himself out, stopping before he did any damage to his mostly healed shoulder. He ached to continue, to say fuck it and beat the hell out of the speed bag until he couldn't stand or feel his limbs, but he'd really be useless if he did that.

He took a shower in the locker room and changed into clean clothes he kept in his locker. He sat on the bench and stared at Samuel's locker, next to Austin's. Samuel's name had been removed, and it appeared as though his things were gone. The locker was dark, empty.

Samuel was being erased.

Austin didn't like the idea of Samuel no longer being a part of the team. Since Austin started working at Rose Protection Agency, others had retired, but no one died on the job. They'd lost clients, before and after they were protecting them, but Austin didn't know of any protectors dying.

Until Samuel.

His throat tightened with grief, knowing he had to process it. Bridget told him so, and so did Montgomery and Zeke. Austin had never been good at that. Emotions weren't allowed. Emotions were signs of weakness, and weakness could be exploited, manipulated, taken advantage of.

Years of abuse took their toll on Austin. It didn't matter that he hadn't seen his father in fifteen years, the bastard's voice rang in Austin's head.

You're weak.

You'll never be anything.

You never should have been born.

Austin closed his eyes and fought back the tears. His father was a piece of shit who reminded Austin every day that he wasn't wanted. His mother wasn't any more of a prize. She left them when Austin was in kindergarten, disappearing one day and never coming back. Austin knew, even then, that his father was abusive. He'd seen the bruises and heard the screaming. He knew it wasn't good, but he didn't really understand it until his father turned the anger on Austin.

There were many times Austin believed every word that came from his father. Times he considered running away or taking his own life. Times he wondered how much worse it could possibly be if he chose one of those two options.

Would Samuel be alive if he had?

It was the first time Austin wondered about his impact on the life of anyone else. Running would have made things easier on his father, and by the time Austin had the courage to seriously consider it, he had no intention of making things easier for his father.

But Samuel deserved better. Samuel was like the father Austin always wanted. Someone who supported him and cared. Someone who offered advice instead of just criticism. Austin found that in Teddy when he joined the Army, but he was a kid then. He was barely old enough to know his own mind, let alone think about his future. Samuel had been the one to show Austin what life could be like.

With a family, a partner, a real chance for something he didn't have growing up. Samuel's family... Austin never knew families could be like that in real life. He saw it on TV, and he heard rumors, but until he met Valerie and Lacey, Austin thought it was fiction.

Now it was again. Austin was no longer welcome in their home. He was an outsider once more, left to his solitude.

Alone in the office with no one around to keep him company.

Austin turned on music in the gym and went to Montgomery's office. The noise was just enough that it drowned out the subtle noises that had been driving him crazy. The buzz of computers, the hum of appliances, the tick of the clock.

Austin laid on the couch and shoved the pillow Montgomery provided under his head. He punched it into place and grabbed the blanket on the end of the couch, tugging it over his feet. He laid back and drew a deep breath, letting it out slowly like Bridget had him doing before she tried to pull up his forgotten memories.

Austin tried to force his mind to clear, but it wasn't working. His thoughts kept drifting to Lacey. His time with her. Making her laugh. Holding her while she slept. Sinking into her warmth and feeling like he was exactly where he was supposed to be.

He hated that he hurt her. It was better if she stayed away from him, but she didn't deserve to be treated like she wasn't important. When all this was over, he would talk to her. Tell her how much their time together meant to him. And explain that he had to leave. Let her heal. Give her a chance to go back to her life without him dragging her down.

All he would do was hold her back from the future she deserved. He had to let her go. But first, he needed to see her once more.

Just once.

He smiled and replayed their time together. Every moment with her was like a dream. One he didn't want to wake up from.

But she was bleeding.

Austin's heart pounded. Lacey was there. In the safe house. No. It wasn't Lacey, it was Hannah.

But he saw Lacey.

Austin reached for her. "Are you okay?"

"You have to remember what happened, Austin. You'll never forgive yourself if you don't."

Austin didn't know what she meant, but before he could ask her, she was Hannah again. Samuel had his arm around Hannah's waist. They were moving to the door.

"You better be on my ass."

Austin chuckled. "That's where you taught me to be."

"Don't forget it."

"Head out, old man. I'll see you in a minute."

Samuel went to the back door. He looked out, then picked Hannah up, carrying her over his shoulders. His steps were unsteady, favoring his left side. He would be fine. He had to be fine.

Bullets pelted the walls and the peninsula Austin hid behind. It was coming from everywhere. Too much. Too close.

He looked back, but Samuel and Hannah were gone. The door left open for Austin to follow. He took two steps, then jerked forward. He fell, grabbing for the door but missing.

The door slammed as he fell against it, closing the door and abandoning Samuel and Hannah in the backyard.

He tried to breathe, but the pain in his back was so intense he felt like he was inhaling fire. The shot caught his vest, but it hit square in the middle of his back. Dead center of his spine. He had to get up. To watch Samuel's back. To—

A gunshot. Just one. In the backyard.

Austin needed to know what happened, but he couldn't move. He tried to draw a full breath but when he did, his vision darkened on the edges.

Another shot. A scream.

Austin crawled forward. Samuel needed him. There were more than two shooters. If Samuel took out two of them, there were still more.

Austin moved slowly, like cement was poured over him. Everything was heavy. His shoulder screamed with pain, but he had to keep going.

Doors closed out front. How many? Tires squealed. Sirens.

Help. Help was coming. They could save Samuel. And Hannah. They would see the car leaving.

Help was coming.

Austin bolted upright on the couch. The blanket wrapped around his feet and slid off the couch when he dropped his feet to the floor. He tugged the blanket away and stood, pacing the office.

The two shots he heard weren't Samuel. It wasn't Samuel killing their attackers. It was Samuel and Hannah being shot.

Austin wiped his hand across his face and was surprised to find his hand wet. Tears overflowed his eyes, and he hadn't realized it. He couldn't stop it either.

Austin went through the office and screamed. He should have been with Samuel. They should have gone together. He told Samuel to go, that he'd be right behind him, but he wasn't.

Because he was shot.

Austin thought the pain in his back was something to do with his surgery. That everything was connected and his struggle to breathe the first few days had to do with being intubated. He never mentioned it to anyone.

There was a part of Austin that was relieved. He was planning to go with Samuel. He hadn't completely abandoned his partner. He still felt responsible, but he didn't leave them to fend for themselves. Not on purpose.

Austin went to his desk and grabbed a notebook. He wrote down every detail he remembered, every piece of what happened. He drew a diagram of the house and where they were when the shooting started. He recorded everything.

Then he watched the security footage of his house being invaded. Over and over again, Austin stared as three men walked into his house and tore it apart. They wore black masks, making it impossible to identify them, but Austin knew they had to be the same men. Austin never saw them the night Samuel died. He couldn't prove they were the same men, but remembering that night solidified the truth in Austin's mind.

The working theory was they worked for Peter Howard. If they did, they didn't happen to find Hannah. They found out where she was somehow.

Austin went back through the footage of his house. He backtracked to before they invaded him. Before the funeral. Before he left—

He stopped. There was a truck sitting outside his house a week before he went to the safe house with Samuel. The windows were down, and the man was definitely watching Austin's house.

Austin had a vague memory of the truck. His neighbors were having work done on their house. Trucks had been there off and on for weeks. Men going in and out of the house. Carrying tools and supplies in and out...

He grabbed screenshots of the driver and kept looking. His video doorbell didn't capture every second of time, but the truck was there at different times of day for six days. Three different men were driving.

No one ever got out of that truck and went inside the neighbor's house. They were using the construction as a cover to watch Austin. And he never noticed it.

It was his job to see things others didn't. To pay attention when there was nothing to pay attention to. He failed. He was being watched, maybe being followed, and he had no idea. He led them right to Hannah.

Austin kept watching his security footage, noting when he stopped going home that they stopped going to his house. They knew. They didn't show up once in the time after Austin went to the safe house.

How did they know he would be the one protecting Hannah?

It didn't entirely matter, but it did. Was there a leak? Did someone inside Rose Protection Agency tell Peter Howard's people about their plans?

It was hard to imagine. Austin couldn't fathom any of his coworkers doing it. They all came to the job for their own reasons, and none of them came in to let the bad guys win.

Austin made a pot of coffee and tried to push away the fog in his brain. There was something he was missing. Something not fitting into place. But he couldn't figure out what it was.

He tried to run through everything again, but the missing pieces didn't appear. Just like his memories, the information was out of reach.

For now.

Austin ached to get out of the office. Get some food and fresh air and a change of scenery. He eyed the keys in Montgomery's office and debated. If he left and something happened to him, they might never bring the men who killed Samuel to justice.

Austin was almost willing to take the risk when the security door unlocked and Montgomery stepped into the office.

His gaze swung through the room until he saw Austin. Montgomery lifted a bag of food. "Hungry?"

Austin nodded and went to where his boss disappeared into the conference room.

Montgomery pulled out bagels and cream cheese, then tossed Austin a cardboard wrapped package.

Austin tore it open, knowing he'd find a breakfast wrap inside. The sausage and bacon scent hit his nose as he took his first bite. It was still hot.

"I figured you probably got as much sleep as I did," Montgomery said, pouring himself a cup of coffee from the pot Austin brewed less than an hour earlier.

"Probably. But I did remember the rest of the night Samuel died."

"You did?" Montgomery asked, turning to Austin with wide eyes.

Austin nodded. "I got hit in the back. My vest caught it, but it knocked me down. I fell, slamming the door closed. Samuel left it open for me to follow him. I was on my way to follow him. He shouldn't have been out there alone."

"You were shot. How can you blame yourself?"

"I should have gone with him."

"Austin, listen to me, we can't save everyone. That's a hard fucking lesson to learn, but it's one we all have to face."

"He was my partner."

"I know."

Austin dropped his food and put his head in his hands. "I don't know if I can forgive myself."

Montgomery laughed without humor. "There are some things that aren't forgivable. Some things... some things we'll never be able to look ourselves in the mirror again and accept. We kill people. People are killed around us. Beaten and abused and tortured. We see the worst the world has to offer. Both here and overseas."

"You sound like you're speaking from experience."

Montgomery only nodded.

"Your sister?"

He breathed a laugh. "She's one."

Austin didn't know what that meant.

"Now that you know it wasn't your fault, we need to figure out how in the hell these guys knew where you were."

"They were watching me."

Montgomery's glare would have frozen Austin in place years ago. Now it had him scrambling to explain.

"I went back through my security footage. My neighbors were having work done. Tons of trucks parked outside. It was one of many, but the men never went into the house."

"How the fuck did they know you were going to be assigned to Hannah?"

"Now that question I don't have an answer for. That's what I've been trying to figure out."

"If they were outside your house, do you have IDs?"

"Not yet, but I have faces."

"Let's see them." Montgomery grabbed his breakfast wrap and coffee and led the way out of the conference room.

Austin pulled up what he had and showed his boss.

Montgomery ran a hand down his face and shook his head. "Well, those two aren't going to give us any information."

"You know who they are?"

Montgomery raised an eyebrow. "Yeah. Jacob Vaughan and Frank Alexander. Peter Howard's men who were in the SUV with him when he was blown up."

"Fuck."

"Yeah. But the other one... We need to find him. And make sure he pays for what they did to Samuel and Hannah."

"And figure out how they knew I was going to be with her."

Montgomery nodded. "Yeah. Because if we have a leak..."

He didn't finish his thought, but he didn't have to. Austin knew the end.

Rose Protection Agency would be done.

TWENTY-ONE

THE DOORBELL RINGING WAS THE FIRST SIGN OF LIFE in the MacNeil household the morning after Lacey's life was turned upside down. Again. She was not in a hurry to go downstairs and see who was bringing them more shitty news. She was perfectly content to stay in bed and ignore the world.

Cocoa's head lifted a second before a knock on the door told Lacey she wasn't going to be so lucky.

"Can I come in?" Maggie asked, opening the door as she spoke.

Lacey was out of bed and across the room before her bestie got one step inside. "You're here! Oh, my God, you're here. Why are you here? How are you here?"

"When you tease the big men with food, they tend to let you inside," Maggie said, hugging Lacey tight.

Lacey's entire body relaxed, and she shuddered in her bestie's arms. "It's so good to see you. Are you wearing a new perfume?"

"You, too. And yeah, Owen got it for me. I haven't decided if I like it or not."

"It's nice. Subtle. Not too overpowering."

"Says the woman who just smelled it on me."

Lacey shrugged. "Maybe I'm just used to what you smell like."

Maggie snorted. "Weirdness of that statement aside, are you okay? I figured you could use some backup this morning. I brought a feast for the grown-ups. And the sexy one with the smirk. Who's he?"

"You're married," Lacey chastised.

"Married, not dead. I don't have a bang list."

"A what?"

"A bang list. A list of people I'm allowed to bang if the opportunity ever arises. Freebie list, cheat list, whatever you want to call it. I don't have one, so I'm not looking to sneak off with the sexy smirker. But he is sexy."

Lacey groaned. "You're crazy."

"Yeah, but you love me. And either he's Austin or..."

Lacey shook her head. "You've met Austin. You know he's not. Brodie is a flirt. He will flirt with a wall."

"Never did anything for you, huh?"

Lacey shrugged.

"Nope. You go for the emotionally unavailable bad boy that your mother doesn't want you to be around. Got it. So, where is Mr. Perfect?"

"Not here."

"I thought for sure you were screwing with me when you texted me yesterday. How is it safe for you to be home and not in some safe house or something?"

"Safe house didn't do my father any favors. And they don't think I'm really in any danger. Kirk and Brodie are staying here since there are still too many questions about who killed my father over a bunch of money."

"Money?" Maggie said. "You're joking. This is all about money?"

"That was pretty much my reaction, too. I can't believe

my father was killed because some asshole wanted to steal money from his own company. But he got what was coming to him, so I guess that's good."

"What do you mean?"

"He's dead. He was also sexually assaulting his sister-in-law, and they think his wife killed him."

Maggie shook her head, her eyes bugging out at the news. "Whoa. I missed a lot."

"It was an eventful night."

"Then I'm even happier I came by. Your texts last night were a little worrying. You sounded slightly unhinged."

Lacey snorted. "That's pretty much my default right now."

"Well, let's go get some of the food I brought before everyone downstairs devours it all."

Lacey looped her arm through Maggie's. Cocoa followed them down the stairs and into the kitchen, where Valerie and Stephanie were enjoying breakfast. Kirk and Brodie were outside on the deck, on the phone.

"Who are they talking to?" Lacey asked.

"Montgomery," Stephanie said.

"Is there news?" Maggie asked.

Valerie shook her head.

"They didn't tell us," Stephanie said. She spotted Maggie and hugged her. "Good to see you, hun."

"You, too. Lacey said you've been staying here?" Maggie hooked her arm around Lacey.

Stephanie nodded. "We have. We didn't want Valerie to be alone."

"I can understand that. It's been such a crazy few weeks."

"Is Owen home with the kids?" Valerie interrupted.

"He is," Maggie said, her entire face softening at the mention of her husband and kids. "I've been missing this one and wanted to check in on both of you. See how you're doing.

Not that there's an option for good, but we've been thinking about you guys."

"Thank you, sweetie. That means a lot." Valerie grabbed Maggie's hand and squeezed.

Lacey called Maggie the Valerie whisperer. No matter what was going on, Maggie always seemed to get Valerie to calm down and be reasonable about it. Sneaking out in high school? Maggie made it okay. Bad grade on an exam? Maggie took the brunt for a lack of studying. Lacey not married with kids? Maggie said everyone had to find their someone, and Lacey wasn't being picky, she was being smart about finding someone who would bring her the joy Samuel brought to Valerie.

Maggie was that good.

"How about some breakfast? The men delivered the food you brought over. Such a treat for us," Stephanie gushed.

Maggie waved her hand as though it was no big deal. Lacey knew it was absolutely a big deal. The amount of food was enough to feed a small army, or at least a house full of hungry adults. And knowing Maggie, she cooked all of it herself.

"Did you make all of this?" Valerie asked.

Maggie blushed. "I wanted to bring you something from home. The muffins are my grandmother's recipe. The egg casserole is something my family makes every year for Easter because it's easy. And the baked French toast is too yummy to not include."

"This is too much," Valerie said, sighing and dragging Maggie in for a hug. "Thank you. This means the world."

"You and Samuel were always so good to me. I wanted to do more, but I didn't know what made sense with everything going on. Lacey texted me last night that she was home, and I knew I had to come this morning."

"You are always welcome here." Valerie patted Maggie's cheek and smiled.

It was the happiest Lacey had seen her mother since her father died. Not that she expected any joy, but it was still tough to know she wasn't the favorite daughter even when she was the only daughter.

Maggie winked at Lacey, as though reading her mind. When Valerie turned back to the food, Maggie pointed to herself and mouthed *favorite*.

Lacey snorted and rolled her eyes. They both knew it wasn't entirely true, and Maggie making a joke of it was the reminder that it had always been that way. Maggie didn't have to worry about disappointing Valerie because she wasn't her kid. Lacey knew that.

But it still stung at times.

"Lacey, are you hungry?" Stephanie asked, offering Lacey a plate with a large slice of baked French toast.

Lacey took the plate and brought it to her nose. The sweet scent of it hit her and turned her stomach.

That was weird.

Lacey loved sweets. She was a huge fan. It had to be something else. Maybe some coffee would help.

Maggie fixed Lacey a mug and handed it over. Lacey brought it to her lips and sipped, but it was... Not right.

Lacey took her coffee and French toast to the table. It had to be in her head. She was anxious. There was a lot going on. And once they heard whatever Montgomery had to say, it would all be okay.

She cut a bite with her fork and brought it to her lips. She took the bite into her mouth and knew she couldn't do it. It was too sweet.

Lacey chewed slowly and swallowed the French toast, but she couldn't eat another bite. She went back to the counter. Maybe a muffin? She grabbed one and brought it to her nose.

Nope.

Just as bad.

She set the muffin down and sliced into the egg casserole. It was savory instead of sweet. The scent of it was tempting. She felt like she could handle that.

With the egg casserole on her plate, Lacey went back to the table where Maggie was entertaining Valerie and Stephanie with stories of her kids. She showed off pictures and told them all about the things that were happening around her house.

Lacey sat and listened to the stories. Maggie was a saint. She loved talking about her kids, but she was doing it to take the pressure off Lacey.

They were besties for life for a reason.

Lacey watched as Kirk and Brodie ended the call and exchanged a look. They spoke to each other, their expressions worried as they discussed whatever news Montgomery had for them.

When they turned to come back inside, Lacey shifted in her seat. Brodie walked in first, heading to Maggie to introduce himself.

"And who is the goddess who treated us to the feast here?"

"I'm Maggie. It's nice to meet you. Brodie, right?" Maggie let him kiss the back of her hand, the one with a ring on it.

"Yes, ma'am. You have one lucky husband."

"He's well aware." Maggie winked at Brodie, and he threw his head back and laughed.

Brodie moved to the side and fixed a plate of food.

"Good to see you again, Maggie," Kirk said, hugging Maggie and squeezing her shoulder.

"You, too. How are you holding up?"

Kirk shrugged, exchanging a meaningful glance with Brodie.

"What did Montgomery want?" Lacey asked, needing to know as much as she dreaded the answer.

"Austin remembered more of what happened." Kirk met Valerie's gaze.

Valerie sank to her chair, and Stephanie took her hand.

"It wasn't his fault," Kirk said.

Valerie sucked in a breath. Her eyes filled with tears. She brought a hand to her mouth.

"He was shot in the back. He had on a vest, but they don't stop the impact. He passed out right before the police arrived. Heard the sirens. He tried to get to Samuel, but he couldn't." Kirk shared a look with Stephanie.

Stephanie put an arm around Valerie and held her as the sobs took over.

Lacey leaned into Maggie, needing her bestie as she heard the news. No one could have done anything. There was nothing to be done.

Lacey knew Austin wasn't to blame, but hearing the proof—

"How do we know he's not lying about what he remembered?" Valerie whispered.

"Valerie," Kirk said with a sigh.

"He was supposed to be there for Samuel. And he wasn't. He got shot? So did Samuel. Except Austin is still here. He's still walking around. And now he's telling us stories that he couldn't remember? Do we believe this?" Valerie's voice bordered on screeching by the time she was done speaking. She had a panicked look in her eyes.

Stephanie stood and went to a cabinet. She took out a bottle of pills and brought one back to Valerie. "Take it and we'll go lie down."

Valerie accepted the pill and broke into another sob. She followed Stephanie without another word, the two of them going upstairs.

"Do you think she's right?" Maggie asked Kirk and Brodie.

Both men shook their heads without hesitation.

"Austin would have done anything for Samuel. He thought the guy walked on water. He's been pretty beside himself. Blaming himself for what happened. He still does according to Montgomery, but damn, all this is just crazy," Brodie said. He swiped his hat off and scratched his head. He slid his hat back on and looked at Lacey. "You know Austin thought of your father as his family. He would never—"

"I know," Lacey said.

Brodie nodded, then dug into his food.

Lacey pushed her French toast around on her plate, fighting against the knot in her stomach. She never thought Austin could have been to blame. It wasn't possible that he would hurt Samuel. Or done anything that could have resulted in his death.

She wished she could talk to him. Tell him she was happy he remembered. Hopefully the memories brought him some relief. Some closure.

Stephanie came back to the kitchen and cleaned up the dirty dishes. She put away the little bit of food that wasn't eaten, then wiped down the counters. "Are you done with this?"

Lacey let Stephanie take her plate with the French toast.

"Want me to save it for you?"

"Yeah. I'll probably eat it later."

Stephanie nodded, covering the plate in plastic wrap.

Maggie studied Lacey closely, then nodded toward the living room.

Lacey sat on the couch, Cocoa on one side and Maggie on the other.

Maggie was quiet for a minute, then leaned closer. "Are you pregnant?"

"Whoa, what? No. Why would you even think that?"

Maggie raised one eyebrow.

"I'm on the pill," Lacey hissed.

"It doesn't always work. There are warnings on them for a reason."

"No. It's not..." Lacey thought back to what day it was.

"That's not the face of no. Are you already late?"

Lacey chewed the inside of her lip.

"How late?"

"Four days, I think. I'd have to check my app to be sure, but..."

"Do you have a test?"

Lacey shook her head. "First, why would I have a test? I haven't had sex in forever before... Austin. And second, why would it be here?"

"Good points." Maggie tapped her lip with her finger and looked around. "You have to do a test. I'll go get one."

"Maggie, you can't." Lacey grabbed her friend's arm.

"Why not?"

"Because... What if it's positive?"

"Then we'll figure out what you're going to do."

"But..." Lacey closed her eyes. She needed the answer, but — "Wait, how did you know?"

Maggie smirked. "When I got pregnant with Adam, I couldn't eat things that were normal for me, like French toast. At all. Even the smell of it made me feel sick."

"Seriously?"

Maggie nodded. "Yep. And you know these hips don't lie. I'll take down anything sweet any day of the week. But when I got pregnant, nope. Just the thought of it was enough to make me gag."

"And you think..."

"The only way we know is if you take a test."

"Do you really think...?"

Maggie shrugged. "I think it's very possible." She stood and grabbed her handbag, then stopped. "Shit."

"What's wrong?"

"I need to go. I set a timer on my phone for when I needed

to leave. I'm going to pop a boob if I don't get it into a mouth soon."

"Ugh, gross," Lacey said, gagging.

"Just wait until it's your precious one. You'll think it's the most beautiful thing ever."

"I'm not—"

"Hey, ladies," Brodie said, walking into the living room.

Lacey rolled her lips in and forced a smile.

"What did I walk into?"

"Breastfeeding talk," Maggie said, taking all the attention on herself. "I have to run home for a few minutes, but if it's okay, I'll be back in about an hour?"

Brodie nodded, sliding a look at Lacey.

Lacey forced a smile, hoping he didn't think anything was up.

"See you then," Brodie said.

Maggie hugged Lacey, then rushed to the door.

"Is she okay?" Brodie asked.

Lacey nodded. "She's fine. Just a little weird."

"The best ones usually are."

HE WATCHED the woman run out of the house and get into the blue minivan. She backed out without checking behind her, peeling down the street in a hurry.

He debated following her, but something told him she would be his way inside the house. His easiest way inside the house. He pulled out onto the road to follow her and tapped his screen to make a call to his brother.

"Yeah."

"I'm following the friend. She ran out in a hurry, but I think I'll be able to convince her to get me inside."

"What makes you think that?"

"She drives a minivan."

His brother snorted. "Easy mark."

"That's what I'm counting on."

"What are you going to do if you get inside the house?"

"Make them pay for what they did to the boss, and Jacob and Frank."

"Keep me posted."

He hung up and pulled onto the street behind the mom's van. She pulled into a garage and closed the door behind her, but he was patient. He could wait.

Thirty minutes later, the garage opened again, and the same minivan backed out of the garage. He watched the mirror and spotted the woman behind the wheel.

Easy mark.

She pulled away from the house, going back the way she came from, toward the other house. He kept his distance but kept her in his sight. She pulled into a pharmacy parking lot and went inside. He thought about getting into her van, but he waited. Patience was key. They'd already waited long enough. They weren't going to fuck it all up now.

The mom came out of the store with a small white bag with the pharmacy logo on it. She got back in her van and once again, turned toward the MacNeil house.

He smiled as she pulled into the driveway and got out. She had no idea she'd been followed. Even up to the front door.

TWENTY-TWO

Lacey heard the doorbell and went to the stairs. She chewed her nails the entire time Maggie was gone. Could she be pregnant? What was she going to do? How did she let it happen? Did she forget a pill? She kept them in her handbag and didn't think she missed any, but something happened.

A shout from the foyer had Lacey stopping on the top stair. The front door was open, and Brodie had his gun pointed at whoever was there, all his usual humor gone as he backed up into the house.

"We're all going to have a little chat," a man said.

Lacey watched as Maggie walked into the house, her hands in the air. A gun was pointed at the back of her head.

"Maggie!"

The man with the gun looked up and flashed a smile of pure evil when he saw Lacey. "Ah, so she is home. I thought she wasn't here." He jabbed the end of his gun into Maggie's neck.

Maggie whimpered.

The man kicked the door closed and jerked his head

toward the living room. "We're all going to have a little chat. You, too, Princess."

Lacey blanched at the term. Coincidence or not? Did it matter? The man had a gun to her bestie's head.

Lacey was already running down the stairs when she saw Kirk behind her. He held a finger to his lips, and she nodded before continuing downstairs.

Maggie tried to go to Lacey, but the man grabbed Maggie around the neck and held her to his front.

"Nuh uh uh. You're not going anywhere. We're going to sit right here. Where I can see anyone trying to sneak down the stairs or through the front door." The man glared at Lacey and Brodie.

"What do you want?" Brodie growled, his gun still trained on the man.

The man's smile was menacing. His gaze slid to Lacey. "Tying up loose ends."

"How does it make sense to come in here? Now you have more loose ends."

Lacey gawked at Brodie. Was he trying to get them all killed?

"True. Maybe we should all have a party. Go out in the backyard. I can fix drinks for everyone," the man said with a smirk.

"Yeah, sure. You first," Brodie said, jerking his gun toward the back.

The man laughed long and loud, his humor falling flat with Lacey.

What did he want? Obviously her, but why drag Maggie in? Why come after her when she was surrounded?

"You have to know you're not going to get out of here," Brodie said. "What's your plan, huh? Take us all hostage and orchestrate a mass suicide?"

"Nah, I'm more of a hands-on kind of guy."

Maggie tried to take a step away, but the man wrapped a hand around her throat and brought her face to look at him.

"You think you can just run? That if you do, I won't just shoot you in the back?"

Maggie cried.

Lacey would have given anything for her bestie. Maggie had kids, a husband, people who counted on her.

Just like Austin said about Samuel.

"Let her go. You have me. I'm the one you want anyway. Just let her go." Lacey stepped forward.

"I'm afraid your new protector is right, though. You're all loose ends now. Maybe I should just start the fun."

Maggie screamed.

Brodie shouted.

Lacey curled her hands around her belly. The precious life inside her was in danger. It was no longer about her. Nothing ever would be again. Everything narrowed to that one point. That one little thing where no one and nothing mattered but the baby growing inside her.

Lacey didn't need a test to know Maggie was right. She was pregnant. She'd felt different for a week, but brushed it off as part grief and part elation at being with Austin, then despair at losing him right after she'd lost her father.

But now... Now Lacey knew what was really going on. She was pregnant. She was carrying Austin's baby.

And just like she couldn't bear to see Maggie's kids lose their mother, she couldn't let her own child die inside her.

Lacey screamed, all her rage and fear zeroing in on the man who was threatening them. His gun at her best friend's head. His threat of killing all of them. What he did to her father and the witness they were protecting. Whatever role he played in protecting the predator that was behind everything.

She rushed the man, her scream drawing his attention as she threw herself at him.

He braced, Maggie rolling to the side as Lacey launched toward the madman with the gun.

Just before she hit him, he jerked, his body turning sideways before sinking to the floor. Her forward progress took her to him, then past him to where Maggie was. Lacey pulled Maggie away from the man who laid on the floor, a pool of blood forming around him as he gasped.

His eyes were wide, no words forming from his open mouth. He gasped, then relaxed, as though instantly falling asleep.

Footsteps rushed toward Lacey and Maggie. Hands pulled them away from the man on the floor.

Kirk.

Brodie kicked the gun away from the man, glaring down at him before pulling out his phone. "Yeah, we need police and medical. A man broke into a home and he's dead."

Maggie gasped, grabbing Lacey's hand.

Lacey looked back at the lifeless eyes of the man on the floor.

Brodie gave the address and asked for Captain Marcus Patrick to be notified. He smiled at whatever the operator said, then hung up. He shot a look at Kirk, who nodded, then Brodie made another call.

"Our third shooter forced his way inside with Lacey's friend. Kirk took him out." Brodie paused for a minute and nodded. "Yeah. Already called. Mackenzie answered. She's sending everyone."

Kirk led Lacey and Maggie to the kitchen. He pointed to the table, and they sat next to each other, hugging and crying.

"I'm so sorry," Maggie said. "I should have been paying attention. He walked up behind me when I was almost to the porch. I thought he worked with your dad until he stuck the gun in my back."

"Are you okay? Are you hurt?"

Maggie shook her head. "I don't think so. Just scared. I don't know how you've handled all of this. I about peed myself."

"I don't think I've handled any of it well. Maybe I'm numb because it started with my dad. I haven't had time to stop and think about it."

"You just rushed that psycho. You were a little crazy. It worked, but why in the world did you do that?"

Lacey breathed a laugh. "I saw this documentary..."

Maggie chuckled. "You and your documentaries. I've never met anyone who watches them like you do."

"I have," Lacey whispered, rubbing her belly again.

Maggie's brows went up. "Really? He does?"

Lacey nodded.

"Oh, the test. I dropped it outside." Maggie got up to go, but before she could get around the table, Stephanie and Valerie walked into the kitchen.

"Are you two okay?" Stephanie asked, hugging Maggie.

Valerie came to Lacey and hugged her. "I thought I was going to lose you, too."

"I'm fine, Mom. Brodie and Kirk took care of us."

"They shouldn't have had to. You should have been safe here," Valerie said.

"We're going to make sure you are all safe," Montgomery said, joining them in the kitchen with a white bag in his hand. "Does this belong to anyone? It was outside the door. It's—"

"Mine!" Maggie shouted, jumping up and rushing to him. She snatched the bag from his hand before he could say anything else. "Thank you. I dropped it when that man put a gun to my head."

Montgomery looked at her and nodded, not arguing but definitely not believing her either. His gaze slid to Lacey.

She ducked her head, not meeting his gaze. She realized she had a hand curled around her belly and removed it, even though it was too late. She closed her eyes and prayed he'd keep his mouth shut. At least until she had a chance to figure out what she was going to tell Austin.

And her mother.

"We need to ask you both a few questions," Montgomery said, his gaze locked on Maggie and Lacey. "Since you were in the room with him, we need to know what he said."

"Brodie was there, too," Lacey said.

Montgomery nodded. "The police need statements from all of you. Kirk, too, since he's the one who killed the man."

"I never saw Kirk," Maggie said.

Montgomery smiled. "If you had seen him, the shooter would have, too. Kirk was on the stairs. He took the shot. But the police need you to tell them what happened. Maggie?"

Maggie nodded.

"Captain Patrick is a friend. Since you were the first one to encounter the man, he'd like to speak to you first. If that's okay?"

Maggie handed the bag to Lacey and said, "Hold that for me."

Lacey nodded, clutching it to her chest.

Maggie followed Montgomery out of the room, leaving Lacey alone with Stephanie and her mother.

"How about some tea?" Stephanie said, going to the stove and grabbing the kettle. She filled it with water without waiting for anyone to answer.

Lacey sat in silence, thinking about the bomb she held in her hand. The test would confirm what she was already sure was true. She could just go to the bathroom and take the test, but she didn't want to do it alone. It felt easier with Maggie by her side.

Lacey wondered what her life would look like. Raising a child alone would be a challenge, but she refused to force Austin to have anything to do with them. He said he was done, and Lacey would honor that. He had a right to know, but other than that, she didn't need anything from him. She loved him, and she would love their child enough for both of them.

If she was pregnant.

Stephanie set a mug in front of Lacey, and she sipped the tea. It was bitter but not sweet, so Lacey could keep it down without feeling like it was going to make her sick. Stephanie and Valerie talked around Lacey while she sipped her tea and ignored everything but the feel of the test in her lap.

When Maggie was done being questioned, it was Lacey's turn. She detailed everything she remembered from hearing the doorbell to seeing Maggie walk in to her choice to rush the man who was threatening them. Lacey left out the part about protecting her possible unborn baby, but she figured that wasn't relevant.

As soon as they were done being questioned, Maggie grabbed Lacey and led her upstairs. "I need to go soon, but I talked them into giving us a minute."

"Are you going to be safe?" Lacey asked.

Maggie nodded. "There's already someone at my house. Montgomery is putting someone with us for the night just because I'm so unsteady. He said everything is over, but he offered to have someone watch the house anyway."

"I'm so sorry I got you wrapped up in all of this," Lacey said.

Maggie shook her head. "We'll be fine. If this was the last of the guys who were after you, there's no reason to worry that more are coming. It's more a precaution than anything else. But you need to take that test. Now."

Lacey's hands shook. "Do I have to?"

Maggie nodded and shoved Lacey toward the bathroom attached to her bedroom. Maggie opened the box and laid everything out. "Have you ever taken one?"

Lacey snorted. "No."

Maggie held up the stick. "Cap off, pee on that. Hold it in the stream for at least ten seconds. Cap on, then set it somewhere flat." Maggie pulled out a bunch of toilet paper. She flattened it and laid it on the counter next to the sink. "Set it here. We have to wait three minutes, so by the time you wash and dry your hands, you'll be a third of the way there."

"Are you going to wait with me?"

"Yes. I'll be here. Always."

Lacey drew a breath and nodded.

Maggie walked out of the bathroom and closed the door.

Lacey stared at the test and knew no matter what, her life had changed. She wanted to be pregnant. She'd always hoped to have a family, a husband and kids. She wouldn't get the husband, but she still wanted the baby.

"Just do it," Maggie said through the door.

"I hate that you know what I'm thinking."

Maggie snickered through the door. "Love you."

"Love you." Lacey pulled the cap off the test and sat down. She counted to ten, slowly, then capped the test and set it on the counter. She finished using the bathroom and washed her hands, staring at the test that had no result yet.

"Open the door," Maggie said.

Lacey opened the door, and Maggie pulled her out of the bathroom.

"Sit. Staring at it isn't going to make it work faster. Trust me."

Lacey chuckled and sat on her bed with Maggie. "I'm scared and excited."

"That's a good thing."

"Montgomery knows," Lacey said.

Maggie snorted. "Yeah, I guess it's part of his job to be able to read people. I just didn't want him telling everyone what was in the bag."

"I think he understood that."

"Do you think he'll tell anyone?"

Lacey shook her head, realizing she didn't. "No. He's pretty discreet. I think—"

A timer went off on Maggie's phone. She silenced it and looked at Lacey. "Are you ready to look?"

Lacey's heart pounded. Her palms were clammy. She felt sick again. "Do I have a choice?"

Maggie laughed. "Not really."

Lacey stood and wiped her hands on her shirt. "Okay, let's see."

AUSTIN DID NOT DO WAITING WELL. He paced and glared at his phone and debated leaving the office against orders. Every time he moved toward the door, one of his teammates stepped in his path. The fuckers.

Montgomery gave everyone orders not to let Austin leave. All Austin wanted to do was find out if Lacey was okay. One of Peter Howard's psychos went to her house. Was going to kill her. It didn't matter that the guy was dead, he was there. Which meant they knew who Lacey was and all Montgomery's assurances that she would be safe were fucking useless.

Austin was going to hurt someone.

The door opened and the man who held all of Austin's anger walked in. Maybe not all, but a fuck ton of it. Austin made a beeline for his boss and got right up in Montgomery's face.

"You said she'd be safe. You said she was not in any danger. How the fuck do you explain someone getting into the house and trying to kill her?"

"How about you back the fuck off?" Montgomery growled.

"Don't give me that. You were wrong. You need to admit it."

"I was wrong. Because I didn't have all the information. But now that I do, you're staying away from Lacey MacNeil. For good."

"What the fuck are you talking about?"

"Did you fuck her?" Montgomery snarled, his not-question low and dangerous.

"What does that have to do with anything?" Austin breathed, taking a step back.

Montgomery exhaled a long breath. He shook his head and rubbed his forehead. "She's fucking pregnant."

"What? No. She's on the pill."

"Yeah, well, then why did her friend buy a pregnancy test?"

"How do you know it's not for the friend?"

"The one who's married with two kids and wouldn't feel the need to sneak around, or to take a test at the MacNeil's? That friend."

Austin took a step back and found a wall behind him. He sank to the floor, leaning against the wall for support. Lacey was pregnant. With his baby.

A smile tilted his lips before he thought about what that meant.

He never wanted kids. He wasn't cut out for them. After the way he was raised, he couldn't trust that kids would be safe with him. Studies showed roughly a third of children who were abused ended up abusing their kids. There was no way for him to know if he would be in the majority or not, and if he added his military record and his propensity for violence because of that, he didn't trust that he would be in the majority.

He couldn't be a father. He couldn't. He couldn't risk it. Not to Lacey, and not to a kid.

"I knew leaving the two of you alone was a bad idea," Montgomery said. "I never thought it was that bad of an idea. I didn't think you were going to take advantage of her like that."

"Everything was completely consensual," Austin growled from his spot on the floor.

"It better have been."

Austin shoved to his feet. "Is that really what you think of me? That I'm that horrible of a man that I would manipulate her into bed? You think that little of her that she would let me?"

"I don't know what to think right now. All I know is this whole fucking thing keeps getting worse."

"Yeah, well, I'll bow out as soon as you let me. Since I'm such a disappointment and a waste, I'll get my shit and leave."

"Don't be a child."

"You just told me you think I tricked her into sleeping with me, then got her pregnant. You're the one who's making this into something ugly. Not me, boss."

"Cool off for a minute. Lacey is like a sister to us."

"Well, your sister is married to your 'brother' so I guess you like keeping it all in the family."

Austin didn't see the punch coming until it was too late to defend himself. He knew his boss held back, but it still knocked Austin on his ass.

Montgomery shook out his hand and walked away, leaving Austin on the floor.

Austin deserved it. He deserved that punch and so much worse. The only thing he could do was close the case and get the hell out of town. Make sure Lacey was safe, then never see her or any of them ever again.

TWENTY-THREE

Lacey stared at the test. It didn't matter that she knew what it was going to say, to see it right there on the stick blew her mind.

"Are you okay?" Maggie asked.

Lacey shook her head. "I don't know."

"Sit down. Just take a breath. What are you thinking?"

Lacey slid a hand over her belly. She sucked in a breath and let her eyes fall closed. Her lips lifted, a lightness settling over her. "I'm happy. Does that make any sense?"

Maggie hugged her tight, nearly tackling her to the bed. They both fell back, laughing. "It makes perfect sense." Maggie let Lacey up and grabbed her hand. "You're going to be an amazing mom."

"Mom. Wow. That's a really big three-letter word."

Maggie snorted. "Only you would say that."

Lacey swung confused eyes to her friend. "What do you mean?"

"Normal people would say that's huge. You have to get all specific."

Lacey laughed. "Yeah, well, it's how my brain works." She

rubbed her stomach again. It wasn't any different from a few hours ago, or a few weeks ago, but she knew everything was different.

"Do you think your dad would be happy?" Maggie whispered.

Lacey inhaled sharply. Joy and disappointment battled inside her. "I wish he was here for this. He would have been such an amazing grandfather."

"He would have been. And I think he would have wanted you and Austin together."

Lacey laughed and shook her head. She lifted the locket she wore every day and wondered if her dad would have come around eventually. "Austin said my dad always told him to stay away from me, so I'm not so sure about that."

"Really? He loved Austin. Why would he tell him to stay away from you?"

Lacey shrugged. "I don't know. My mom threatened him. Told him not to come to the funeral. I don't think this is going to be happy news for her."

"You don't have to tell her or anyone anything for a while. Usually the doctors say until the end of the first trimester, you should keep quiet. The risk of miscarriage is higher this early."

Lacey nodded. "I know. I'm only what? Four-and-a-half weeks? I'm almost surprised the test showed anything, but I have a long way to go before I'm going to want to tell anyone."

"What about Austin?"

"He needs to know. Even though he doesn't want to be with me, he has a right to know."

"What if he tells you he doesn't want the baby?"

"I'm not giving it up. He doesn't need to be involved."

"What if he wants to be?"

Lacey breathed a humorless laugh. "I'm not really worried about that one. If he wants to be, I won't keep him away, but he was pretty clear about how he feels."

"I'm sorry, Lace. I wanted this to be different for you."

"Me, too."

A knock on the door brought both of their heads up.

"Yeah?"

Brodie walked in, peering around the door before opening it all the way. "Hey. I'm going to head back to the office. Kirk and Stephanie are staying with your mom, but Montgomery wants a meeting."

"No more threat, so no more need for protection," Lacey said. She stood and walked over to Brodie. She wrapped her arms around his neck and hugged him tight. "Thank you for being here. For me and for Maggie."

Brodie hugged her back. "You're welcome. We're happy this is all behind us. That you and Valerie can move forward and finally get some closure. We'll keep an eye out in case we missed anything, but no one else was on our radar. The police are still looking into Kimberly Howard, but this guy didn't seem to work with her, so we think everything is good."

Lacey nodded, feeling sorry for the woman who went through her own kind of hell. "Sounds good."

Brodie waved to Maggie, then tried to close the door, getting stopped by Cocoa. "Looks like he wants to join you two. Is that okay?"

"Of course. Thanks, Brodie."

"Any time." He stopped and shook his head. "I hope not ever again, but we'll be here if you need us."

"Thanks."

Brodie closed the door.

Cocoa jumped up on the bed. He stretched out behind Lacey and Maggie, puffing a breath like the day had worn him out, too.

Lacey and Maggie looked at Cocoa and burst out laughing.

"Same, Cocoa," Maggie said. "Which means I should probably get home."

"I'm surprised you haven't popped yet," Lacey teased.

Maggie looked down. "Thankfully not yet. Soon, though. You'll understand in a few months."

Lacey stopped, yet another thing sinking in. "How am I going to do this all on my own?"

"You always figure things out. And you'll never be alone. Your mom will help, I'll be here, and maybe Austin will, too. Even if he doesn't, you're not alone."

Lacey hugged Maggie tight. "Thanks, Mags."

"Always. I'll see you soon. Are you staying here for a little longer?"

Lacey nodded. "Probably another night, maybe two. If everything is done, I can go back to work. Figure out what normal looks like again."

"And maybe tell Austin?"

Lacey nodded. "Yeah. I need to."

"When you're ready."

"When I'm ready."

AUSTIN CLIMBED the stairs to Lance's apartment with a bag of groceries thrown over his good shoulder. Lance offered him a place to stay while his house was under construction. Austin wanted to cut his losses and skip town, but he needed to sell the house before he could do that, and the only way to sell the house for a decent price was to make it look like it was not used in a set for a shoot-out.

Austin pulled out his keys and slid the new one into the lock just as the door next to Lance's opened.

A brunette woman stepped out, a smile on her face as she looked over. It faltered when she Austin. "Um, hi."

"Hi."

"Are you moving in?"

Austin shook his head. "No, just staying with my buddy for a little while."

Her face brightened. "Oh, so Lance didn't move?"

"Nope. He'll be home later. Did you need something? I'm Austin."

She took a step forward, then stopped. "Claudia. Nice to meet you. I was just going to ask Lance for a favor, but I'll catch him later. Bye." She waved and went back inside her apartment, locking the door before Austin could process her immediate disappearance.

That was weird.

Austin shook off the thought and made a mental note to ask Lance about his neighbor later. Austin carried the groceries to the kitchen and put everything away. He added a few things he hadn't realized they were out of to the list on his phone for next time. Lance wouldn't take money for rent, so Austin was buying all the groceries while he was staying there.

Not that Lance agreed to that either, but he didn't have a choice when Austin kept stocking the kitchen before Lance could go to the store.

Montgomery wasn't letting Austin back in the field until he was cleared by the surgeon. Austin had kept up with his physical therapy and was pushing himself to exercise, but he had no intention of returning to Rose Protection Agency. Especially not after the bombshell Montgomery dropped on him a week earlier.

If it was even true.

Austin expected to hear from Lacey if she was pregnant, and in the eight days since Montgomery told Austin Lacey was pregnant, all he'd gotten was silence. It was good. Austin wasn't meant to be a father. Montgomery was wrong, which was going to make leaving town easier on Austin.

Austin rolled his shoulder, stretching the tightness that he didn't think would ever go away. He had to do another round of PT and wanted to go for a run. Finding things to fill his days with had become mundane and frustrating, but going into the office wasn't a better alternative for him. Going into the office meant seeing Montgomery, and with his black eye almost healed, Austin wasn't looking to get another one.

Even if Montgomery was right.

Lance tried to talk Austin into returning to work, patching things up with Montgomery, but Austin wasn't sure that was possible. Even with all three shooters dead and the police getting closer to arresting Kimberly Howard, Austin was more of a liability than an asset to the team.

The team uncovered footage of others on the team being watched, too. Austin wasn't the only one who missed that he was under surveillance, but it didn't make it easier to accept that Howard's men figured out Austin and Samuel would be the ones protecting Hannah. Montgomery confirmed there was no leak within their systems, but he wanted everyone to be more aware of their surroundings or there would be more tragedies on their hands.

Austin shook off the thought as someone knocked on the door. He figured it was the neighbor, changing her mind about asking Austin for help instead of waiting for Lance, and opened the door.

To find Lacey.

"Lacey," Austin breathed. Fuck. Seeing her took his breath away. He wanted to pull her into his arms and never let go. It had been too long since he was allowed to see her, touch her, love her.

She looked like heaven standing there, her floral dress

hitting her knees. It hugged across her breasts and curved around her belly. A belly Austin couldn't help but stare at.

There was no way for him to tell if she was pregnant so early, he knew that, but his brain, and his dick, didn't get that memo. Both ached to claim her. To put a baby in her if there wasn't already one in there. To make her his again and never let her go.

"How... How are you?" she asked, clasping her hands together over her belly and snapping him out of his reverie.

Austin shook his head and fought against the panic that overwhelmed the desire. She wasn't his. She'd never be his. She couldn't be his. He stepped out into the hall and closed the door behind him, locking it before he turned to her.

She'd taken a few steps back. The faint smile that had been on her face when he opened the door morphed into a look of confusion.

"I was just about to run out," Austin said, moving toward the stairs.

"I was... I wanted to talk."

Austin pushed past her, not sticking around. His throat squeezed. "Sorry. Later?" He didn't wait for her to answer before he turned to go down the stairs.

"I'm pregnant," she blurted.

He stopped halfway down the stairs. His gut sank to his toes, dread and regret and crushing agony filling his body where his organs should have been. He forced a smile and looked up at her.

The light from the hallway cast her in a glow that seemed to radiate from her. He'd heard about pregnant women having a glow, but he'd never seen it. She was stunning. More beautiful than any woman he'd ever known.

"Congratulations." He nodded, then continued down the stairs.

"You're not... That's it?" She chased after him, half a flight above him as he hurried away from her.

He couldn't be within reach of her. If he was, he would do something stupid like ask her to forgive him for telling her he couldn't handle things between them or touch her or kiss her or admit he loved her.

None of those were options. She was better off without him. Everyone knew it.

"What do you want me to say, Lacey?"

She scoffed. "I don't know. I guess I thought you'd care. It's yours, you know."

"Okay. Do you want money or something?"

She swallowed, a flush rising up on her neck. She cupped her hands around her belly, the belly that was growing his child. She was protecting it from him. Protecting both of them from him.

That was what she needed to do.

"No. I... I don't want money. I don't want anything. I just thought you should know. It felt wrong to keep this from you, but I don't need anything from you. I can take care of the baby."

"You're keeping it?" he blurted. That might have been the biggest surprise of all. Not that he thought one way or the other about what she would do.

Just every time he took a breath.

Leaving town was definitely his only option. Seeing Lacey with their baby would destroy him. Absolutely gut him. He'd cave, he'd ask for another chance.

Leaving would stop that. He could go somewhere no one knew him. Let Lacey and the baby have the life they deserved without him fucking it up.

She stood up straighter and met his gaze. "Yes, I'm keeping it. I have a secure job that comes with benefits. I have family and friends that will help me out. I'll be fine. We will be fine."

Austin almost took a step toward her. Almost. His feet wanted to move. His hands wanted to reach for her. His entire being ached to be close enough to her to have her again.

But he didn't. She didn't need him. She didn't even want him. Austin knew what happened when he wasn't needed. If he had a purpose, if he had value, things were fine. As soon as his purpose was met, everything was over.

The same thing happened with Montgomery. Austin didn't protect Samuel. His partner was gone. He'd failed. And Montgomery tried to say he didn't blame Austin, but the truth came out when he knocked him on his ass.

Austin didn't need to stick around to see Lacey not need him. She was independent. She always had been. Samuel told stories of her taking care of herself when she was young. Keeping her room clean, her toys picked up. She was always the kind of woman who didn't need anyone.

Especially some loser who wouldn't be able to give her all the things she deserved.

"Okay, then. Sounds good. Good luck, I guess."

Lacey rolled her lips in. That flush crept all the way to her cheeks. She nodded. One tear slid down her cheek, but she swiped it away. As another one fell, she raced down the stairs past Austin and shoved her way out of the building.

Austin followed her, staring after her. He should apologize. He should tell her he loved her.

But what good would it do?

She said she didn't need him. He had to take her word for it.

All he would do was drag her down. Make her life harder. Make her hate him for not being the man she deserved to have in her life.

She backed out of a visitor parking space and drove to the edge of the parking lot. She stopped, using her signal to indicate where she was going. She waited as a vehicle passed.

He chuckled to himself. She followed every rule. She was going to be a great mom. To his kid. A kid he'd never meet.

His throat tightened with the thought. No. He couldn't.

Austin continued to the parking lot. He could go for a drive or something. Maybe stop at a park and get in his run. He just needed to not be in the apartment. Alone. With his thoughts about Lacey and their baby.

He was almost to his SUV when a man stepped in his way.

Austin moved to step around the man, but he moved with Austin.

Austin looked up to apologize and stopped. He looked just like the man Kirk killed. The man who'd gone after Lacey.

The man smirked. He pointed a gun in Austin's face.

Austin took a reflexive step back.

"So glad your girlfriend could show me where you were staying. Get in the car."

Austin glanced at the car, a white nondescript sedan that would blend in with every other vehicle that looked similar. It would be impossible to find and follow.

He thought of Lacey. He told her to go away, but if he got in the car, he'd never see her again.

Voices sounded on the far side of the parking lot. Kids.

"I can take one of them instead," the man said, stepping close enough to Austin to let him smell the cologne he bathed in that morning. "Or you can get in now."

Austin couldn't let anymore innocent people pay for his mistakes. He had to end this. Even if it meant the end of his life.

He did as the man said and got in the vehicle, hoping watching Lacey drive away wasn't the last time he ever saw her.

TWENTY-FOUR

Getting away from the guy driving was Austin's first priority. If he rolled out of the car, the guy would be pissed, but chances were good someone would notice and call the police before he could toss Austin back in the car or grab someone else.

Then Austin realized where the guy was going.

He drove down the street toward the library where Lacey worked, pulling into the parking lot and tucking into a space toward the back.

Lacey was walking inside.

"You do anything stupid, and this is my first stop. I'll grab your girl, but she won't have a choice to get in herself. I'll drag her ass into the back. And when she's begging me to kill her, maybe I'll do it. Or maybe I'll just hurt her enough that she won't survive, but she'll have a little bit of hope that you'll find her before she dies. You never will, though. You run, no one will ever see her alive again."

Austin stared at Lacey as she opened the door to the library and smiled at a young mother holding hands with a toddler. They exchanged words, and Lacey laughed, her entire face brightening.

He wanted to share moments like that with her. To have been good enough for her. To have told her he loved her, even though he knew it wouldn't have changed things. He didn't deserve her, but he wished she knew he loved her, not for who she could be, but for exactly who she was.

But she'd never know.

He told himself he'd tell her, but after he learned she was pregnant, he couldn't do it. He couldn't give her any hope. Not when she deserved more than him. So much more.

The door closed behind Lacey, and the man turned to Austin. "Toss your phone out the window."

"I don't have my phone with me," Austin lied.

The man reached for his door handle.

"What are you doing?"

"If you're going to lie to me, I'm going to ask your girl-friend to tell me the truth."

Austin dug his phone out and tossed it before the man could finish.

He grinned and settled in his seat again. He pulled out of the parking space and left the way they drove in. He turned onto the main road, heading out of town.

Austin had no idea how he was going to get away. The threats were one thing, and likely empty, to a point, but could he take the chance? The man knew where Lacey worked, probably where she lived, too. Lance would figure out something was wrong eventually, but would it be too late?

Probably.

Austin tried to pay attention to where they were going with every turn, but the longer the man drove away from the city, the less familiar Austin was with the area.

The man finally pulled into a long, dirt driveway with a rundown barn at the end. The sedan bounced down the rutted driveway, tossing Austin side-to-side. The man didn't move much, anticipating each hole as though he was familiar with where they were going.

It gave Austin a spark of hope. If there was a connection, his team would find it.

"Are you going to kill me?" Austin asked.

The guy smirked at him and slid the sedan into park. "Not yet."

Austin didn't love that answer, but better him than Lacey.

The guy got out of the car and came around to Austin's side, as if Austin had plans to run into the wide open field that surrounded them. He grabbed the back of Austin's shirt and shoved him toward the barn door.

It was obvious the barn hadn't been used in years as soon as they stepped inside. Rusty tools hung on the walls. Broken stall doors dangled on failing hinges or rested on the floor where they used to contain the animals inside. The scent of hay filled the space, like a memory within the wood.

Austin searched for any signs or identifying markers, but it could have been a barn anywhere. There was nothing to tell him where he was. He turned back toward the man and came face to face with a fist. Everything went fuzzy, and Austin learned just how hard the floor of a barn was.

"That was for my brother," the man growled.

"I didn't have anything to do with your brother. He was the one who forced his way inside the house."

"Because of you. Because you were a loose end. And your girlfriend was the way to get to you."

"Your boss got out of jail. Why even bother with us?"

"Why bother? Were you going to stop looking for us?"

Austin couldn't argue that point. "Your boss is dead. Does that mean you're calling the shots?"

"You think you're so smart? That you have it all figured out?"

"No. I don't have anything figured out."

"When your boss killed my boss, we knew we couldn't walk away."

"My boss? No. We had nothing to do with Peter Howard being killed."

"You're lying."

Austin shook his head. "No, I'm not. I was on my way to talk to him when his SUV blew up. We had nothing to do with that."

"It was revenge. We know it was revenge!"

The man accentuated his words with another punch that sent Austin to his knees. He doubled over, choking for air. "That's not how we operate."

"Then who the hell killed him?"

Austin almost laughed at the confusion on the guy's face. He had no idea what the hell was going on. He bought the line someone sold him and hadn't stopped to think if it made sense.

The guy raised his gun and pointed it at Austin. "Who killed him?"

"If we knew that, the police would have arrested someone."

"The cops are corrupt."

Austin raised an eyebrow. Life lessons from a man pointing a gun at someone. "The cops are trying to make sure people are held accountable for their actions. Like kidnapping."

The man looked around as if he hadn't considered what he was doing before. Then he shrugged, and his face transformed. "You'll be dead long before they even know you're missing. And I'll be long gone."

Well fuck.

LACEY WAS READY FOR A NAP. Maggie warned her the first trimester was hard and that she might feel that way, but Lacey knew it was more than the pregnancy.

It was Austin.

Going to talk to him... She didn't know what she thought he would say, but she wasn't prepared for such cold dismissal. She thought he would care. Instead, he was indifferent.

Better to know before the baby was born instead of after. Once the baby arrived, Lacey would make sure they always knew love. They always knew they were wanted. Even if it wasn't by their father.

The front door to the library dinged, and Lacey looked up to see Zeke walk in, full gear like the day he showed up to tell her about her father.

"No. Don't... You can't be here to give me more bad news," she cried when his gaze landed on her and he made his way toward her.

"Austin's missing."

"What?"

"The police got an anonymous tip that they saw him get into a car outside Lance's apartment with a man holding a gun on him."

"No." Tears flooded her eyes, pouring onto her cheeks before she could stop them.

"We tracked his phone, and it was here. We found it in the parking lot. What time was he here?"

"Here? He wasn't here." Lacey shook her head.

"His phone was in the parking lot, at the back near the grass. It looked like it was tossed out a window. The police are going to check for prints, but we thought you might have been able to tell us what time he was here to narrow down our window."

"He wasn't here. I haven't seen him since I was at his apartment. At Lance's."

"Wait, you were there?" Zeke asked.

"I went to talk to him. I... He said he was on his way out. I left and came here."

Zeke rubbed his jaw. "What time was that?"

Lacey looked at the clock above the door. "Three hours ago? I went there on my way in."

Zeke checked his phone, then tapped the desktop. "Thanks, Lacey." He headed for the door quickly.

"Zeke!"

"Yeah?" He stopped and met her gaze.

"Will you... Will you let me know when you find him?"

Zeke nodded. "Of course."

Lacey watched Zeke go, a bad feeling in her belly.

It didn't matter that Austin didn't want her, she didn't want anything to happen to him.

She just hoped they found him. Fast.

DEVLIN PULLED off the road by the old barn and stared at the white sedan parked in front. Nothing stood between the road and the barn, meaning he'd be completely exposed if he went in.

But he had no other option.

He grabbed his phone from the cupholder and called Kimberly.

"Did you find them?"

"Yeah. Just where you said. I'm here now."

"What are you going to do?"

"You know what I'm going to do. I'm going to end this. Then you'll be safe. And so will Nicole."

Kimberly's soft sob cracked his heart open. When he took the job working for Peter Howard, he expected another position as security with a little muscle thrown in. In another life, he'd been a bouncer, and the skills came naturally to him. Toss people around if they needed it, protect the boss, and keep your mouth shut.

What he never expected was to meet Kimberly. A woman who made him question everything he'd ever done with his life.

Getting assigned to protect her was the best-case scenario. She was kind and beautiful, and she treated him like a human. Unlike her piece of shit husband. The man her father forced her to marry in order to secure the family business.

Devlin wondered if Kimberly's father knew what would come of his life's work when he pushed his daughter into a marriage like the one she had with Peter. Embezzlement, assault on her sister, and an unhappy life for Kimberly. She insisted Peter never hurt her, but she never loved him either.

"You're coming with us, right?" Kimberly asked, her words whisper soft.

"If you want me to," he said, his chest swelling. He'd never told her how he felt, never crossed any lines with her. She was married, and for all his faults, he wasn't going to push her into something she didn't want.

Kimberly was good. She was kind and loving and giving. She took care of people, like her sister. She would have done well with her father's company, if he'd trusted her to do it. Instead, he thought rich and successful Peter Howard was better suited to take control and grow the business.

"Yes, I want you to come with us. I want... I care about you. I know you don't feel the same, so I understand—"

"Who said I don't feel the same?" he blurted.

"I just... You've never said anything."

He chuckled. "I don't blow up husbands for just anyone, sweetheart. That was only for you."

She breathed a laugh. "Well, that's good to know."

"I'll call you as soon as I leave here. We'll head for the border, all three of us, and we'll disappear. You and Nicole will be safe from now on. I won't let anyone touch either of you again."

"Thank you," she said, her voice full of relief and maybe a touch of joy.

"Get Nicole ready. I should be to you in no more than an hour."

"I'll see you soon."

"Yes, you will."

She hung up, and he smiled. One thing left to do, then they were free. As free as fugitives could be. He knew the police were closing in him. They'd already questioned Kimberly about the bomb that killed her husband. She was with Nicole in the hospital, so her alibi was solid, but they asked her if she paid someone to do it.

Devlin never took a cent from her. He was happy to rid the world of the son-of-a-bitch who ruined Kimberly's life. And now, he was getting the best gift of all and Kimberly would be his.

He got out of his SUV and closed the door quietly. The road was deserted, nothing around for miles. It would make getting away easier since he wouldn't have to worry about someone calling the cops before he did. Just like he called in the tip about Austin Ward being taken.

The easy thing to do would have been to take the asshole out from the road, but the old barn wasn't decrepit enough to get a clear line of sight through the walls. He had to get closer in order to see what was going on and make sure he took out the right man.

The walk up the driveway was not as bad as he anticipated. Dusk was settling in, leaving shadows all around for him to move between. He was at the edge of the barn without anyone knowing he was there.

He hoped.

A shout came from inside, toward the back of the barn. The shout was followed by a shuffling and a thud. Someone was getting his ass handed to him.

He moved toward the noises, ready to take his shot if he had one. If he could get in and out without being seen, all the better.

Austin Ward was being held up by the collar of his shirt. Blood ran down his arm and coated the front of his shirt. His head bobbed to the side, like he was losing consciousness.

"If you'd just died with your partner, you wouldn't be here right now. You would have gotten a big funeral. Instead, your girlfriend is going to think you just ran off. You're going to break her heart."

"My team will find me," Ward hissed, his breath coming out in a wheeze.

Reggie laughed loudly.

Fuck, Devlin hated that asshole. Cocky fucker who thought he was entitled to whatever the fuck he wanted just because his brother worked for Howard. Helped himself to any and all perks of the job, especially the drugs.

Reggie punched Ward again, letting go of him. Ward fell to the floor, crumpling into a heap.

Was he toying with Reggie, or was he really that bad off?

Kimberly didn't want anyone else hurt. Anyone innocent. Ward had only been doing his job, a job that would have kept Nicole safe if Howard's grunts hadn't taken out the witness. A witness Kimberly created when she left reports on Hannah's desk. The first of three executive assistants to take the bait and go to the authorities. Kimberly planned to run the business when her husband went to jail, but Hannah's murder before the trail screwed everything up.

And then Nicole... Everything Kimberly planned went out the window when she learned what Peter had done to Nicole. All Kimberly cared about was keeping her sister safe from Peter.

Which meant all Devlin cared about was keeping Nicole safe from Peter. And anyone who felt an allegiance to the dead man.

Devlin moved back to the door and pushed his way inside, the screech drawing Reggie's attention.

"What—Dev? What are you doing here? I thought you were with the wife?"

"Her name is Kimberly, and she sent me."

"Why? I didn't think she cared about all this." Reggie swung his gun back to Ward. "This fucker seems to think she's the one who had the boss killed." Reggie's laughter echoed around the empty barn.

Devlin did not join in.

Reggie noticed and turned back to Devlin. "He can't be right. Why the fuck would she kill her husband?"

"She didn't," Devlin said. "I did." He pointed his gun before Reggie could process the words and pulled the trigger.

Reggie's eyes went wide as the bullet hit him. He fell, dropping to his knees before the blood pumping out of his heart emptied onto his shirt. Reggie fell face-forward onto the wooden floor, limbs going limp.

Austin Ward groaned. He faced Reggie, fighting to push himself back when he saw Reggie's lifeless body.

"I'm not here to kill you, but it's better if you don't know who I am," Devlin said.

"Why?"

"Because none of this should have happened. I'm sorry about your partner," Devlin said.

"What?"

Devlin took the nine-millimeter from his waistband and laid it next to Reggie. It was the gun used to kill Samuel MacNeil. Reggie's fingerprints were on it, thanks to the idiot's inability to do something simple like wipe a gun clean after he used it to kill a man.

Ward watched Devlin, his eyes wide with confusion.

"You'll never see us again, Mr. Ward. Take care of that baby. Your medical bills and Mr. MacNeil's funeral expenses have been covered."

"Do you actually work for Peter Howard's wife?"

Devlin smiled and shook his head. "Not anymore."

Devlin turned and walked away, trusting that the man behind him wouldn't use the loaded gun at his side to shoot.

When Devlin got to his SUV, he called in another tip to nine-one-one about spotting the white sedan at the barn. Before they could get anything else from him, he hung up and pulled away from the barn.

He called Kimberly. "I'm on my way to you."

"Is Austin Ward alive?"

"Police are on the way to him now."

"And Reggie?"

"All loose ends are tied."

"Thank you, Dev." A breath shuddered from her. "We'll be outside when you get here."

"Can't wait."

Devlin hung up the phone and drove straight to the hospital. Kimberly and Nicole walked out as he pulled up. Devlin helped Nicole settle in the backseat of the SUV, then opened the passenger door for Kimberly. He climbed in next to her and reached for her hand as he pulled away from the hospital.

She clasped his hand between hers and smiled at him.

Devlin smiled and drove toward their new life. Gone forever without a trace.

TWENTY-FIVE

Austin listened as the silence pressed in around him. He knew he was going in and out of consciousness. He didn't know how long he'd been there, or if anyone was looking for him, despite the assurances of the man who killed his kidnapper.

Austin tried to pull himself closer to Reggie's body, hoping to find a phone he could use to call the police. He didn't know where he was, but if he was lucky, they would be able to trace the call and get to him.

Sirens woke him up, consciousness filtering in around the edges. Had he called? Austin lifted his head and was still five feet away from Reggie.

The man named Devlin kept his word.

Lights pierced his eyes and shouts echoed in his brain. Austin tried to call out, but his voice was gone.

"Hands!" the first man shouted.

Austin tried to lift his hands, but before he could, he heard a familiar voice.

"That's our victim."

"Thank God," Austin breathed, letting the darkness come in again.

THE NEXT TIME Austin woke up, the scents of bleach and fresh linens assailed him. He groaned, wishing they'd give him something for the crashing headache.

"Just relax."

Austin tried to look at whoever was talking, but he couldn't find him. He knew the voice, though, and knew he was safe. He would be fine.

"Lacey," he whispered, then fell asleep again.

"Good morning, Mr. Ward. How are you doing today?" a woman said. She was far too happy to be waking him up, and he was ready to tell her.

"He's not a morning person."

Austin's eyes flickered open and found Lance in a chair next to his bed.

Lance nodded at him.

"Well, he needs to get up and moving. It'll help him heal faster so he can get out of here. And get back to whoever Lacey is."

Lance chuckled.

Austin glared at his former friend. Lance didn't know what happened before Austin was kidnapped, but it didn't matter. Lance did know how badly Austin screwed up with Lacey before.

"I see your eyes are open. If you're going to be able to get out of bed, I can remove your catheter, Mr. Ward."

"And that's my cue to go," Lance said, jumping out of his chair like he'd been threatened with the device.

Austin nodded, letting the nurse help him swing his feet over the edge of the bed. "How long have I been here?"

"Fourteen hours or so. They wanted you to sleep overnight, but today, you need to get moving."

"I didn't have a catheter after my last surgery. Why did they put one in now?"

The nurse snickered. "You don't have one. I just figured you might want some privacy to get out of bed the first time. You were unconscious when you were brought in. The doctors gave you blood and fluid, then knocked you out. You're probably a little unsteady, and some men are funny about needing help to the bathroom."

Austin shook his head. "I need to watch out for you."

"Just taking care of my patient." She offered an arm for Austin to hold as he stood.

She was right, and he was unsteady. If she hadn't wrapped an arm around him right away, he would have fallen when he stood. She held him still until he felt steady, then shuffled with him to the bathroom.

"You're not going to want to hear this, but you need to sit down. It's for your safety. And the bathroom door doesn't lock, but I won't come in until you tell me you're ready or you open the door."

"Sitting sounds like a good idea right now," Austin confessed.

She chuckled and released her hold on him.

Austin used the sink and the rails around the toilet to help sit. When he was done, he was able to stand and wash his hands without help, which he thought was a good thing. He opened the door to the nurse smiling.

"All set?"

Austin nodded. "Thank you."

"It's my job. You have a big family waiting to see you. If you're feeling a little better, I can send some of the others in."

"They're here?"

She nodded and shuffled with him back to bed. She pulled the blankets over his feet and up to his waist, then patted his feet. "Are you ready to see them?"

Austin nodded. "Yeah. Thanks."

"You got it."

She left the room and said something to someone in the hall. Before the door closed behind her, Montgomery and Teddy were walking in.

Teddy clasped his hand and pulled Austin in for a hug. "How are you feeling?"

"Like I got my ass handed to me."

"Pretty much how you look, too."

Austin chuckled, wincing when he did.

"Two broken ribs, broken nose, and bruised windpipe. Stitches on your arm. No surgeries," Montgomery reported.

Austin nodded.

"You had us worried," Montgomery said.

Austin shrugged. He wasn't sure where things stood with Montgomery or the team. He wasn't too excited about getting fired while he was in a hospital bed in his boxers, but he didn't have a lot of choices. "How did you find me?"

"Police got a tip. Two, actually. One saying you got into a sedan at gunpoint. That led us to Lacey's library."

"Lacey. Is she—"

"She's safe," Teddy said.

Austin closed his eyes and thanked God, and Samuel, for watching out for her.

"A second call came in that led us to your location. You were almost gone. Lost a lot of blood," Montgomery said, his face pinched.

"Not enough. I'm still here, boss."

"Fucking asshole, I don't want you dead. I never did."

Austin swallowed. "Look, about what I said—"

"Forgotten. Just get better and get back to work."

Austin didn't answer.

Montgomery didn't notice, but Teddy did.

"Can we have a minute, boss?" Teddy asked Montgomery.

Montgomery nodded and headed for the door. "See you soon."

Austin nodded again, not saying a word.

"I know that look. Why are you running?"

"I've made too many mistakes here lately. I can't... It's better for everyone if I just disappear."

"Everyone or you? Because last I checked, no one is trying to push you away."

"You will when you find out what I did."

"You and Lacey? We all know you were with her. That's your choice. You don't owe anyone an explanation. You've loved that girl for years."

"You knew that?"

Teddy rolled his eyes. "You thought you were so sneaky, but I've been there. It's been a minute, but I've been there. Now it's up to you if you're going to be a man and tell her how you feel or run and have her wonder what she did."

"I can't... She deserves better than me."

"Of course she does. She deserves the moon. But the thing with love is it's not about what we deserve. It's about what's right for us. If you're half the man I know you are, half the man Samuel knew you were, you'll stop at nothing to make that girl the happiest woman on earth."

"Samuel always told me to stay away from her."

Teddy chuckled. "Of course he did. Why would he give you his blessing outright? That would have made you run. But knowing you weren't allowed to love her made you want her even more."

"You... No. I don't think so. He threatened me."

Teddy shrugged. "Maybe you're right. I guess you'll never know if you run, though."

A knock on the door came a second before Zeke stuck his head into the room. "There are people out here waiting. You can't monopolize all the time."

Teddy moved toward the door, trading places with Zeke and Brodie.

Austin shook hands and spoke to all his teammates. When he started to fade, they filtered out of the room and let him rest. Austin wanted to ask if Lacey had been there, but he didn't have the guts. He told her he didn't want her, and she took his word for it and left.

Like he asked.

OVER THE NEXT DAY, Austin answered questions from the police about the man who took him and about how he died. Austin didn't think Devlin was the other man's real name, but he shared it with the cops. A part of him wanted to protect the man who helped him, but it wasn't in him to cover up someone's crimes.

Kimberly Howard and her sister were gone before Austin made it to the hospital, walked right out the front door of the hospital where Nicole was being treated. They got into a black SUV with no plates and disappeared. No one knew where they were, and Austin was fairly sure no one ever would.

A week after he was released from the hospital, Austin got a call from the crew working on his house that the work was done. Their projection had been for two more weeks, but Austin wasn't disappointed to find out it was done early and he could go home.

Lance went with Austin to meet with the foreman, Antonio, and go through the house. Driving up, it looked mostly the same, but the last time Austin was there was felt like a lifetime.

"Shit," Lance said when he got out. "I haven't been here since Samuel's funeral."

"Yeah," Austin agreed.

"Are you ready?"

Austin shrugged. "Don't really have a choice."

They walked up the driveway to the front door. The door opened when they got close, and Austin got the first peek of his remodeled house.

The door had been replaced with a solid steel door, one that was heavy and damn near impenetrable. It was painted a light blue color that Lacey picked out when they were in the hotel. The floors were in good shape, but the walls had been littered with bullet holes. The walls were repaired and all the furniture replaced.

"Damn, I didn't know you could afford to do it up like this," Lance said.

"I didn't either," Austin said. He looked around, trying to figure out how all the things that were done fit into his budget. Lights were replaced, the kitchen upgraded, collapsible sliders added to the back leading to a new deck. It was what he'd always wanted to do to the house, but he didn't have the funds for it.

"We got a call last week," Antonio said. "Told us to go ahead with the rest of the things we'd talked about. She said you were okay with all of this."

"Did she tell you her name? Or if she has a sister?" Lance asked.

Austin chuckled to himself.

"Do you know who it was?" Lance asked.

"I have a guess."

"Wait, is it Lacey? Are you... I thought that was done."

"She said her name was Kim Weston," Antonio said. "She was a representative with a local organization that helps veterans with things like medical bills, home renovations, and funeral expenses. Sent a second crew to help and everything so it would be done sooner. I didn't realize it was a surprise, though. She said you were in the hospital, and I saw it on the news and didn't want to bother you. We set up the second bedroom like she said, and added a whole bunch of things she thought would be nice additions to the house."

"Wow," Austin breathed as Lance's eyes went wide.

"So, it's all good?"

Austin nodded. "Yeah. It's great. Thanks. It might take me a while to pay you the balance, though."

"It's all taken care of, Mr. Ward. The organization paid for all of it."

Austin chuckled. "Seriously?"

Antonio nodded and shook Austin's hand, then let himself out.

Lance waited for the door to close, then turned to Austin. "Okay, what the fuck happened in that barn and why in the hell is Kimberly Howard footing the bill for your renovation?"

Austin smiled. "You heard Antonio. It was a charity."

"Fuck you. I know that's not the whole story."

Austin sighed. "The guy who killed Reggie? He was working for Kimberly. Sounded like he started working for Peter, but he's the one who took Peter out. Said Kimberly never wanted anyone to get hurt. She was sorry about Samuel."

"Did you tell the cops all of that?" Lance asked.

"Of course. They killed people. Even if the people they killed were horrible, I'm not going to help them."

"A fugitive who killed someone paid for your home renovation."

"She also paid for my hospital bills and Samuel's funeral."

Lance chuckled. "Are you kidding me?"

Austin shook his head. "That's what the guy Devlin told me before he left the barn. It's the same organization. It's a legit company. They had a huge donation come in recently. Montgomery looked into it already and said the donor specifically requested some of the money was set aside for Samuel's and my bills, but I didn't realize this was part of it."

"Wow. This is pretty damn sweet."

Austin looked around the room as the rest of what the foreman said came back to him. "Yeah. Uh, give me a minute."

Lance stared after him as Austin headed for the hallway.

The second bedroom wasn't a place Austin used much. He had a bed in there in case anyone needed a place to crash for the night, but it was mostly wasted space.

Austin pushed open the door and stopped when he found a fully decked out nursery. A wooden crib sat on the far wall, away from the window and the door. A neutral gray color scheme outfitted the space, with tiny bits of color throughout the space. It was peaceful and soothing, just like a baby's room should be.

"What the fuck is this?" Lance asked, following Austin into the room.

Austin didn't have words, but the look on Lance's face said they weren't necessary.

"Lacey's pregnant."

Austin nodded.

"That's why you walked away from her."

"No. I walked away from her before I knew. She... Fuck, she deserves so much more than I can ever be for her."

"What do you mean?"

"She's... She's fucking perfect. She's everything, man. She's sweet and kind and so damn good. She came from a family that loves each other and supports each other. And I'm so far from that it's fucking crazy."

"What's fucking crazy is you thinking your past gets to define you."

"You know it does. It always has. And her being pregnant is even more of a reason for me to stay away from her."

"What? What the hell does that have to do with anything? You should be there for her, and your kid. What is wrong with you?"

"What if I'm like him?" Austin whispered.

All the fight left Lance. He drew a breath and closed his eyes. He understood Austin's worries, and his words.

"I can't risk that."

"Then don't be that," Lance growled. "Be better. Be more. You've never wanted to be like him, and you're going to choose to walk away from the woman you love and your child in order to prove you're not? I gotta say, at least he stuck around. He raised you. He was a piece of shit, but he was there. Your kid's not even going to be able to say that about you. They're just going to say you're a piece of shit who fucking bailed."

"Fuck you," Austin growled.

"When did you find out she's pregnant?"

"The day I was taken. She showed up at your place to tell me. But I already knew. Montgomery told me."

"How the fuck did he know?"

Austin shook his head. "Said something about a test at the house the day that guy forced his way inside."

"Lacey told him it was hers?"

"No. Montgomery assumed since her friend claimed it was hers."

"Fucker can read people like a book."

"Yeah."

"Okay, so you've known for two-and-a-half weeks?"

Austin nodded.

"And you still haven't pulled your head out of your ass?"

"Let me ask you something... Do you think it's possible Samuel told me to stay away from Lacey because he knew it would make me want her more?"

"What are you talking about?"

"Teddy said Samuel wanted me and Lacey together. That he always told me to stay away from her because if he gave me permission, I would have dismissed her. Do you think he's right?"

Lance snickered. "He was pretty damn smart. I wouldn't be surprised if he did exactly that."

"I don't know. I just..." Austin's gaze landed on a picture of him and Samuel. It was a day he'd forgotten about. They'd only been working together a year or so, and Samuel told Austin he thought of him as family. As a symbol of that, he gave Austin a key.

A tiny key.

The kind of key that didn't fit a door.

Austin asked Samuel what it opened, and Samuel said it was symbolic, but that one day, Austin might find a need for it.

"Dude, what is going on in your head?" Lance asked.

Austin pulled his wallet from his pocket and opened the tiny zippered section where he kept that key.

"What is that to?"

"I think it might be the key to my future."

TWENTY-SIX

Austin stared at the MacNeil house. His first step forward was inside that house. Where everything began for him.

Where his future was.

Austin walked up the walk, rubbing his hands on his shorts before he rang the bell. He waited, wondering if Valerie was going to leave him standing outside in the early summer heat. When the door opened, she looked surprised to see him.

"Austin? What are you doing here?"

"Can we talk? Inside?"

Valerie hesitated but nodded. She stepped back to let Austin inside.

He closed the door and followed her to the kitchen. He hadn't ever been in the house without Samuel there. It hit Austin all over again that he'd never see Samuel again.

But in the last few weeks, he'd begun to come to grips with that. And his part in the death of his partner.

"Do you want something to drink?" Valerie asked, pulling out a pitcher of tea. She smiled at him.

Austin chuckled. Samuel found out Austin liked Valerie's

tea and ever since, there was always a pitcher in their fridge, even when Austin dropped by unannounced. "Thank you." Austin never expected Valerie to continue with the ritual nearly two months after Samuel died.

"I guess I was hoping you would stop by sometime." Valerie poured two glasses and joined Austin at the table.

"I wasn't sure you'd be willing to see me."

"I was angry. And upset. I never should have said the things I said to you. I know you weren't to blame for Samuel's death."

"You do?" Austin blurted. He shook his head. "Right. Montgomery said he was going to tell you what happened."

Valerie shook her head and put her hand over his. "That's not why I know you weren't to blame. I know because I know you, Austin. I know the man you are. Samuel was right about you. For years, he's told me how good of a man you are. I lashed out, and I hope you can forgive me."

Austin nodded. "Of course. I blamed myself, too. I... I still do."

"No. You have to let go of that. Samuel's death was a tragedy. It was horrible and traumatic, and the only ones to blame are the man who pulled the trigger and the one who sent them. You could have been right beside Samuel in a coffin, and that wouldn't have been better."

"Thank you, Valerie."

"I will always wish he was still here, but that doesn't mean I would trade your places. And I know Samuel would feel the same. If you'd died and he'd survived, he would have blamed himself and wished he'd been the one gone."

Austin breathed a laugh. "He always said the same thing. He wanted me to be here for you if anything ever happened to him. I'm sorry I wasn't."

"You were there for Lacey, and I'm grateful for that."

"I know I haven't been around for her the last few weeks,

but I'm ready to be who she needs. I wanted to speak to you first, but I want to be there for her and the baby. I want to be a father."

"Father?"

Austin nodded. "I know you're going to think this is coming from nowhere, but I love Lacey. I have for a long time. I didn't mean for this to happen, but I want to be in her life. And I want to be in the baby's life. It's up to Lacey if she wants us to be together, but that's what I want."

"Lacey's pregnant?" Valerie breathed.

"Oh, shit. I thought... Um..." Austin stood, backing away. "I was never here. I said nothing."

"Sit your ass back down this minute, young man," Valerie snarled.

Austin crept back over, sinking into the chair. His shoulders curled in. He'd never been scolded before.

"My daughter is pregnant? And you're the father?"

"Um, yeah?"

"Is that a question or an answer?" Valerie snapped.

Austin exhaled and sat up. "It's an answer. And I'm sorry, Valerie. I... I do love her. I want to be a part of her life. The last time I saw Lacey... I wasn't in a good place. I was blaming myself and thought she'd be better off without me in her life. Maybe she would be, but I love her. I really do."

Valerie reached for his hand and squeezed it again. "Samuel always said you loved her. I thought he was crazy." She chuckled. "He would be dancing around right now and telling me he was right."

Austin laughed at the thought. "He knew me better than I knew myself most of the time."

"He was that way for all of us." Valerie sniffed and wiped a tear from her eye. "He would have been so excited to be a grandfather."

"I know. I've been thinking about that since I found out."

Valerie smiled. Tears streamed freely down her cheeks.

"I'm sorry you found out like this. I just assumed Lacey would have told you by now."

Valerie shook her head. "She was always closer to her father. He would have been the first person she told. I always let him talk to her when she needed something. I knew she was more comfortable with him, but I never pushed for us to have a better relationship. If I had, maybe she would have told me about the baby."

"I didn't mean to make all of this harder on you. I just wanted to own up to my part in it. I wanted you to know how sorry I am about Samuel and to see if you could ever forgive me—"

"There's nothing to forgive, Austin."

He swallowed roughly. "Thank you. I know things aren't ever going to be the same again, but I do still want to see you. To be here if you need anything."

"It sounds like I'm going to need a father for my future-grandchild."

He laughed. "I'm up for that one."

"Good."

LACEY GRABBED her handbag and checked her phone. She was going to be late if she didn't get out the door. It wasn't that she was delaying. No. Definitely not. Of course not.

She groaned, frustrated with herself. She had to get used to doing things alone. No one was coming. It was just her.

She pulled her keys out of her bag and opened her door, stepping back when Austin almost hit her in the face.

"Lacey," he said, sounding as surprised as she was.

"What are you doing here?"

"I was... I wanted to talk to you."

Lacey moved into the hall and turned her back on him. She took two tries to get her key into the lock. "I'm on my way out."

"I guess I deserve that."

She swirled to face him. "You think I'm just sitting around here waiting for you to show up? I have a life, Austin. I have things going on."

"I'm sorry. I didn't mean... You're right. I shouldn't have just shown up. Maybe we can set up a time to talk?"

Lacey brushed past him, barely holding herself together. He looked good, and he smelled even better, damn him. All she wanted to do was sink into his arms and not be alone. Not be a single mother. Not have to do all of this by herself.

But she couldn't let her heart lead the way. Not anymore.

"What is there to say? You were pretty clear how you feel."

"I love you," he blurted.

Lacey stopped. She shook her head, a mirthless laugh falling out. "Wow. Okay. I don't know what you think it's going to do telling me that, but it's just... Don't. I don't want the pity, or whatever this is."

"Pity? You think I'm telling you I love you out of pity?"

"I don't know why you're saying that, Austin. I really don't. What I do know is you said you couldn't handle us, and you disappeared. It's been weeks since I've seen you. Now, you're here telling me you love me. Just leave me alone, Austin." She swallowed the tightness in her throat and pushed out of the building. If she could just get to her car—

Austin grabbed her arm and spun her around. His lips crashed down on hers.

Lacey whimpered, hating how easy it was to fall into him. To let her body take over and lose herself in the man she loved. The man who was breaking her heart by saying he loved her.

No. She couldn't.

Lacey pushed him away, putting her hand over her mouth. He kissed her. He actually kissed her. Like he thought that would do anything.

She was furious. And hurt.

"Stay away from me."

"Lacey."

"No, Austin. You..." She swallowed. "What happened between us was a mistake for you. I get it. You weren't looking for forever, and you're off the hook. I told you I don't need anything from you. We're good." Lacey moved toward the parking lot again.

"The first time I saw you, I couldn't breathe. The first time you laughed, I wanted to cut off my arm to hear it again. For years, I've been looking for any scraps I get from you. God, I'd do anything to see you smile, even just for a minute."

"Austin."

"No, Lacey, let me... Let me say this. I know you don't need me. God, you've never needed anyone. You're so... amazing. You can do anything, Lace. I know you can. I've watched it. But being with you... Shit, none of that was a mistake for me. Or a regret. My only regret is that I pushed you away because I was scared. I'm still scared, but I know I can't just be scared and walk away. Because I don't want that. I want a life with you. With our baby. I want to watch documentaries with you and rub your feet when you're tired. I want to talk about baby names and make more babies. I want to have a life with you, Lacey MacNeil."

Tears ran down Lacey's cheeks. She wasn't sure if he was serious, but he was damn convincing. "Are you... How...?"

Austin stepped closer, cupping her cheeks. "I love you, Lacey MacNeil. I've loved you for years. And being with you for a few weeks was... Fuck, those were the best weeks of my life. I know that's horrible because it was right after your dad died, but I think... I think he wanted us together. Even if he didn't, I want to be with you."

"What about everything you said? About not being able to handle us."

"I thought it was the only way to keep you safe. I couldn't imagine losing you, too. It was easier for me to think about not being with you instead of you being gone for good. If I pushed you away... If I pushed you away, you'd still be alive. I wouldn't let you down or get you hurt or hurt you myself."

"Austin."

"I know that was the wrong thing to do, and I'd love to tell you I won't do anything like that again, but I've never been in love before. I've never been a father before. I will make mistakes. I will screw up. But I want to be a father and a husband, one day, if you'll have me."

"What?"

"I'm not proposing right now, but one day, I will. Until then, I hope we can get to know each other better, and I hope maybe I can convince you to love me back."

Lacey chewed on her lip. She wasn't ready to ignore the pain he caused, but maybe they could take a small step forward. "Do you want to go somewhere with me?"

Austin hesitated a minute, then nodded.

Lacey pointed to her car, getting in behind the wheel. She let everything he said roll around in her mind. She thought she was seeing things all those times she caught Austin watching her. She convinced herself she was the one chasing him.

But he said he loved her. He wanted to marry her. Be a father to the baby.

She pulled into the parking lot and turned off the car.

He looked at the building, then at her. He didn't say anything.

Lacey got out, leaving Austin to decide if he was going to follow her.

He did.

Lacey gave her name at the desk and took a seat in the waiting room. Austin sat next to her, and damn him, he did not look out of place at all.

Someone called her name, and she got up. He didn't move, so she looked at him. "Are you coming with me?"

"Do you want me to?"

Lacey nodded. Baby steps.

The technician led them to a room, and Lacey laid on the exam table.

"Are you excited to hear the baby's heartbeat today?" the technician asked.

Lacey nodded.

"What?" Austin breathed.

The technician looked up at him. "Surprise for dad? You'll enjoy this. Let's see what we can find."

Lacey stared at the screen that was no more than fuzzy blobs to her. She tried to figure out what something was, but there was no making sense of the—

A whooshing sound echoed through the room, and the technician smiled. "There we go. That's our heartbeat. Nice and strong."

"Oh my God," Austin breathed. He moved closer, reaching for her hand. "That's our baby."

Lacey squeezed his hand.

He looked down at her, his eyes bright with tears. "We did that."

Lacey nodded. "Yes, we did."

The technician clicked a few more things, then pointed to the screen. "That's the baby. It's roughly the size of a strawberry right now, so too small to see a lot of features, but everything looks good." She turned off the monitor and wiped Lacey's belly. "We have a few pictures for you to take with you. You can schedule your next appointment on the way out."

"Thank you so much," Lacey said. She followed the technician out of the room and went to the desk. She scheduled another appointment, not trying to hide it from Austin and smiling to herself when he appeared to be putting it in his calendar.

Austin followed her to her car and got in without a word.

Lacey stared straight ahead, wondering what Austin was thinking. She didn't have to wonder for long.

"Why did you bring me here?"

"You said you want to be a father. I figured you should be here for this. If you want to be."

He sucked in a breath. "You're going to let me be involved?"

Lacey exhaled a laugh. "You're really a fool, aren't you, Austin Ward?"

"Excuse me?"

"Are you really that oblivious? You really think I don't love you?"

"You love me?" Austin breathed.

Lacey shook her head. "You silly man."

"You love me."

Lacey nodded. "I love you."

Austin leaned toward her, closing the distance between them. "You love me."

Lacey chuckled. "You love me."

"Hell, yes, I do." He sealed his lips over hers and kissed her.

For a long damn time.

AUSTIN SMILED as Lacey rushed past him for the third time in five minutes. She was nervous. He was, too, but there was a calmness that had settled over him. Like when he was going out on an assignment and knew he was ready.

It had taken a little while to get used to a new partner, but working with Teddy again was great. Montgomery had given them some easy assignments over the last few months, letting Austin ease back into things and still have off plenty of time for Lacey's appointments.

Including the latest one. And the reason for Lacey's anxiousness.

"Maybe we should put this over there," she said, grabbing a centerpiece from the kitchen island.

"Stop," Austin said, taking it from her hand and wrapping her arms around his neck. The baby bump between them thumped him, and they both smiled.

"Someone else is just as anxious about today as I am," Lacey said.

"Or maybe that little someone is just telling me to back off their mommy."

Lacey chuckled. Every time Austin got close, the baby kicked. She teased that it was a back off thing. Austin thought it was a hello. Either way, it wasn't going to deter him from showing her how much he loved her.

Austin leaned closer and kissed Lacey, licking into her mouth and teasing her until she finally relaxed. She sighed and a tiny moan slipped out. That was what he was waiting for.

Lacey had been very interested in sex the last few weeks, a perk of the second trimester she confessed, and Austin was not complaining. But she'd been worried about the party and tense for days. He was ready for it to be behind them so she could rest.

Austin pulled back just enough to smile at the peaceful look on her face. Which was eliminated when the doorbell rang.

"We're not ready."

Austin stopped her before she could rush away. "Yes, we are. Everyone coming is family. They aren't worried about perfection. They just want to celebrate the baby."

Lacey drew a breath and nodded. She took his breath away in her maternity dress, the delicate purple hugging her bump and accentuating her more full than usual breasts. She smiled at him, then went to let in their first guest.

The next twenty minutes were a flurry of activity with guests arriving and gifts Lacey insisted no one bring being found a place to live. Valerie played hostess right along with Lacey, making sure people had food and drinks and were comfortable.

Lance sidled up to Austin with a beer, which Austin accepted gratefully. "How's everything going?"

Austin sipped the beer and nodded. "Good. She's stressing, but I think she's okay."

"And she has no idea?"

Austin chuckled. "I don't think so. She was surprised when you were willing to take the lead on the gender reveal."

Lance tapped his bottle to Austin's. "Sounds like mission success to me."

Austin nodded. "How are you? Neighbor still bugging you?"

Lance growled. "Every damn day she needs something. And if she isn't asking for something, she's running into me as I'm coming home or leaving. If I didn't know any better, I'd think she was targeting me."

Austin chuckled. "For what? You think she wants a husband?"

Lance shook his head. "Fuck if I know, but the woman wants something."

"Maybe she just wants you."

Lance barked a laugh. "Yeah, no. Not happening."

"Doesn't mean she's not interested."

"Whatever. Are we going to do this or what?"

Austin nodded, letting Lance change the subject. Austin clapped his hands to get everyone's attention. "I'd like to thank you all for being here with us today to celebrate. And for all the amazing things you brought."

Lacey walked over and joined Austin, sliding right under his arm and circling hers around his waist.

"You are all family to us, and we will forever miss Samuel, but we know he's here, too, waiting, just like the rest of us, to find out the gender of this little one." Austin rubbed Lacey's belly. "Is everyone ready?"

Lance set the box in front of Austin and Lacey, then stepped to the side.

Lacey grinned, looking at Austin. She grabbed the tab on the box and pulled, releasing the...

Blue balloons!

The balloons obscured her from his view and gave Austin a second to drop to one knee. As their guests cheered, Lacey grabbed the balloons, spotting the ring weighing them down.

"What..." Lacey finally noticed Austin kneeling. Her eyes went wide. Her hands flew to her face. "Austin?"

Austin grabbed the ring where it floated between them. "Lacey MacNeil, I've loved you for years. I've loved getting to know you over these last few months. Over all that time, I've found something I never thought I'd have. A family. I know I'll never be worthy of you. But I'm going to spend the rest of my days trying to be. And I hope I can do that by your side. As your husband. Will you marry me?"

Lacey nodded. "Yes, you crazy man!"

Austin surged to his feet and kissed her, getting a swift kick from their son.

Their son.

"He's saying hello," she said against Austin's lips.

"Yeah, he is."

"What's his name?" someone asked.

Austin and Lacey didn't break eye contact as they answered together. "Samuel."

THANK **you** so much for reading Lacey and Austin's story! I have always enjoyed protector romances, and creating a series of them has been so much fun for me. And these two... They put me through it, but I'm so happy they found their way to each other.

The series continues with Lance and Claudia's story. She didn't move into the apartment next to him by chance. She needs protection. And who better to get it from than the man who is always looking out for others and could snap a grown man in two if needed. Because it might be needed if Claudia's brother finds out where she is. Preorder Searching For His Curvy Girl now and read on August 12.

WONDERING if Austin's key fits Lacey's locket? Find out in their bonus scene now. Available only to subscribers.

LOOKING FOR MORE ROMANTIC SUSPENSE? His career is over. His brother is missing. He has nothing left. Except his brother's best friend. And she's off-limits. Freedom is available now.

ABOUT THE AUTHOR

USA TODAY Bestselling Author Mary E Thompson spent most of her childhood wishing she had a few less curves. She hid in the pages of books because her favorite characters never cared what size her clothes were. Now, neither does Mary, and she writes stories that celebrate women like her. Real women who have curves, chase dreams, and find love, because we should all be happy, no matter our dress size.

Mary spends her non-writing time with her husband and two kids, watching too much TV, cheering for her hometown football team (Go Bills!), and hiding chocolate from her family.

Visit https://MaryEThompson.com/ to sign up for Mary's newsletter, **Romancing the Curves**. Subscribers get free ebooks and other fun stuff, like exclusive, members only content and giveaways, plus are the first to know about new releases and sales!

www.ingramcontent.com/pod-product-compliance
Lightning Source LLC
Chambersburg PA
CBHW020744310726
48969CB00002B/404